MINCE PIES AND MURDER

J. R. LEIGH

B
Boldwood

First published in Great Britain in 2025 by Boldwood Books Ltd.

Copyright © J. R. Leigh, 2025

Cover Design by Rachel Lawston

Cover Illustration: Rachel Lawston

The moral right of J. R. Leigh to be identified as the author of this work has been asserted in accordance with the Copyright, Designs and Patents Act 1988.

All rights reserved. No part of this book may be reproduced in any form or by any electronic or mechanical means, including information storage and retrieval systems, without written permission from the author, except for the use of brief quotations in a book review. This book is a work of fiction and, except in the case of historical fact, any resemblance to actual persons, living or dead, is purely coincidental.

Every effort has been made to obtain the necessary permissions with reference to copyright material, both illustrative and quoted. We apologise for any omissions in this respect and will be pleased to make the appropriate acknowledgements in any future edition.

A CIP catalogue record for this book is available from the British Library.

Paperback ISBN 978-1-83751-488-5

Large Print ISBN 978-1-83751-489-2

Hardback ISBN 978-1-83751-487-8

Ebook ISBN 978-1-83751-490-8

Kindle ISBN 978-1-83751-491-5

Audio CD ISBN 978-1-83751-482-3

MP3 CD ISBN 978-1-83751-483-0

Digital audio download ISBN 978-1-83751-485-4

This book is printed on certified sustainable paper. Boldwood Books is dedicated to putting sustainability at the heart of our business. For more information please visit https://www.boldwoodbooks.com/about-us/sustainability/

Boldwood Books Ltd, 23 Bowerdean Street, London, SW6 3TN

www.boldwoodbooks.com

*For Norman, who read all my books.
With thanks and love and happy memories.*

There's nothing more beautiful than the way the ocean refuses to stop kissing the shoreline, no matter how many times it's sent away.

— SARAH KAY, POET

WHO DUNNIT...?

Morwenna Mutton – our sleuth
Lamorna Mutton – her mother
Tamsin Pascoe – her daughter
Elowen Pascoe – her granddaughter
Ruan Pascoe – her ex, a fisherman
Jane Choy – Police Constable, Devon and Cornwall Police, Morwenna's friend
Rick Tremayne – Detective Inspector, Devon and Cornwall Police
Sally Tremayne – Rick's wife
Blessed Barnarde – Detective Chief Inspector, Devon and Cornwall Police
Louise Piper – Morwenna's friend from the library in Seal Bay
Steve Piper – Louise's husband
Donald Stewart – library assistant
Pawly Yelland – local writer and historian
Becca Hawkins – Tamsin's friend from the gift shop
Susan and Barb Grundy – sisters from the pop-up charity shop

Barnaby Stone – Morwenna's sometime boyfriend, a surgeon from London
Pam Truscott – Barnaby's sister
Damien Woon – owner, Woon's boatyard
Beverley Okoro – Damien's partner, an artist
Mike Sheridan – DJ, Bay Radio
Trudi Smith – assistant, Bay Radio
Julian Pengellen – from the manor house
Pippa Pengellen – from the manor house
Tristan Pengellen – their son
Faye Bryce – Pippa's friend
Lady Elizabeth Pengellen – a ghost from the Victorian era
Seb Chivers – from London, Tristan's friend
Carole Taylor – from the B & B
Vic Taylor – her husband, runs Taylor Made cars
Britney Taylor – their daughter, in Elowen's class
Billy Crocker – in Elowen's class
Milan Buvač – a fisherman
Rosie Buvač – Milan's wife
Maya Buvač – one of their six children
Fernanda Pérez – Tristan's ex
Justin Kidd – a photographer
Ms Stark – Elowen's teacher
Sheppy – Kyle Sheppard, beach entertainer and magician
Courtenay Lamb – from Camp Dynamo
Imogen Bruce – a student working in the tearoom
Zach Barr – a student working in the tearoom
Shaela Carmody – a medium

GLOSSARY

Ansom, ansum – Nice, handsome, good.
Backalong – In previous times, a while ago.
Bleddy – Local pronunciation of 'bloody' as an emphasising adjective.
Dreckly – At some point in the future; soon, but not immediately.
Emmet – A tourist. It actually means an ant.
Giss on! – Stop talking rubbish!
Gurt – Large, great.
Heller – Lively, troublesome child.
Jumping – Angry.
Maid – Any girl or woman, often used as a form of address.
My bewty – My beauty, a term of affection. Bewty can also be substituted with ansom.
Oggy – Pasty (from Cornish language *hogen*).
Proper – Satisfactory, good.
Quilkin, Guilkin, Kuilkin – Frog.
Rufazrats – Not feeling great.
Teazy, teasy – Bad-tempered.
Tuss – An obnoxious person.
Yeghes da! – Cheers in Cornish.

FRIDAY 12 DECEMBER

1

Bad things sometimes happened when you least expected them.

So, as far as Morwenna Mutton was concerned, today was just another ordinary Cornish winter's day. The skies over Seal Bay were already dark indigo. The raw wind from the sea buffeted her face as jangling music burst from shop doorways. It reminded her that Christmas was less than two weeks away. Typically, she hadn't bought a single present or eaten a solitary mince pie yet.

Gaudy lights flashed in windows and jovial plastic Santas twinkled on rooftops. Even the post boxes had all been decorated for Christmas. This year, the same as every year, an anonymous person gifted in the art of crochet had covered all the post boxes in Seal Bay with little woollen Santas clutching a wine glass in one hand and an envelope in the other. No-one in Seal Bay had any idea who made them. It was a Seal Bay mystery. Last year, Morwenna remembered, she was asked to sleuth who the phantom crocheter was. Someone had even accused her of making them, but it definitely wasn't her. She couldn't knit for toffee.

It was hard to escape the fact that Seal Bay was in festive

mood, even though Morwenna hadn't caught up with the Christmas spirit yet. Elowen was bursting with excitement though. Her mittened hand clutched Morwenna's cold one as they walked from the primary school towards the Proper Ansom Tearoom. She had started to skip, an irregular hop and a jump, her dark curls bouncing. Her eyes shone as the words tumbled from her mouth; she was desperate to talk about all the exciting things that had happened that day.

'I've got to sing a solo in "Away in a Manger". Ms Stark says I'm the best singer in the class. Lots better than Britney.'

'Did she really say that, Elowen?' Morwenna asked lightly. Now Elowen was seven, fibs had become one of her mischievous habits. Thankfully, it had replaced her incessant request for a dog. And that, in turn, had replaced her obsession with her invisible friend, Oggy, and the purple knitted toy, Oggy Two.

She was growing up too fast. Morwenna smiled; she'd be bringing boys home next. Then the trouble would really start.

'Well, she didn't say that exactly, Grandma. Ms Stark said I had a loud voice, but that's nearly the same as a good one, isn't it?'

'I suppose it depends who's listening.' Morwenna changed the subject. 'How's football going?'

'Great. I'm the best centre forward. Coach has got us playing mixed teams. I like tackling Billy Crocker. I score lots of goals when I play against Billy because he can't run fast. Grandad comes to watch me. You should come, Grandma.'

'Perhaps I should.' Morwenna's mind drifted to Ruan, her ex. She hadn't seen him for a few days, despite him living across the road.

In truth, her emotions were still in boomerang mode since what happened back in the summer. Her feelings had shifted up dramatically to the next notch; she fiercely wanted to hang onto her independence, but there were moments with Ruan when her heart knocked ferociously.

There were these strange echoes of the past, when he'd been the person she cared for most in the world. Before the arguments, before the big split.

She didn't understand it at all.

And anyway, men were nothing but trouble. She'd tell Elowen that one day. Of course, Tamsin knew that already.

'Sorry, what was that, my bewty?' Morwenna asked. Elowen was pulling at her hand, drawing her attention to something in a shop window. The door to The Celtic Knot gift shop was open. Becca Hawkins, Tamsin's best friend, was already doing great Christmas business.

'Can we go in and look at presents? I want to get something.'

'We're nearly home,' Morwenna said.

Elowen scuffed her shoes on the ground. 'I need some money.'

'You need to earn money, Elowen. It doesn't come free,' Morwenna said firmly. They were a few seconds' stroll from the tearoom.

Elowen held back and made a face. 'If I had a proper dad, he'd give me pocket money.'

Morwenna took her granddaughter's hand gently. 'Let's go home. You can have a warm drink and a mince pie, and we'll do your homework.'

'I hate mince pies.' Elowen sniffed. Changing the subject hadn't worked. 'I wish I had a dad.'

'I wish I had one.' Morwenna regretted the words as soon as they came from her mouth. She hadn't seen or heard of Freddie Quick since she was four years old.

Elowen wasn't listening. 'Other people in my class have a dad.

Maya Buvač has a dad. Britney Taylor has a dad. Billy Crocker has two dads. Why can't I have one?'

'We'll talk about it when we get inside.' Morwenna was playing for time.

Elowen pulled Morwenna's arm to get her attention. 'When I ask Mummy, she says everyone has a biological daddy, but she left mine behind in the Caribbean when she went on holiday.'

'Well, you can ask your mum again later.'

'She said she'll tell me when I'm older, but I'm seven already.'

'You need to be patient and wait until she's ready.'

'I hate being patient. I want to know what his name is. I want to see a photo of him. And I want to go to the Caribbean and meet him.'

'We'll talk about it in good time,' Morwenna said. They had reached the Proper Ansom Tearoom. The doorbell clanged as Morwenna pushed the door open.

'I know. But I bet if I ask Great-Grandma, she'll tell me now.'

Morwenna knew Lamorna had no idea about Elowen's father. No one did, except Tamsin. It had been tacitly decided not to ask.

'Let's get a hot drink.' Morwenna ushered Elowen inside and watched as she rushed towards the counter where Tamsin was filling mugs. Morwenna looked around. There were twinkling fairy lights in the window. A red sign flashed Merry Christmas on the door. A small tree hid in the corner, the plastic one she'd bought last year. Several people were huddled around tables over drinks, talking loudly.

Tamsin came over and hugged Morwenna, who sank down gratefully at an empty table.

Tamsin said, 'You look shattered.'

'Today's been busy.' Morwenna wrapped her fingers around the steaming mug Tamsin placed in front of her. 'Preparations for tonight are full on.'

'The writer's talk?'

'Pawly Yelland.'

'Have you sold many tickets?'

'It's a total sell-out, Tam. I've got to be back there in an hour or so, to set up mince pies and urns.'

'Carole and Vic are going. I'll look after Britney. She and Elowen will play in her room.' Tamsin glanced towards Elowen, who was helping herself to a banana. She picked up on Morwenna's mood. 'Was Elowen OK on the way home?'

'Yes. She's a little heller though.'

'It was good of you to pick her up.'

'She's been asking about her dad.'

'Oh?' Tamsin froze. 'She said something to me earlier this week. I thought I'd fobbed her off.'

'She's like a dog with a bone.'

'She is,' Tamsin admitted. 'I didn't know where to start. I just said he's best forgotten.'

'She was asking to see photos.'

'I don't think I have any,' Tamsin said enigmatically. 'Anyway, he was a bad holiday fling. A biological father, nothing more. Oh, Mum, I meant to ask,' Tamsin changed the subject quickly, 'have you got your costume for tomorrow night?'

'The Pengellens' party?' Morwenna shook her head. 'I'd forgotten about it, what with this Pawly talk. I'll find something, like a pair of reindeer antlers and a red nose.'

'Becca and I are going to town on our costumes.' Tamsin was suddenly animated. 'It's going to be brilliant. Half of Seal Bay are going. I love Pengellen Manor. The view from the windows across the top of that cliff is incredible, apparently. And they'll put on a big show. Money's no object.'

Morwenna looked around. 'How's business?'

'Not bad. Zach's mince pies are selling faster than they come out the oven. I'm doing a pumpkin latte. Imogen's back from uni soon and she'll take on the waitressing.'

'So you won't need my help. That's good.' Morwenna put her head in her hands. 'Maybe I'll start to feel Christmassy soon.' Her expression suggested that she doubted it.

'Dad's going to the Pengellen fancy-dress too,' Tamsin said meaningfully. 'Perhaps he'll give us all a lift.'

'I might just not go.' Morwenna felt her spirits sink. She had no idea why. Perhaps it was too early to feel Christmassy. Perhaps the mention of Ruan reminded her of happy Christmases long ago.

'It'll be great. Mince pies, wine, dancing under the mistletoe.'

'I used to love mistletoe...' Morwenna looked up. 'And who are you thinking of sharing mistletoe with? Eh?'

Tamsin laughed a bit too loudly. 'Any random. It's Christmas after all, Mum.'

Morwenna was about to tell her daughter that it was snogging randoms in the Caribbean that had led to Elowen being born. She thought better of it. Tamsin was twenty-nine, a single parent, devoted to Elowen. She hadn't had it easy either, running a business, juggling childcare. She deserved to let her hair down.

Morwenna was full of sympathy. 'So – who are you dressing up as?'

'Becca and I are Cinderellas, before and after. She's the one in tatters and I'm the princess at the ball.'

'Of course you are,' Morwenna said. Elowen clearly took inspiration from her mother.

'And Grandma's going as the fairy godmother.'

Morwenna covered a smile. Lamorna wasn't much better. Any excuse to glam up. Morwenna wondered if the love of flaunting oneself had missed a generation. Her mother had wanted her to go as a tinselly fairy too, but she'd be happier going dressed as something less ostentatious, something funny like a Christmas pudding. The truth was, her own glitz and glam extended to her favourite rainbow leggings, a knitted cardigan in the design of a Cornish flag and the funky wetsuit she'd had her eye on in Quilkin's. She dressed to please herself, not to attract attention.

Morwenna finished her tea. 'I'd better be going, Tam. I'm walking back. I left the bike up at the house. Brenda will be hungry.' She sighed. 'That hill's hell in the dark.'

'Ring Dad. He'll come down and give you a lift.'

'No, I won't,' Morwenna didn't want to depend on Ruan. She had an idea he'd be at the talk tonight. So many people would be there. Pawly was discussing his new book, due to be published next year. It was called *More Hidden Secrets of Seal Bay*. The event promised to be popular – Pawly had implied that he had a few secrets to share.

Morwenna probably wouldn't get time to talk to Ruan. Anyway, Louise's Steve would give her a lift home at the end of the evening.

Stretching tired muscles, she struggled into her coat, a purple duffel with a big hood. Tamsin had moved back to the counter, taking customers' payments. Elowen waved a quick goodbye and disappeared upstairs to the flat.

Morwenna picked up her bag, an old favourite knitted in the shape of a chicken, and made for the door. It pinged as she pushed forward into the biting wind that made her eyes water, then she picked her way through the darkness towards the hill that led to Harbour Cottages.

2

The evening began normally, with lots of bustle. Morwenna had no idea of the tangle of events that might follow.

There was an air of expectancy in the library. The space filled quickly, and people were talking in hushed voices. Morwenna stood by the table heaped with mince pies and clotted cream, watching more guests arrive.

The library had been decked out with twinkling lights, a tall festive tree in the corner and a teddy bear in a Santa Claus outfit reading a book. Holly leaves and mistletoe berries gleaming like pearls were tied with red ribbons over the stockroom door. Several library tables had been pushed together for refreshments, with an arrangement of cups and saucers, a steaming urn with a rattling lid. Susan and Barb Grundy from the pop-up charity shop heaved another table next to Morwenna and began to lay out piles of woollen offerings: hats, gloves, scarves, toys.

Barb winked. 'All right, maid? We thought we'd join you. It's all for the Lifeboats.'

'We whacked the prices up,' Susan cackled. 'For Christmas.'

'I think we should whack them down again,' Barb said glumly.

'The other fundraisers in the shop, the Christmas cards and confectionary, are selling more than we are.'

Susan looked unsure. 'The knit-your-own-cake patterns are going well.'

'Not as well as the Christmas willy sweets.' Barb groaned. 'At least all the money goes to the Lifeboats.'

Morwenna decided to help out. 'I could do with a scarf. How much is that purple and green one?'

'Twelve pounds,' Barb said, ever the businesswoman.

'Giss on! It's ten quid to you, Morwenna,' Susan interrupted. 'You can wear it after the swim on Sunday.'

'You're on.' Morwenna reached into her chicken bag for her purse as Susan wound the scarf around her neck. 'Here's fifteen. Keep the change.'

Morwenna looked around. The library was filling up with recognisable faces, and a few she didn't know. Louise, neat in a smart suit, was showing Julian and Pippa Pengellen to their seats in the second row. Her husband, Steve Piper, sat at the front, shoulders hunched, clearly feeling like a spare part. Damien Woon from the boatyard and Beverley, his partner, were holding hands at the back. The entire Buvač family had arrived apart from Tommy, who was touring with Spriggan Travelling Theatre Company as their technician. Carole and Vic Taylor were there; Morwenna could hear Vic complaining that he was missing the sport on TV to listen to some half-baked author banging on about Cornwall. Carole shushed him, her face red.

Morwenna gazed around for Pawly Yelland. He hadn't arrived yet. It was seven twenty, and the talk was due to start at half past.

'He's cutting it a bit fine, Pawly.' Susan read Morwenna's thoughts.

'He is.' Morwenna noticed Louise's eyes move towards the door for the third time in five minutes.

'I hear he's one for the ladies,' Barb said. 'Perhaps he'll be here in a minute with lipstick all over his face.'

'You've been reading those bodice-rippers again.' Susan nudged her sister playfully.

Morwenna didn't like listening to local gossip. She knew Pawly was unmarried. He'd had a few difficult relationships. She remembered Irina Bacheva from Bay Radio and felt suddenly sad.

'Pawly's a big flirt. He bought a woolly hat off me and he couldn't keep his eyes off my cleavage.' Barb folded her arms across her chest.

'Are you looking for a fifty-something toyboy, Barb?' Susan cackled.

'You're only jealous because he wasn't eyeing you up.' Barb rearranged the pile of gloves again. Her neck had flushed a strawberry pink.

Morwenna watched the last members of the audience straggle in: the local GP and her husband; Jenny Stark, Elowen's teacher. Beattie Harris, the florist, waved as she hurried in, followed by Sheila from Walters and Moffatt solicitors. There were only a few empty seats left.

Donald Stewart, in a tartan suit that smelled of mothballs, appeared by Morwenna's side. He put his mouth close to her ear. 'Pawly's not arrived yet and it's almost half past.'

'Perhaps he's been held up,' Morwenna said encouragingly.

'Louise has texted him three times.' Donald frowned. 'He's going to let us down.'

'I expect he's just late,' Morwenna said.

'A novel was on the table, left open today.' Donald's voice was morbidly low. '*The Man who Disappeared* by Clare Morrall.'

'Coincidence.'

'No, Morwenna, Lady Elizabeth has left us a message.'

'The library ghost?' Susan was quick to catch on. 'What's she saying?'

'Pawly isn't coming tonight,' Donald said, wide eyed. 'Perhaps he's met with a terrible accident.'

'He'll be here any minute,' Morwenna said.

Louise rushed over. 'It's half past. Shall I make an announcement? I could say Pawly's running late.'

'He'll be here,' Morwenna sounded more confident than she felt.

'What will we do if he doesn't come? Steve already wants to go home. He's been in a foul temper all evening. He's overworked, what with all the extra Christmas deliveries.' Louise looked around nervously.

'I'll do a speech about the Lifeboats, if you like,' Susan said.

'And we'll ask for donations,' Barb added.

'Or you could do a talk about being a sleuth?' Louise tugged Morwenna's arm.

'I'm hardly a sleuth.' Morwenna shook her head. 'I've just helped Jane out a couple of times.'

'He's really late,' Louise whispered.

There was a noise in the doorway, someone blustering in. Morwenna saw Ruan and Pawly. Pawly was laughing, his shoulder bag swinging awkwardly as he bumped into the refreshments table, almost knocking over a Victoria sponge.

'Sorry I'm late, Louise,' he spluttered, and his breath smelled of whisky.

'Are you ready to start? Or do you need a coffee first?' Louise asked worriedly. She could smell the alcohol too.

'I was born ready, Louise.' Pawly grabbed a mince pie from the table and wrapped an arm around her. 'Lead me to my doom, darlin'.'

'I put you at the desk at the front.' Louise looked uncomfortable as she removed his arm from her shoulder. He lurched towards her unsteadily and she noticed his empty bag. 'Haven't you brought books? Notes?'

'I'll improvise.' Pawly took her arm again.

Ruan leaned towards Morwenna. He was wearing a dark jacket, and he smelled of something sweet that might have been aftershave. He said, 'Pawly was in The Smugglers. I brought him over.'

'Is he drunk?' Morwenna asked.

'No, he's had a whisky or two, but he'll be all right.'

'Dutch courage? He doesn't seem the nervous type,' Morwenna observed.

'He had a bust-up with a girlfriend.' Ruan met her eyes, his own twinkling. 'He was winding up for a long session.'

At the front table, Pawly was stuffing another whole mince pie into his mouth. His legs appeared to give way, and he tumbled back into the seat. Louise's wide smile covered how nervous she was; Morwenna knew the look well.

Louise beamed in the direction of the audience, gave a small cough for attention, and said 'Good evening, everyone. It's my pleasure to welcome you here tonight and—'

'Pleasure,' Pawly guffawed. '"Pleasure is the only thing one should live for; nothing ages like happiness."'

'Oscar Wilde,' Morwenna whispered to Ruan and he gave a complicit wink. He smelled lovely.

Louise tried again. 'So, many of you know our local author, Pawly Yelland, who writes books about the history of Cornwall. We have several copies of his last one, *Hidden Secrets of Seal Bay,* but I'm sure you're all looking forward to buying a signed copy of your own.'

Pawly grinned sheepishly. His bag was almost empty. He'd forgotten to bring any books. He delved in and brought out a thin jotter, pretending to sift through the pages. There was nothing in it.

Louise gazed around the audience. 'Pawly's currently writing a follow-up – *More Hidden Secrets of Seal Bay*. Although he's originally from Redruth, Pawly's a resident here and he's always shown a great interest in our library.'

'And its ghost,' Donald added with an encouraging nod.

'So, he's been researching the bay's history. I know Julian and Pippa—' Louise indicated the Pengellens, who were sitting near the front '—have given him access to Pengellen Manor, where he's had a very useful time researching the last few centuries.'

'And the present one,' Pawly added enigmatically.

Louise carried on with her introduction. 'Pawly's a graduate of Bristol University, and he has lectured at UWE, Bath and Plymouth.'

Morwenna met Ruan's gaze, both thinking of her friend Irina. Pawly had met her at Plymouth when she'd been a student and he a visiting lecturer. Their brief relationship hadn't ended well.

Louise was coming to the end of her speech. 'But I'm delighted he's here tonight to tell us about his book – and, of course, to sign copies.'

Morwenna noticed Pawly staring into his bag again to see if there were any books. She knew there weren't.

'Please give a warm Seal Bay welcome to Pawly Yelland,' Louise said, and she was met by a round of polite applause.

Pawly stood up for a moment then he sat down with a plonk as if he thought better of it. For a moment, he gaped ahead, as if he'd forgotten what to say. He wiped a hand across his brow. Morwenna thought he might say something inappropriate. Her instinct was right.

'Well, thank you for coming out tonight in the bitter cold to this dusty old library when I'm sure you'd all rather be down the pub. I know I would.'

There was a trickle of polite laughter. Vic Taylor could be heard saying, 'I'm missing the football for this.'

'I've just come from The Smugglers.' Pawly glanced towards Ruan for support. 'Talking of smugglers, that's what my research has been about. The pub itself was a hive of illegal activity in Seal Bay in the seventeen hundreds. John Carter – the famous eighteenth-century pirate from Perranporth – used to do his deals there. Shipwrecks were often discovered on Seal Bay beach. The local clergy were not exempt from illicit activities either.'

Pawly looked around and seemed surprised that the audience were rapt. He was gaining confidence. 'Gangs of wreckers and pirates operated on the Cornish coast in the early nineteenth century. Cornwall was a haven for smugglers due to its rocky coves, sheltered bays and wild, tumultuous waves. Seal Bay was a popular location for the smuggling of silks, tea, tobacco and brandy into England. You've all seen Pengellen Manor, on Pettarock Head. Did you know it was built between 1540 and 1545 to protect Seal Bay against invasion from the French and the Spanish? The house was originally called *Chi an Mor*, the house by the sea. The Pengellen family changed the name – Pengellens have lived in the manor house since the sixteenth century. Oh yes – the Pengellens... ha ha.' He nodded towards Julian, wiping a hand across his brow. 'They've let me delve into the history of the manor and I've uncovered a few sordid little facts. It might surprise you to know that Caradoc Pengellen, born in 1732, was one of the most notorious smugglers in Cornwall.'

There was a light gasp of surprise from the audience.

'Oh, yes. So, it's time for some home truths,' Pawly continued. 'Caradoc Pengellen was a nasty piece of work. He clashed with the Customs men on countless occasions. He and his team were responsible for wrecking, stealing and even murder. It's all on record, Julian.' Pawly had a gleam in his eye. 'The Pengellens are a dodgy bunch. It'll be in the book. And not much has changed, has it, Julian, mate?' Pawly was staring into the audience. 'Your deals in London, eh? I mean, what exactly does "venture capitalism" mean, Julian? We all know that you get into bed with some bent businessmen – and women, probably.'

There was a louder gasp from the audience. Julian Pengellen said, 'That's nonsense.'

Pippa made an exclamation that sounded like, 'Don't be silly.'

'Ah.' Pawly turned his attention to Pippa. 'Mrs Pengellen. Let's talk about you, shall we? Butter wouldn't melt. All the charity work you do. They should give you an award. Perhaps they will. But what about your surname before you made this lucrative marriage to Julian here? You were a Lambert.'

'Everyone knows I was Pippa Lambert,' Pippa said quickly.

'A Seal Bay family that goes back years. In fact, your ancestor Edmund Lambert was a landowner who benefited from the slave trade. He had hundreds of slaves, a staunch anti-abolitionist. In 1832, he wrote a defence entitled *Pledges on Colonial Slavery*.'

Somebody's voice was heard to whisper, 'That's disgusting.'

Pippa said, 'I was aware of Edmund's activities, Pawly. But I can hardly be held responsible for my ancestors, can I? All the same, I try to redress the balance by my work for—'

'What about Pengellen Manor?' Pawly interrupted, a look of revulsion on his face. 'A place of privilege and power. Oh, it's very easy, Mrs Pengellen, to offer mealy-mouthed excuses for your racist ancestors. But—' he turned to the audience '—it'll be in my next book, all the juicy goss. *More Hidden Secrets of Seal Bay*. And it won't be just about the past, either. Oh, no. There are plenty of stories about Seal Bay today that will raise a few eyebrows, believe you me.' His eyes flickered around the room. 'You may all think you're safe but—' His eyes fell on Damien Woon, at the back of the room. 'Woon's boatyard, for instance. There are a few tales I could tell about that place and—' Pawly seemed to notice the audience, shocked faces, open mouths. 'This is the bit where the author says you'll have to wait to read it. But I won't spare the blushes. This next book will be a hellraiser.'

'Pawly, could you tell us about the ghost of Lady Elizabeth?' Donald was trying to change the subject. 'I'm fascinated by stories of her haunting the library. And her curse.'

'It's all hogwash.' Pawly laughed. 'I'd like to see her curse me.'

Louise stepped in professionally. 'Well, Mr Yelland. Pawly. I wonder if we should pause for – for refreshments.' She signalled to Morwenna. 'There will be teas, coffees, mince pies. And there's a knitted goods stall, proceeds to the RNLI.'

'I need a slash.' Pawly stumbled to his feet. 'Where's the toilet?' He set off at pace towards the storeroom. Louise rushed after him with the intention of redirecting him. Morwenna watched carefully, ignoring the queue of customers who had thronged to the table. Pawly threw the door open and walked into the dark cupboard. Louise was grabbing at his arm urgently, doing her best to point out that the gents was in the other direction. As she touched him on the shoulder, he whirled round, a sprig of mistletoe in his hand.

'Giss a kiss,' he slobbered, his mouth on hers.

Steve, on the front row, was suddenly wide awake, on his feet, hurtling towards the cupboard, roaring like an angry bull. He grabbed Pawly by his shirt. Morwenna flinched as Steve threw a punch, Louise screamed and Pawly fell.

It happened in slow motion. Blood bloomed like a rose on Pawly's nose as he scrambled up, laughing. 'Well, you can't blame a bloke for trying.'

SATURDAY 13 DECEMBER

3

Lamorna was delighted to hear about the fisticuffs. 'I wish I'd been there. I'd have paid good money to see Steve and Pawly fighting.'

'It was over in a flash. Hang on, Mum – can you just turn round ninety degrees?' Morwenna was kneeling at her mother's feet in her bedroom at Tregenna Gardens, pinning up the hem of the pink tulle skirt. 'No, that's a hundred and eighty – turn back a bit.'

'I will grant your every wish, Cinderella.' Lamorna shot out her arms in a pose as if waving a wand. 'I hope I'll be the only fairy godmother tonight. I don't want anyone stealing my thunder.' She looked down. 'What are you going as?'

'I don't know yet,' Morwenna said. 'I could wear a dressing gown and go as Scrooge?'

Lamorna had an idea. 'Why don't you put a raincoat on and go as Miss Marple? You could carry one of those big magnifying glasses.'

'And how is Miss Marple Christmassy? The theme's Christmas.' Morwenna laughed. 'I might find a big box, put a ribbon on my head and go as a present.'

'You should wear something sexy. And take some mistletoe. Ruan's coming.' Lamorna shot her a look.

'It was mistletoe that caused the problems last night.' Morwenna decided that was the end of the subject of Ruan or romance. Lamorna hadn't given up.

'Do you ever hear from that plastic surgeon? The one you were going out with in the summer?' When Morwenna didn't reply, Lamorna continued. 'Pam Truscott's brother. The one who took you out on his fancy boat.'

'Barnaby's in Barbados. He and Pam bought a house. He's thinking of retiring. Pam's son, Simon, works in a bar out there.'

Lamorna's eyes twinkled with mischief. 'Didn't he invite you to go with him?'

'You know he did.'

'Why didn't you go?'

Morwenna knew exactly why. She'd agreed to go, at first. She'd convinced herself that she needed a break and that it would help her decide how she felt about Barnaby. Then Ruan had kissed her on the beach and in an instant, she'd changed her mind.

She'd spent the last five months trying to work out why.

Barnaby had been very sweet about it. He understood that she needed time to work out her feelings. He'd left for Christ Church, and she hadn't heard from him since.

'I didn't really fancy Barbados,' Morwenna lied. 'Seal Bay has everything they have.'

'Except the weather.' Lamorna was unconvinced. 'Well, we have this Christmas bash at Pengellen Manor tonight.' She thought for a moment. 'Do you think Pawly Yelland will turn up after what happened?'

'The library punch-up?' Morwenna made a face. 'I'm nearly done with your hem.'

'So did he apologise?'

'Pawly? Yes, he did. Steve stood there glaring and poor Louise was nearly hysterical.'

'Did the police come down?'

'No, Jane was on duty. But Pawly and Steve shook hands, although from the look on Steve's face, Pawly's not forgiven. If looks could kill.'

'Why?' Lamorna said mischievously. 'A Christmas snog under the mistletoe never hurt anybody.'

'Louise was furious. Pawly was drunk – he insulted half the audience. Apparently, he's having a bad time with a relationship.'

'Oh?' Lamorna was all ears.

'Ruan said that's why Pawly was drinking. He'd had a tiff with someone.'

'Ruan was there?' Lamorna arched an eyebrow.

'Yes. I always talk to Ruan, Mum. He's Tam's father. He lives across the road.' Morwenna made a humph noise and changed the subject. 'Are you coming swimming tomorrow?'

'It's too bleddy cold.' Lamorna grunted.

'I might buy a new wetsuit. I could get you one?' Morwenna asked hopefully.

'My hip's playing up.'

Morwenna laughed. 'When did you ever actually get in the water?'

'It'll give me arthritis. Gout.' It was Lamorna's turn to change the subject. 'Are you all done? I've got two pasties warming.'

* * *

Later, they sat at the table in Lamorna's living room sharing lunch. Lamorna still wanted to talk about the antics in the library.

'So, has Pawly always been single?'

'I don't know much about his past, Mum, except that he has disastrous relationships. Irina Bacheva had a fling with him once.'

'Oh?' Lamorna shook her head. 'It was a shame, what happened to her.'

'It was.' Morwenna took a bite of pasty. She wasn't really hungry now.

'What time are you calling for me tonight?'

'Ruan's giving us all a lift – me, you, Tam and Becca.'

'Who's babysitting Elowen?'

'She's having a sleepover at Britney Taylor's.'

'Is Carole looking after her?'

'They've got a babysitter.'

'Good luck to her, looking after those two girls. Elowen's a right handful.'

'She's adorable.' Morwenna exhaled sharply. 'You know she's been asking about her father.'

'Well, it was bound to happen.' Lamorna was halfway through the pasty. 'Tam doesn't ever say who he was, not to anyone.' Her eyes lit up. 'You're a sleuth. Can't you find out?'

'If Tam doesn't want to tell us, I won't ask.'

'I know but – eight years ago, she goes to Jamaica with her friends and comes back in the pudding club, and she's never said a word. The father probably has no idea that he has a child back in Cornwall. I think he must have been a local though.'

'What makes you think that?'

'Just a hunch: if she's left him behind in Jamaica, he won't come to look for her, will he?' Lamorna shrugged. 'Tam and I have no luck with men. There was that dreadful man she was engaged to, Jack—'

'Don't.' Morwenna shuddered at the memory of Jack Greenwood. She wanted to forget the whole episode. 'We Mutton maids are cursed when it comes to men.'

'I am. What with Morrie Edwards who asked me to marry him eight times, and Harry Woon who could snog for England, and your dad, Freddie Quick, all the charm of an alley cat on heat, here today and gone tomorrow. Then I lost Daniel.' Lamorna looked upset. 'And then there's you.'

'Me?' Morwenna asked.

'You've got two men in love with you and you're too stubborn to pick either of them.'

'Maybe you're right, Mum,' Morwenna said. 'But what about Elowen? She's desperate to find out about her dad.'

'You'll have to talk to Tam.'

'Why me?' Morwenna made a face.

'You're her mother.'

'What about grandmothers stepping in to help?'

'I'm no role model.' Lamorna finished her pasty. 'You could ask Ruan.'

'The only thing I ever heard Ruan say on the matter of Elowen's father is that he'd like to kill him. And Ruan's a pacifist,' Morwenna said. 'I'll sort it out.'

Lamorna pushed her plate away. 'I'm sure you'll find a way to talk to Tam. Now how about a bit of pudding? I've got some trifle in the fridge.'

Morwenna shook her head. 'No, thanks, I'd best get off. I said I'd pop into the tearoom on the way home. And I'd better work out what I'm wearing tonight.'

* * *

It was six o'clock and Morwenna still had no idea what she'd do for a costume. The afternoon had been busy. Now she was flaked out on the sofa with her feet up, Brenda purring on her knee. It was pure bliss.

The phone rang, interrupting her moment's calm, and she snatched it up.

'Hi, Louise.'

Brenda looked up quizzically, as if wanting to know the latest on the Pawly saga.

'Umm. No, I think it was a great evening, memorable, yes, I agree that everyone got their money's worth. What?' Morwenna listened for a moment. 'No, Louise, no one thinks you're having a fling with Pawly. Why would they?' She held the phone closer to her ear. 'Oh, Steve doesn't believe for a minute that you and Pawly – yes, he was just being protective. No, I don't think Pawly will show up after everything he said about Julian and Pippa.'

Louise was talking nineteen to the dozen. Morwenna pushed back her silver hair and adjusted Brenda on her knee.

'Donald said what?' She stifled a laugh. 'Well, I'm sure Pawly didn't intend to insult Lady Eliz—Yes, I'll see you there. What? No, I've no idea what I'm wearing – oh, right, Steve's Father Christmas? Well, it is the season of goodwill – ha ha, right, I'll see you both later.'

The call ended and Morwenna reached out a hand to stroke Brenda's fur. As the cat rolled onto her back to have her tummy rubbed, Morwenna closed her eyes in an attempt to regain her moment of peace.

The phone rang again and Morwenna almost knocked it from the sofa arm.

'Hi, Jane, yes, how's work? Oh, right. The Christmas rush hasn't started yet?' Morwenna relaxed into the sofa, listening to Jane monologuing about how her day had been mostly paperwork, how Rick had been grumbling about deadlines and how Blessed had brought in several teenage shoplifters and read them the Riot Act.

Morwenna asked, 'Are you going to the party? Oh, Blessed's going as what? Oh, you're Dick Whittington and she's the cat? And Rick's going as a – no, he isn't! Giss on! A parsnip? I've got to see that.'

Morwenna sat up. 'No, I've no idea. I'll see you there. Yes, I'm looking forward to it.' There was a knock at the door. 'Sorry, Jane, I have to go – it's like Clapham Junction here. Yes, later, right.'

Morwenna put the phone down and eased Brenda from her knee. The knock came again, a steady thump, thump. She knew who was there before she opened it.

'Ruan.'

She noticed that warm glimmer in his eye that usually meant he had a surprise for her. He held out a brown paper bag. 'A little bird told me you had no costume for tonight.'

'Oh?'

'Lamorna rang me. I brought you this.'

'What is it?'

'Open it.'

Morwenna peered inside. 'It's all red material.'

'That's because it's a Santa costume.'

'With a beard?'

'No beard. Just a hat and a jacket and trousers. Ms Santa doesn't have a beard.'

'Oh, that's kind of you, Ruan.' She met his eyes and time ticked for a moment. 'What are you going as?'

'Santa Claus. We'll be a pair. His and hers Santa suits.'

'Ah. Well... I expect we won't be the only ones.' Morwenna searched for something witty to say, but nothing came. 'Thanks.'

'I'll pick you up later.'

'Are you sure you don't mind driving us all?'
'Not at all.'
'I'll see you.'
'Right.'
'Right.'
'Bye, then.'
'Bye.'

Morwenna closed the door and clutched the brown paper bag tightly. That was typical of Ruan. Generous. Practical. Thoughtful. She made her way back to the warmth of the living room. Brenda was staring at her with questioning green eyes.

'What?' Morwenna asked the cat. She was suddenly feeling in the mood for the Pengellens' party, now she had something to wear.

Her instincts told her that it was a mistake to expect everything to go smoothly, that Christmas parties had the potential for the unexpected, but she ignored the voice in her head. Instead, she began to hum a little tune.

'It's Beginning to Look a Lot Like Christmas...'

4

Ruan sat in the front of his van with Lamorna, who was in a party mood, flouncing in her fairy godmother dress and tiara, waving her wand. In the back, Morwenna was squashed between the two Cinderellas. Becca's ragged Cinders was sporting a low-necked tattered number and Tamsin had gone to town with the fluffy pink princess theme.

Morwenna's Santa suit was far too big, but a belt and a pair of boots had somehow brought the look together. She'd do, although she thought Ruan looked a much more eye-catching Santa Claus.

Ruan drove up the winding hill that led to the top of Pettarock Head. Pengellen Manor was accessed through tall iron gates, along a stone drive, an enormous Gothic-looking house with arches and tall windows, turrets and a tower. The impressive frontage was illuminated by butter-coloured lights that led to the oak door.

Becca caught her breath. 'This place is awesome.'

Tyres crunched against gravel as Ruan brought the van to a halt next to a line of cars. Everyone clambered out and hurried towards the door. A cold wind blew in from the headland. The sound of the sea whispered from beyond the cliffs. Above, the sky was black velvet with milky clouds.

Inside, music trickled from a far room, mellow Christmas hits. Tamsin led the way through the vast hall with its chequered floor, past a sweeping staircase and tall pillars into a dimly lit room with high ceilings and heavy velvet drapes. People were clustered in groups, and there was light chatter and tinkling of glasses.

Pippa Pengellen, wearing a layered green dress and a delicate little pointed hat with twinkling lights, rushed over, grasping Morwenna's hand. 'I'm so glad you could all come. Down the stairs to the left, you'll find food and drink in the drawing room. Julian's in charge. Help yourself.'

'Thanks.' Morwenna spotted someone who might be Rick Tremayne standing in the corner with someone who might be Sally, but she hardly recognised them. Rick was wearing a big white parsnip costume with a crest of leaves on his head. Sally was dressed in something similar, but orange. Of course, she was a carrot. Morwenna waved greetings, reminding herself that she and Rick had a sort of understanding now, and was relieved when he waved back.

There were some incredible costumes. One woman was dressed as a Christmas pudding; there were several Miss Santas with white fluffy hats and short red skirts; there was a man covered in Christmas wrapping paper. Morwenna counted two Christmas crackers, three turkeys, five snowmen and one man in a costume patterned with Brussels sprouts.

There were several more Santa Clauses, including one with a piggyback Rudolph stitched between his legs. Elves were everywhere, smart ones, sexy ones and grotesque ones, piskies and spriggans. One young man wore a Rudolphkini: antlers and a strategically placed pouch. He didn't appear to feel the cold.

Lamorna looked Pippa up and down, taking in the layers of net. Her dress was expensive. 'What are you supposed to be?'

'A Christmas Tree,' Pippa laughed, and pressed a button on her shoulder. Her dress twinkled.

'Lovely. I think I'll get a drink,' Lamorna said and took off towards the stairs, followed by the two Cinderellas.

Morwenna said, 'Shall I get you a something, Ruan?'

'Yes, please,' He pointed to a couple dressed as Mary and Joseph. 'There's Damien over there, with Bev. I need to talk to him.'

'Right,' Morwenna said, and was on her way. She paused to gaze at the collection of portraits on the walls, Pengellens through the ages. Morwenna recalled what Pawly had said last night about the Pengellens' history, all pirates and smugglers.

She reached a vast room with dark panels lit by candles, where a dozen people in festive clothes were helping themselves to food and drink. Dry heat blazed from the roaring fire in the inglenook. Julian Pengellen was playing host, dressed suavely as a snowman in a top hat and dapper white suit.

Morwenna heard a happy shriek. Louise, an elf with scarlet lipstick, tugging a grumpy Santa, made a beeline for her. She raised a glass.

'The best champagne. Would you believe it? Poor Steve's driving.'

'Fruit punch.' Steve held up a cup of pale liquid to prove his point.

'And that's the only punch we need around here tonight.' Louise was clearly a bit tipsy.

'I told you, Lou.' Steve looked chastised. 'I'm not having that silly tuss kissing my wife.'

'It's in the past, Steve,' Louise trilled. 'Have you seen Jane and

Blessed? They've come as Dick Whittington and the cat. And Donald's dressed in a kilt.'

'As long as Yelland doesn't show up.' Steve frowned into his fruit cup.

Louise tugged his arm. 'We just had a stroll upstairs. There's a balcony and a tower and you can see the bay.'

'I might take a look,' Morwenna said as Louise pulled Steve away. She approached Julian Pengellen, who held up a bottle of bubbly.

'Morwenna. Welcome. Moët?'

'I don't mind if I do.' Morwenna watched the fizz rise as he poured. A wedding ring with a single diamond gleamed on his finger.

'Help yourself to nibbles,' Julian said.

'I will.' Morwenna picked up a small pastry. 'Mmm. Did you make these?'

'Outside caterers,' Julian said. 'I don't cook much. Although if Pawly shows his face, I might make an exception.' He winked. 'After that ridiculous speech yesterday, I'd give him a poisoned mince pie.'

'He didn't cover himself in glory,' Morwenna said.

'I have to say, I feel betrayed after opening my home to him. Pippa's furious. She works hard with her charities and she could get recognition for it. But that damned fool might have put a spoke in the wheel.'

'Oh?' Morwenna asked.

Julian held out the plate of canapés. 'I've already said too much.'

'No, thanks.' Morwenna recalled his comment about poisoned pies. 'But I'll take a fruit punch for Ruan, if I may.'

'Be my guest.' Julian pointed to the glasses. 'I'm on drinks duty for the duration.'

Morwenna turned and almost cannoned into a tall blonde woman wearing a flimsy white dress, feathered wings and a gold halo.

She said, 'Pam.'

'Morwenna.' Pam Truscott hugged her. 'I hoped we'd bump into each other.'

'I thought you were in Barbados.'

'I'm back.' Pam hugged her again and Morwenna stood on tiptoes to peer over her shoulder to see if anyone was standing behind her.

She thought she'd better ask. 'And Barnaby – is he back too?'

'He's tying up a few loose ends. He'll be here for Christmas. Prospect Bay is heaven. You'd adore it.' Pam stood back and glared momentarily. 'So, what happened between you two last summer?'

'We're just friends.'

'No one's *just* friends,' Pam said bluntly.

'It's complicated.'

'Ah. Well, I'm sure you can meet up and *un*complicate things.' Pam had the look of a woman who always got what she wanted. 'My brother's fond of you.'

'He's a nice man.'

'He's much more than that, and don't you forget it.' Pam tapped her nose. 'I hope we'll be seeing you at Mirador over the festive period.'

'That would be lovely,' Morwenna said, not knowing how to answer the Barnaby question. She took her champagne and Ruan's drink and made a quick exit.

As she paused in the hall, familiar laughter tinkled in her ears. Two Cinderellas were loitering on the bottom step with a smartly dressed Santa Claus and the man in the Brussels sprout suit. It was Tristan Pengellen and his friend Seb, chattering animatedly to Tamsin and Becca. Seb was carrying a bottle of champagne. Morwenna recalled that Becca had a 'thing' for both of them – what had she said? 'I like a bit of posh.' But Tamsin was equally engrossed in a conversation before Tristan led the way up the vast staircase, intent on showing them round his mansion.

Morwenna felt maternal anxiety creeping across her skin and she pushed it away.

They passed a couple coming downstairs: a dark-haired woman in a cute blue and yellow dress, a red bow in her hair, and a man in a green cap, who was taking photos with a digital camera of everyone he passed. The woman paused to say something to the group on the stairs. Her laughter rang out before she and the man (who might have been Peter Pan or Robin Hood) hurried into the main room.

Morwenna watched the party in full swing. Ruan was talking to Damien and Bev. Lamorna was chatting to Louise and Steve, who was still talking about Pawly's antics. Dick Whittington and the cat were in deep conversation with the parsnip and the carrot. Morwenna wondered if the police officers were talking shop. More people had arrived and were bopping to the Christmas tunes, smooching, dad-dancing, boogieing, waving their arms. The man in the Rudolphkini was embracing a blonde female Santa in a ra-ra skirt.

Morwenna noticed Mike Sheridan, one of the DJs at Bay Radio, dressed as a turkey, bopping with a woman who seemed to be wearing a box of stuffing. Pippa was dancing with a woman dressed as Red Riding Hood. A man in a Santa Claus suit burst from the throng, placed himself between Pippa and Red Riding Hood and began wiggling his hips in a most suggestive way.

Morwenna looked closely: it was Pawly.

Pippa looked unimpressed and her friend, a tall woman with smooth dark hair, seemed even more unhappy as Pawly lurched towards her and snogged her as he'd snogged Louise the night before.

'He's sex mad,' Morwenna murmured. 'What's got into him all of a sudden?'

Pawly was all over Red Riding Hood, stuck to her face while she struggled backwards. Pippa looked alarmed. Red Riding Hood slapped Pawly hard and rushed past Morwenna in tears. Pippa followed her, calling out, 'Don't worry, Faye. The man's an arse.'

Pawly reached Morwenna in the doorway, panting. She noticed he had a half-empty bottle of champagne in one hand, a mince pie in the other. She asked kindly, 'Pawly? Are you all right?'

'No.' Encased in a hood and snowy beard, Pawly was sweating. He grasped the door jamb and breathed heavily. 'To be honest, Morwenna, it's not going well.'

'I'm surprised you came,' Morwenna said. 'After last night.'

'I messed up.' Pawly turned to Morwenna and, from what she could see of his face, he looked upset. 'I've let it get to me.'

'Let what get to you?'

'Women. One woman.' Pawly gazed after Red Riding Hood and the frothy Christmas tree. They had disappeared.

'Pippa, you mean?' Morwenna asked.

'Faye.'

'Oh?'

'We had a thing. She meant a lot.'

'You were together?'

'Faye and I, yes. We hooked up at the end of the summer. Hot evenings. Great sex. Then—' Pawly remembered his bottle and took a swig '—I told her I loved her. And she told me that she loved me too, but not in *that* way.'

'What way?' Morwenna frowned. Relationships were complicated.

'She dumped me and went back to her old man. Pippa stuck her nose in and said she'd have me arrested for stalking.'

'I see.'

'I want her back.'

Morwenna shot him a look. 'By getting drunk and trying to snog her face off?'

Pawly looked sorry for himself. 'I've ruined everything.'

'You've drunk too much.' Morwenna stated the obvious. 'Tomorrow's another day. Reset.'

'You're right.' Pawly was still holding himself up against the door.

'Go home, Pawly.'

'Yes. I'll get a taxi. But perhaps before I go, I might just tell Faye that—'

'Go home,' Morwenna said firmly. 'It's for the best.'

Pawly waved the mince pie. 'You have a point. I'll go.'

He lurched forward, almost knocking her backwards, and took off at a lope. Morwenna hoped he was going towards the entrance, but he mumbled something about the toilet, changed direction and began to lumber up the stairs. Morwenna looked at the drinks she held in both hands. She was about to take one to Ruan, when Louise and Steve pushed through the dancers, followed by Lamorna.

Louise said, 'Will you give it a rest, Steve?'

'It makes my blood boil. I could punch his lights out.' Steve was puffing beneath his Santa Claus suit.

Lamorna put her hands on her hips. 'He's just a bleddy fool.'

'Pawly?' Morwenna asked gently.

'Don't mention that man's name,' Steve said crossly. He turned to Louise. 'Will you be all right here for a minute, Lou?'

'Of course.' Louise looked confused. 'Where are you going?'
'For a slash,' Steve said and took off towards the stairs.

5

Ruan was still deep in conversation with Damien. Morwenna handed him a glass of fruit punch. He said, 'We've been talking boats.'

'There's a surprise,' Morwenna replied, her eyes twinkling.

Ruan looked serious. 'I'm thinking of getting a motorboat.'

'What for?' Morwenna asked.

'To do a bit of fishing when I retire,' he said.

'Surely you *stop* fishing.' Morwenna smiled.

'But it would be my own boat, my own fish.'

'That's a good definition of socialism.' Damien laughed.

Beverley had been watching Morwenna steadily. 'Retirement. More free time. Would you two get back together?'

'I don't know.' Morwenna was surprised by Beverley's lack of tact.

'But what about the plastic surgeon you've been dating? I saw you together on his boat. Are you still seeing him?' Beverley asked.

Morwenna thought she was like a dog with a bone. 'Barnaby's in Barbados.'

'Pam's back though,' Ruan said. 'She was just discussing her boat with us.'

'I think she has her eye on you, Ruan.' Beverley was definitely in the mood for stirring things up. 'She invited him on the *Pammy*, Morwenna.'

'She needs a few jobs doing,' Ruan said simply.

'I bet she does,' Beverley said with an expression that suggested something that went beyond sailing. Damien placed a hand on her arm.

'Come on, Bev.'

Morwenna watched him drag her away and in seconds, Bev and Damien were locked in each other's arms, her head against his shoulder. There was no sign of Pawly, although there were several Santas in the room. Carole and Vic Taylor had appeared, wearing matching red and green Christmas cracker costumes with the slogan Taylor Made Motors on them. Carole was dancing energetically, mouthing the words of the song 'I Wish It Could Be Christmas Every Day', while Vic shuffled his feet and looked around to check if anyone was watching him.

Pippa and her friend hadn't reappeared. Steve was nowhere to be seen; Louise was dancing with Lamorna. Morwenna wondered if Ruan would ask her to dance. Instead, he said, 'I was talking to Tam before.'

'Where is she?' Morwenna gazed around at the dancers but couldn't see her daughter.

'She and Becca were with Tristan. I think Becca has a thing for his friend. But there was a bit of an argument.'

'Oh?'

'Tam just told me a few minutes ago. Tristan's ex turned up. She's from Mexico but she lives in London. She came with her photographer. He's a big name apparently. Tristan wanted to know who invited her and the ex got stroppy and said that Pippa had asked her. I think Tristan's taken a fancy to Tam.'

'But Tam's not interested in a boyfriend, not after—' Morwenna pushed Jack Greenwood from her thoughts again.

'Becca can't keep her hands off his friend.'

Morwenna was concerned. 'Elowen's been asking about her real father, Ruan.'

'I know. She mentioned it when I took her to football. We need to ask Tam what she wants us to say.'

'We do. Where do you think she is now?'

Ruan shrugged. 'This is a big house. Lots of rooms. The party's going on all over the place.'

'You never stop worrying about your kids.'

'You don't.' Ruan saw the concern on her face and changed the subject. 'Apparently there's a balcony that looks out over the headland.'

'I bet you can see right across Seal Bay.'

Ruan drained his cup. 'The punch was nice. I might get another one.'

'I'll come with you,' Morwenna said.

Back in the drawing room, people were helping themselves. Julian had disappeared. Ruan pushed his way through the various elves, panto characters and snowmen, coming back with two cups of punch. 'Well. Are you up for a look round?'

'All right.' Morwenna sipped sweet punch.

Ruan pointed to the stairs. 'Come on, let's find that spectacular view.'

Two Santas, one small with a belted suit and the other tall, lean and muscled, walked up the grand staircase side by side. Pengellen portraits watched them from the walls. At the top, the stairs split, one going left and the other right. Ruan raised an eyebrow. 'Which way?'

Morwenna pointed to the left and they walked down a dark corridor, lit only by amber wall lamps. The walls were mahogany panels, and the air smelled somehow ancient. Morwenna's voice was a whisper. 'It's a bit eerie.'

'This place is hundreds of years old,' Ruan said.

Morwenna said, 'I bet it's seen some drama over the centuries.'

'Life, death, love,' Ruan whispered.

They passed a gaping door; inside a light shone, the colour of bronze. A woman's voice could be heard, a man's whisper, a low laugh. Morwenna glimpsed two figures inside on a bed, their arms around each other. She was fairly sure one of them was a tattered Cinderella. She tugged Ruan's arm. 'You'd think they'd shut the door.' She met his eyes. 'Where do you think Tam is?'

'Not in the next room, I hope,' Ruan said. They exchanged looks. No matter how old your child was, being a protective parent was a hard habit to shake.

The following doors were firmly closed. They hurried past. At the end of the corridor, there was another large room, the door ajar, lights blazing inside.

Morwenna faced Ruan. 'What do you think's in there?'

She pushed the door wide and looked into a large library, filled with shelf upon shelf of books. There were paperbacks and heavy reference books, ancient tomes.

Morwenna caught her breath. 'I've no idea why Lady Elizabeth would want to haunt Seal Bay library. Look at the size of this one. And all those books.'

There was a small movement in the corner. A man dressed as a pantomime dame was sitting in an armchair, legs crossed, blowing his vape.

Morwenna tugged Ruan's sleeve. 'Let's explore.'

They turned a corner, and the corridor narrowed, dark panels closing in on either side. Amber wall lights glimmered. Shadows loomed at the far end, shifting in the flickering light of the sconces.

Morwenna said, 'Where do you think this leads?'

Ruan shook his head. 'Up.'

As they turned right, there was a flight of twisting narrow stone stairs, leading to the next floor. Ruan said, 'I bet that's where the view is.'

'Right,' Morwenna said and led the way, her feet resounding on stone.

On the next level, the corridor was lit by one single sconce. There were two large rooms with heavy oak doors, one on either side. Ruan pushed one door open and they went in. It was filled with darkness and the shadows of furniture, but at the end of the room there was blue light from a vast arched window.

Morwenna's voice was hushed. 'What an amazing house.'

They walked towards the window and stared out onto the bay, a half-moon of lights glimmering, making zigzag patterns on the dark water. Morwenna held her breath, taking in the twinkling jewel-encrusted sea, diamonds on black velvet.

Ruan said, 'Wouldn't it be something to live here?'

'Here?' Morwenna made a face that implied he was joking.

'We'd have loved this house, back in the old days,' Ruan said.

'We couldn't have afforded it,' Morwenna began.

'No, but imagine how life might have been – me, you and Tam here.'

'On fisherman's wages? And what Mum and I earned from the tearoom?'

'We'd have been happy.'

'Mmm.' Morwenna knew what was coming.

'We could be happy again.'

'Ruan—'

'You remember when I kissed you? In the summer.'

'On the beach.'

'It meant something,' Ruan said, his face serious. 'It was my way of saying, I wish we could be together, like we used to be.'

'Before all the arguing?'

'We lost our way.'

'We did.' Morwenna took a deep breath.

'I miss you every day.' For a moment, Ruan looked as if he would take her hand. Then he didn't. 'We were good.'

'We were.'

'I still love you. I always will,' Ruan said.

They were standing in shadows, staring out of the window into the night. Morwenna turned away from the inky spread of the sea and sky, facing Ruan. Her breathing was shallow; words stuck in her throat. Time stopped: she was being pulled into the softness of his gaze. She wondered if Ruan would kiss her. It would be perfect. Just as it had always been.

Another feeling rushed in. Morwenna felt a moment of panic. She couldn't risk the cycle starting again: blissful happiness, then another breaking of her heart. She and Ruan were safer apart. She was safer.

'You know how I feel but—'

'But?'

'When we broke up, it changed me.'

'I'm sorry.' Ruan nodded. His voice was a breath on the air. 'We hurt each other. But what we have—'

Her feelings shifted again, softened. They were definitely going to kiss and she wanted it as much as he did. At that moment, all past hurt melted away. The future didn't matter. The moment was everything – now, one meeting of lips and she'd be lost again, but Morwenna felt she couldn't stop the inevitable. His arm was around her, his breath on her cheek. Their lips almost brushed and she closed her eyes.

There was a thud in the corridor outside, as if something had fallen. A wallop that stopped as quickly as it had started, then silence.

They both jerked back at the same time, wide-eyed.

'What was that?' Morwenna heard the urgency in her own voice. The silence was broken as hurried footsteps rang out, feet pattering against stone, fading to nothing.

They rushed into the corridor and looked both ways. The darkness on one side was illuminated by the tawny gleam of wall lights. The stone stairs twisted downwards. Morwenna noticed a dull shape at the bottom.

They were both cannoning down the steps. A red figure lay huddled in a heap, limbs twisted. It was a tall man in a Santa Claus suit, a mince pie still clutched in his hand.

Ruan arrived at his side first and knelt beside him, turning him gently, lifting a wrist, placing two fingers against the pulse. Morwenna held her breath.

'It's Pawly.' Ruan's gaze met Morwenna's. His fingers moved to his neck. 'I don't think he's breathing.'

6

Morwenna tugged her phone from the pocket of her Santa Claus trousers and pressed a button.

'Jane, can you come up to the first floor? Yes, right now. Stairs, go right, then keep going. Bring Blessed. And Rick. What? No, an accident. Get an ambulance. OK. See you...' She stood back. 'Ruan, he's...'

'Dead? I think so.' Ruan looked up the stairs and back to Morwenna. 'I expect he fell.'

'No, there was someone else here.' Morwenna had heard footsteps.

'That might have been Pawly though.' Ruan watched as she pointed her phone and started taking photos of the body. 'Do you think you should...?'

'It's a bit disrespectful but...' Morwenna snapped away '...later on, we might be glad I did.'

'Why?'

'Just in case.' Morwenna leaned forward, taking more pictures of Pawly, the way he had fallen, the ground around him. She said, 'Sorry, Pawly.'

She pushed her phone in her pocket as she heard pelting footsteps. Jane and Blessed appeared together, Dick Whittington and cat, followed by a panting parsnip. Jane watched as Rick and Blessed crouched next to the body and turned to Morwenna. 'The ambulance is on its way. Right. Tell me what you saw.'

'We were in the room upstairs, looking at the view of the bay.' Morwenna wondered why she felt so guilty. 'We heard a thump. Footsteps.'

'The thump first? Or afterwards?' Jane asked. 'How many people?'

'Two, maybe,' Morwenna said.

'Or it could have just been Pawly.' Ruan seemed less sure.

Blessed looked over her shoulder. 'Jane, I think his neck's broken.'

'A fall in a darkened corridor,' Rick said. 'He'd certainly been drinking.'

Jane whispered something about a post-mortem and a call to the coroner's office.

'I'll speak to the Pengellens,' Blessed said quickly. 'The ambulance is on its way. I'll have to ask you to come down with me, Morwenna and Ruan—' She was suddenly on duty despite her cat ears and tail. 'We have to establish what happened.'

Morwenna glanced back to Pawly. He was sprawled on his front. Did it look like a fall or was he propelled downstairs? If he was pushed, might there be bruising? What about the trajectory associated with a simple fall, and are there any impact injuries? She was no expert, but the photos might help.

There were more footsteps. Two paramedics arrived, followed by a third with a case. Morwenna stood back, listening to what they were saying. Blessed wanted to know about any injuries the deceased might have sustained.

Deceased?

Pawly was dead. Just like that.

She felt Ruan's reassuring hand on her shoulder and heard him say, 'Are you all right?' She was still taking in the rush of activity, police, paramedics and the thump, thump of her own heart.

Jane's voice cut through the buzz in her ears. 'Morwenna, we're asking everyone to go to the main room. Blessed's going to talk to the Pengellens.'

'Do you think it was accidental?' Morwenna heard herself say.

'Could be.' Jane put her lips close to Morwenna's ear. 'But I'll see you tomorrow morning at the swim. We can talk more.'

'Right,' Morwenna said. She found herself being led along the sconce-lit corridor.

Back in the main room, the music had stopped but so many voices were bubbling with anxious questions. Lamorna appeared by Morwenna's side. Her face was a picture of concern.

'I saw flashing lights outside.' She clutched Morwenna's hand, as she'd done so often when Morwenna was a child. It was both protection and support, solidarity. 'Someone's saying there's been an accident. We saw Jane and Rick going out of here like the clappers, but nobody knows what's going on.'

Morwenna's lips wouldn't move. She looked around the room, forcing herself to notice details. So many people had it in for Pawly. And all of them were at the party.

She needed to spot anything that might be useful later. Was there anything unusual? Was anyone missing?

The Christmas tree and the persistently winking fairy lights were the only festive things left. The atmosphere was filled with concern and speculation. Everyone was standing in clusters, asking questions, voices raised in alarm.

Louise was by her side, grabbing her sleeve. 'What's gone on? I heard that the paramedics are here. Steve's been gone ages.'

Morwenna was still dazed. A few feet away, Pippa and Julian were talking to Blessed, who was back in the room in her professional capacity, speaking to them as the owners of the house. Morwenna read her lips. 'We'll be asking for everyone to remain here, just for a while...'

Steve arrived, out of breath, wrapping an arm round Louise. She eyed him suspiciously. 'Where have you been?'

'Call of nature.'

'You've been ages.'

'I couldn't help it.' Steve turned to Morwenna. 'What's going on?'

'I don't know.'

She felt Ruan next to her, pushing a cup of water into her hand, and she drank thirstily. A thought came to her. 'Have you just been in the drawing room?'

'Yes.'

'Who was there?'

Ruan paused, thinking. 'The man taking the photos, Peter Pan.'

'Who else was there?'

'The man in the Brussels sprout costume and Damien and Bev, Pam Truscott.'

Morwenna looked around again, looking for suspects, examining faces. The woman he'd tried to kiss, Red Riding Hood, was in the corner, gulping champagne as if it had gone out of fashion. Morwenna reminded herself that she was called Faye.

Becca was missing, and Tristan's friend, Seb. Morwenna remembered that they'd been in the bedroom together. Carole and Vic Taylor had probably gone home. It was almost midnight, and they had a babysitter.

She reminded herself to file the information for later. Sleuth's instinct.

Ruan placed a calm hand against her back. 'Are you all right?'

'Fine,' Morwenna lied.

'Tell me who—' Lamorna began but she was interrupted by the appearance of a man in a turkey costume. 'Morwenna, just the person.' It was Mike Sheridan, the DJ from Bay Radio. 'I've heard a body's been found, clutching a mince pie.'

Lamorna was alarmed. 'Who's died?'

Mike ignored her and continued to question Morwenna. 'One of the coppers said you were a witness.'

Ruan stepped in. 'The police will talk to everyone.'

'I've got a breakfast show first thing tomorrow,' Mike persisted. 'Listeners want to know. Who's died? Did you see them? You're the Seal Bay sleuth.'

'Now's not a good time, Mike,' Ruan said calmly.

The room was suddenly quiet, and everyone turned to look as Rick Tremayne arrived in the doorway, still wearing his parsnip costume, flanked by Dick Whittington and the cat. He spoke up.

'Ladies and gentlemen. There's been an incident.'

Julian pushed his way towards Rick. 'Can these people go home?'

Rick's eyes narrowed. 'I'd like everyone to stay briefly. I'll need to speak to you and Pippa. Everyone else' – he raised his voice – 'I'm afraid we need to complete our checks. Morwenna.' He assumed a professionally serious expression. 'Can I ask you a few questions?'

Morwenna heard Mike Sheridan mutter, 'I knew she'd have something to do with it.' Then she was following Rick down the hallway, her body already aching with tiredness.

* * *

After dropping Tamsin and Becca off, then Lamorna, Ruan drove back to Harbour Cottages and paused outside number four, the engine idling. It was late and Morwenna could hardly keep her eyes open. Her limbs ached.

She clambered out of the van. 'Thanks, Ruan.'

'I'll come in with you, shall I?'

'It's late.'

'I think you need a glass of brandy.'

Morwenna met his eyes. 'Yes, I do. Thanks.'

'Me too.'

It was bitterly cold. A frost had settled on the garden gate and sparkled on the path, diamonds in the dark. She pushed the key into the lock and walked into the warmth of her little cottage. Ruan knew where the brandy was kept in the kitchen cupboard. He poured them a glass each and they sat on the sofa, shoulders touching. Brenda immediately sprang on Morwenna's knee and began to purr, as if she knew instinctively that her human needed comfort. Morwenna took a deep gulp of the amber liquid that swirled in her glass and Ruan did the same.

'I can't believe it.' She took a deep breath. 'Pawly's dead.'

Ruan made a low sound that meant that he shared her disbelief. 'He didn't seem himself, that night I spoke to him in The Smugglers.'

'Why?' Morwenna was dog-tired, but Ruan's words interested her. 'How was he different?'

Ruan thought for a moment. 'He was always professional and calm; he had a sense of humour. And he was a man with a mission. He was a writer, a historian, a bit of an eco-warrior.'

'But?'

'That night he seemed troubled. I suppose it was the problem with his girlfriend.'

'Faye? Red Riding Hood?' Morwenna asked.

'I don't know.' Ruan shook his head. 'He wasn't thinking straight. He was drowning his sorrows.'

'The night at the library.' Morwenna gazed into the brandy glass. 'He upset a few people.'

'He did.'

'Enough to push him down the stairs?'

'When I was talking to Rick, after he'd spoken to you, he seemed to think Pawly drank too much and slipped.'

Morwenna recalled her conversation with Rick in the drawing room, his sweaty forehead, the dark rings around his eyes. She knew him well enough to recognise the weight of responsibility that pressed on his shoulders.

Ruan looked tired. 'I think Pawly fell out with his girlfriend, drank too much and tumbled down the stairs.'

'What makes you so sure?' Morwenna faced him.

'It's logical. Who'd kill him?'

'We heard footsteps.'

'They were probably Pawly's.'

'Do you think so?'

Morwenna could think of a few people who disliked Pawly. All the suspects had been at the party. They had grudges against him of one sort or another, but she was fairly sure that none of them were the sort of people who'd murder someone.

She counted them on her fingers. Steve. He had a temper. Julian and Pippa. They were certainly angry. Faye?

'You're probably right,' she said.

'I ought to go.' Ruan finished his drink and stood up. 'You must be bushed. I know I am.'

'Yes.' Morwenna didn't move. She ruffled the fur behind Brenda's ears. It felt soothing.

'It's been a long evening.'

'It has.'

'Well, I'll say goodnight.'

'Can you see yourself out?'

'Of course.' Ruan paused, as if he wanted to kiss the top of Morwenna's head. He seemed to think better of it. 'I'll see you later tomorrow. I'm taking Elowen to Hippity Hoppers.'

'I'm swimming.'

'We'll catch up with each other.'

'We will.' Morwenna twisted round, watching him go. 'Thanks, Ruan.'

'Take care.' His voice came from the hall; she heard the door click shut.

Morwenna closed her eyes, thinking back to the party, to when she'd explored the house. As she'd stood with Ruan in the upstairs room, she'd heard a thud, followed by footsteps. There must have been two people.

Pawly and *someone else*.

Morwenna would talk to Jane tomorrow, at swimming. Perhaps the problem of Pawly's death could be easily explained. Morwenna ought to go to bed. She'd be exhausted tomorrow, but a swim in the freezing ocean always did her the world of good.

She smoothed Brenda's fur again, feeling the vibration of the cat's purr through her fingers. A sudden thought came, a moment's pang of guilt.

She plunged her hand into her Santa pocket and brought out a small digital camera. It had been left on the table in the Pengellens' drawing room, and she'd picked it up at the end of her conversation with Rick and pushed it into her Santa trousers. Rick hadn't noticed.

It had been the one Peter Pan was using to take photos throughout the evening. He'd left it lying around. There would be some interesting pictures. There might be a clue.

Yes. it was stealing. And no, Rick wouldn't be pleased if he knew, but he didn't. Jane would be furious. Peter Pan would certainly be looking for it.

Morwenna promised herself she'd return it. Or she'd give it to Jane tomorrow and apologise. It had been a long night, she'd say – she'd been tired, she'd picked it up by mistake.

But she'd download the pictures first and check the movements of all the suspects.

SUNDAY 14 DECEMBER

7

There was a large crowd assembled at the seafront when Morwenna arrived, her old wetsuit beneath her clothes. The freezing weather usually put swimmers off – last week, it had just been Morwenna, Jane and Blessed. But this Sunday's meeting of the SWANS – Seal Bay Wild Aquatic Natation – was well attended.

As Morwenna secured her bike, she noticed that Susan and Barb Grundy were buttonholing Louise and Jane; Donald Stewart was perched on the sea wall listening, wrapped in several towels, Blessed Barnarde was already in the water – being a Detective Chief Inspector of Police and from London, she had no intention of listening to gossip.

Carole Taylor was in a thin swimsuit. She wouldn't last long in the freezing water. She hurried towards Morwenna.

'Have you heard the latest?'

'No.' Morwenna reached Jane, Louise and the Grundy sisters. 'What's new?'

'Someone definitely killed him,' Susan interrupted.

'Jane was saying it could be murder,' Barb added.

'I didn't say that,' Jane said firmly. 'There'll be a post-mortem, then we'll know more.'

'But someone pushed Pawly,' Louise said nervously. 'I hope no one thinks it was Steve.'

'He thumped Pawly after he kissed you,' Donald said from beneath the heap of towels. 'Is that a motive for murder?'

'Half of Seal Bay had a motive,' Barb added. 'Pawly had a fancy woman and she ditched him. Perhaps she pushed him down the stairs.'

'We don't know that's what happened,' Jane said.

'Do you think it was an accident, Morwenna?' Carole asked.

'The coroner will find out,' Morwenna said.

'Yes, let's leave it to the coroner.' Jane gave her a look that meant she didn't want to say too much.

'Steve was in the toilet, so he has no alibi,' Louise said nervously. 'What if the police ask him about his whereabouts at the time of death?'

Morwenna thought about the digital camera on the small table in the living room. She wouldn't mention it yet.

'It's not good to jump to conclusions,' Jane said. 'That's why I'm so cross with Mike Sheridan.'

'The DJ?' Susan's mouth was already open with shock.

'What's he done?' Barb asked.

'I heard him this morning on his breakfast show. Vic always has it on.' Carole was shivering but her eyes gleamed with interest. 'Pawly was found in a Santa Claus suit in a crumpled heap at the bottom of the stairs, with a mince pie in his hand, and he was pushed. Mike said the police are looking for a local killer.'

'It's unwise of Mike,' Jane said crossly. 'Such talk brings the wrong type of interest. Right. Let's go in the water.' She glanced to where Blessed was already swimming.

'We should.' Morwenna hugged herself. 'We'll get cold.'

'Mike mentioned you too, Morwenna.' Carole didn't move. 'He told the whole of Seal Bay that you found the body. He said that as the Seal Bay sleuth, you'd be helping the police.'

'As a suspect?' Louise asked.

'As an investigator.' Carole was enjoying telling the news.

'Mike said that?' Morwenna shook her head.

Jane gazed at the water again. 'I'm going in.'

'Me too. We'll catch our deaths.' Morwenna made a grim face at her unfortunate choice of words. She caught up with Jane as they hurried across the sand. 'So, do you think it was an accident?'

'It's best if people think so, for the time being at least,' Jane said, breaking into a run.

Morwenna panted to keep up with her. 'But you think someone might have killed Pawly?'

'He'd been drinking. You could smell it on him as he lay on the floor.'

'So?'

'So he might have fallen. If he was pushed – and he probably wasn't – there would be several suspects.' Jane looked away. 'Local people.'

'Such as?'

'Pawly was very confrontational at the library event. He upset people.'

'And you think someone saw an opportunity?' Morwenna said as they rushed into the sea. 'Somone who was at his library event?'

'We'll see,' Jane panted as the cold waves lapped around their ankles, bee-sting cold. 'The coroner will rule whether death was accidental, natural causes, or potential murder.'

Morwenna was up to her knees in the water. 'When's the post-mortem?'

'This week.'

Morwenna asked, 'What's your instinct?'

'There was something about how Pawly's body was lying on the ground.' Jane launched herself into the cold water. 'Twisted. I don't know. I wouldn't be surprised to hear that he'd had some help falling down.'

'Right.' Morwenna dived in. The shock of the cold made her heart knock. Her skin prickled. She swam harder out to sea and felt a burning sensation in her fingers. Blinking water from her eyes, she saw Blessed and Jane together, sleek as two frolicking seals. In the other direction, Louise was shivering at the water's edge with Donald. Carole, Susan and Barb were still talking by the sea wall.

Morwenna came up spluttering, her silver mane of hair slick like a mermaid's. A rush of energy tingled through her body and suddenly her mind was clear. The facts came to her as if they were being spat from a machine.

Pawly was dead. It might have been an accident.

But if it wasn't, everyone at the party was a suspect. Her instincts cried out that something didn't feel right.

Pawly had been acting erratically. He'd made enemies.

Morwenna wondered who hated him enough to harm him. Anyone could have walked into the party in fancy dress and pushed him downstairs. An outsider. Who would have noticed?

The answer came immediately. The man with the digital camera. Peter Pan. And the camera was now sitting on the low table in her living room. She needed to download the contents. Then she had to return it to the Pengellens' house, unnoticed. A plan was forming. Morwenna swam towards Jane and Blessed and called out, 'I'm going to head back now.'

'It's getting cold,' Blessed agreed.

'Aren't you coming for coffee at the tearoom?' Jane yelled.

'No, I've got things to do. I'll catch up with you soon.' She swam closer. 'Do you want me to keep my ear close to the ground?'

'It's a police matter, strictly,' Blessed said. 'But we're always grateful for your local knowledge.' She tapped her nose with her finger.

'Morwenna's very discreet,' Jane said defensively.

'I know.' Blessed nodded. 'It's an emotional time of year, and we need to make sure the locals don't get involved.'

'We have to play things down,' Jane advised.

'Of course.' Morwenna splashed in the water.

'It's a shame Mike didn't keep his nose out,' Jane said.

'Hopefully, the post-mortem will reveal accidental death.' Blessed shook water from her swimming cap, sending droplets flying. 'We can concentrate on enjoying a normal Christmas.'

'I hope so,' Morwenna said. She struck off for shore, passing a floundering Donald. On the beach, Carole, Susan and Barb were still talking. She thought again about Pawly's death. There had been someone there with him.

Something was definitely not right.

* * *

In the living room, Morwenna sat at her laptop, her hair still damp from the shower, while the digital camera downloaded the photos. Brenda pushed her nose in, desperate to see what was on the screen. Morwenna fondled the cat's whiskers and Brenda buffeted her impatiently.

'I'm on it, Bren. We'll have some really good images.' Brenda pushed her head against Morwenna's cheek. 'What? No, I don't feel guilty. Well, maybe a bit – but we'll get the camera back to Peter Pan dreckly.'

She watched as the photos popped up on the screen, leaning forward. 'Oh, he's taken videos too. That's useful.' Brenda clambered onto her knee and patted her face with a paw. 'You think I shouldn't have taken the camera? I'll have a look at the photos, then I'll come clean to Jane. Now – how am I going to get this camera back to Pengellen Manor? I'll deal with that first, then we'll take a proper look at what we've got here.'

She eased herself up from the chair and went into the kitchen, Brenda at her heels. The cat looked up, round-eyed, and Morwenna sprinkled a few biscuits into a bowl in the corner. Brenda began munching.

Morwenna shivered at the thought of Pettarock Head. The headwind from the bay always made the climb hard, but at least her bike had a motor. She was already picking out the things she needed. Warm clothes, especially a hat and gloves. A bag to conceal the camera. And a bunch of flowers.

She gazed at the jar in the window. There was a bunch of carnations that Louise had given her two days ago, for all the extra work she'd done for the author talk. It would be all right to use them.

Morwenna lifted the carnations from the vase and shook the excess water into the sink. Some pretty wrapping paper, and they'd do fine. A card thanking the Pengellens for the party and wishing them a happy Christmas. Morwenna wouldn't mention Pawly, but she'd imply sympathy.

With thanks for the party invitation and good cheer. Thinking of you this Christmas, Morwenna.

Something like that.

Half an hour later, in a woollen hat and scarf, her duffel coat, warm leggings and the knitted Cornwall cardigan she'd bought from Susan and Barb Grundy, she pushed the bike outside. She glanced towards Ruan's house, number nine. The van was gone.

He'd taken Elowen to Hippity Hoppers earlier, though he'd probably be at the tearoom by now, chatting to Tamsin.

She clambered onto the saddle and set off at pace. The sea sparkled in the distance, a turquoise bowl in the winter sunlight. The sight of it always lifted her spirits. Thoughts of Pawly's death dampened them again. He was a nice man. Troubled, though. She owed it to him to find out what had happened.

She cycled through the town centre, following the traffic. There wasn't much about, a few cars, families out for the day. She cycled past a few shops that were open on a Sunday for Christmas trade. The Quilkin Emporium, a small old-fashioned department store, was advertising Santa's grotto in flashing red and green lights. Morwenna thought briefly that Elowen might like to go next Saturday. There was a row of B & Bs with 'Vacancies' signs in the window: business at Carole's Blue Dolphin was usually slack this time of year. The Smugglers Inn was busy though, the doors flung wide. The smell of old hops filled Morwenna's nose as she cycled past, turning the corner. To the left was Camp Dynamo, the caravan site that the surfers used in the summer, and to the right, the road twisted uphill to the headland. Morwenna put her head down and pushed on.

The view of the coast was spectacular from Pettarock Head; Morwenna looked down at the rushing ocean, the expanse of pale sand. She reached the tall iron gates of the manor house and clambered off her bike. It was best to push it across the dense gravel. There were several cars in the car park: a Land Rover, an Audi, a white BMW, a couple of sporty models. Morwenna wondered if Julian had friends over for Sunday lunch, if she'd be interrupting.

She reached the heavy brass knocker in the shape of a wonky house on a bridge, and the words 'Props – Polperro' beneath. Morwenna studied it – Polperro had once been an isolated

Cornish fishing community, where smuggling was a traditional occupation. The original Props Cottage boasted a secret staircase that allowed smugglers easy access to the beach. Pawly Yelland would have known all about that. No wonder he'd found the Pengellens an interesting bunch.

She took a deep breath and knocked hard.

8

Morwenna knocked again. The breeze from the sea stung her cheeks. Her ears were cold beneath the woollen hat. She was about to knock again when the door opened and Pippa stood there, smart in a cream suit, her dark hair tied back revealing pretty gold earrings with red stones. She smiled politely at Morwenna. 'Hello. How nice of you to drop in.'

'Hello.' Morwenna smiled back. She tugged the carnations from her bag, wrapped in pink paper. 'To say thanks for last night.'

Pippa's smile disappeared. 'Oh, what an evening. I can hardly bring myself to think about it.'

'I know.' Morwenna nodded vigorously. 'That's why I brought you these.' She produced the card.

'That's kind.' Pippa didn't budge. Morwenna expected her to step back, offer her a few moments' shelter from the cold, a coffee even. Pippa noticed the electric bicycle leaning against the wall. 'You didn't ride up here?'

'I did.' Morwenna wafted a hand in front of her face in the

hope that Pippa would think she was cold or thirsty, and invite her in. Pippa stayed where she was.

'I'm in a meeting,' she said by way of explanation.

'On a Sunday? You're keen,' Morwenna said. She intended to be so nice that Pippa couldn't refuse her a cup of something.

'I run several charities across Cornwall.' Pippa took a breath as if she was exhausted. 'Rough Sleepers, Birth and Baby, Food Banks, Seal Bay, Point Break, the Surfer Therapy for Young People.'

'My goodness.' Morwenna thought it was no wonder that Pippa looked tired, but she needed to get inside. 'You do a lot of good work.'

Pippa closed her eyes for a moment. 'I'm on the verge of being recognised for it. That's why I was so furious about what Pawly said, in public too.'

'I expect your charities will take your mind off – you know – last night.' Morwenna watched Pippa's expression carefully.

'Oh, that was horrendous. The police came earlier. This place is a total disaster area. We haven't cleaned up yet. The photographer who came with Tristan's ex is grumbling that he's lost his camera – he's here looking for it now. We've got food deliveries due and we're all at sixes and sevens. Julian's had to go to London.'

'So you're on your own?'

'Tristan's here, and Seb. His dreadful ex and her friend are staying on somewhere in the bay, although why anyone would want to after...' Pippa gasped as if the next words were unspeakable. 'Pawly made enemies, though. I can't help wondering if he brought it on himself.'

'No one deserves that,' Morwenna said kindly. 'Do you need any help clearing up?'

'No, no.' Pippa frowned harder. 'I ought to get back to my meeting – but thanks for the flowers, Morwenna.' She was about to close the door. As an afterthought she said, 'We must have coffee some time, when all this awful business is behind us...'

'Coffee?' Morwenna winced suddenly as if in pain. Pippa was about to close the door and she couldn't let her do that. 'I drank too much of it earlier. It's a diuretic, you know – it goes straight through.' She crossed her legs quickly and jumped about frantically. 'The cold's got to me and...'

Pippa looked puzzled. Then recognition crossed her brow. 'Oh, you need the bathroom? Of course.' She finally took a step back.

'At my age, you know – the bladder's not what it was... ha ha.' Morwenna squeezed past her. 'Thanks, Pippa. You don't mind?'

'Not at all.'

'I know where it is. I'll just rush up.'

'Oh, of course.' Pippa suddenly looked alarmed as Morwenna was about to dart upstairs. 'Oh – wait – do avoid the area where – you know – the thing happened.'

'Of course. I'll use the one on the first floor,' Morwenna said. She dashed across the thick carpet: she was inside the house. And halfway up the grand staircase.

She passed the gold-framed Pengellen portraits on the walls. At the top, the stairs split, one going left and the other right. Morwenna paused: she couldn't leave the camera upstairs. It needed to be back in the room where she'd found it.

She crept back down. Everywhere was quiet. She peered around the expanse of hallway and moved mouse-like towards the large room where the party had been held. Silently, she stepped inside and blinked in the half-light. No one was about.

Nothing had been touched. The tall Christmas tree, the

flashing lights, garlands of mistletoe and ivy, empty glasses, plates, bits of uneaten food were strewn everywhere. The furniture was still moved back, sofas and chairs against the wall. A piece of tinsel had come down from the roof. Curtains were closed and specs of dust danced in the air where the thin shard of light pierced the gap.

Morwenna looked around. On the wooden floor, a huge ceramic plant pot housed a green leafy cheese plant. She delved into her bag and tugged out the camera, dropping it into the pot. Someone would find it there. On her toes, she made for the door.

The sound of voices made her pull back quickly. She flattened herself behind the door, breathing shallowly, hoping no one would come in.

A woman was talking loudly in an accent that Morwenna thought was Spanish. She sounded irritated. A man replied quickly, a soothing English tone. Morwenna thought she recognised Tristan's name and assumed it was his ex-girlfriend, the model. Pippa had referred to her as the 'dreadful ex'.

Briefly, Morwenna remembered Seb and Becca in the bedroom. She wondered if they'd still been there when Pawly tumbled down the stairs. They had no alibi either, apart from each other. There was so much she needed to find out.

The couple had gone. Morwenna ducked around the corner and watched them disappear into the drawing room, a tall dark-haired woman and a slim man, both in costume. She assumed they were dressed as Snow White and Peter Pan.

He'd find his camera later. He'd have no idea that Morwenna had copied the photos. If there was anything that pointed to the killer, she'd show Jane, and Jane could seize his camera as evidence. She was clutching at straws, perhaps.

At full speed, she made a dash for the door, tugging it open, feeling the rush of cold sea air.

She was outside, clambering onto her bicycle and setting off towards the tall iron gates. The first part of her mission was accomplished.

* * *

Morwenna sat at the laptop into the evening, staring at one picture after another. Peter Pan had taken lots of video footage of guests, and Morwenna watched each one several times, looking for clues. On the surface, there was nothing obvious. As the clock ticked on, the cottage grew cold and she hugged her cardigan for warmth.

The most interesting thing about the photos was that most of the subjects were oblivious of a photographer. Morwenna assumed that made him good at his job. There was a brief video of Tamsin and Tristan, Seb and Becca climbing the stairs that caught her eye and she watched it three times. Seb was carrying a bottle of champagne, laughing loudly. Tamsin's voice was crystal clear. 'I want to see the view.'

Becca clung to Seb's arm and laughed nervously. 'It's not haunted, is it?'

Tristan was saying, 'I'd like to show you the west wing – apparently, the smugglers hid there. Caradoc Pengellen in the eighteenth century...'

Tamsin sounded impressed. 'Was he a Cornish rebel?' There was no reply. Peter Pan had finished filming.

Morwenna wondered if Tamsin and Tristan were a couple now. She had no idea. There was so much she didn't know about her daughter. Morwenna reminded herself to have a chat with her at the earliest opportunity. She promised herself she'd mention Elowen's comments about her father again. It certainly needed discussing.

Back to the pictures. There were far too many, and Morwenna's vision was becoming blurred. Most of them were of couples dancing, a few people posing for the camera. There were lots of snaps of Pippa and Julian Pengellen, separately, with other people and together. Morwenna examined a photo of Pippa, in her glitzy fir-tree costume, dancing with Faye in her Red Riding Hood outfit. There was no love lost between them and Pawly.

Morwenna leaned forward, examining their expressions carefully. Pippa looked oblivious, a champagne flute in her hand. Faye seemed happy enough, as if she hadn't a care in the world. She didn't look like a woman who planned to shove her ex-boyfriend down the stairs.

Morwenna changed tack. She started at the beginning again, with the intention of following Pawly's movements throughout the evening. Surely that was the key to what had happened. She wanted to see who he spoke to; there had to be something. A clue.

The first problem was that so many people were dressed as Santa Claus: it was hard to tell which one was Pawly.

She noticed two Santas speaking together on the staircase. Pawly and Steve Piper, both in red suits. Morwenna leaned forward to get a better look. Steve was carrying a bottle of sparkling water. Of course, he was driving. His expression was hard to discern, what with the huge beard, but Pawly's pose was interesting. He had a hand on Steve's shoulder and appeared to be telling him something. Their eyes were locked like bulls in combat.

Or, on the other hand, they could be two men who had reached a truce. It was impossible to be sure.

There was a photo of Pawly with Damien Woon and Beverley Okoro, his arm too tightly around them. Pawly was saying something, his mouth wide, but Damien was looking the other way, as if angry. Beverley seemed uncomfortable: Pawly's embrace was unwelcome. Morwenna resolved to find out more about Pawly and Damien. Something had caused a rift between them. Ruan would know.

She gazed at the clock. It was past six. She was hungry. For a moment she thought about going over to Ruan's house, where there would be hot food and a warm fire. She hadn't bothered to light the one in the hearth yet.

Something patted her leg gently, a small paw. Brenda leaped on her knee, demanding food too. Morwenna closed the laptop screen and rubbed her eyes. She was tired.

She wandered into the kitchen, placed some dried cat food in a bowl, listened to Brenda crunching and wondered what to cook. There was always cheese on toast. She'd had cheese and bread for lunch. Soup, then. There were a few old vegetables, a few curly carrots, but it didn't sound appetising. There might be a pasty in the freezer. Morwenna told herself off. She needed to take more care of herself.

Her phone rang and she picked it up. 'Hi, Mum. All right?'

Lamorna sounded weary on the other end. 'Where were you this afternoon?'

'Why?' Morwenna felt suddenly caught out. How could her mother know she had stolen the camera and returned it to the manor? Of course she didn't. Her mum always had the ability to make her feel guilty.

Lamorna wasn't finished. 'We sat in the tearooms and waited for you to show up.'

'We?'

'Me, Tam, Elowen, Ruan. We were going to have a walk on the beach.'

'Was I supposed to be there?' Morwenna was horrified. 'Did I forget?'

'Oh no, maid, but we thought you'd turn up. What have you been up to?' Lamorna's voice cracked a little.

'Sorry.' Morwenna felt awful. She'd neglected her mum.

'It doesn't matter. Ruan took care of me,' Lamorna said and Morwenna could almost see her mother's crafty smile.

'Oh, he did, did he?'

'The thing is, I've been feeling a bit down in the dumps since...' Lamorna's voice trailed off. 'I don't know. It's my age. And I was in the corner shop and this funny thing happened.'

'What?'

'Oh, I'll tell you when I see you.' Lamorna's voice took on a mischievous tone. 'Will you be in the tearoom tomorrow afternoon or will I get stood up all over again?'

'I'll be there to help Tam.'

'No need. Imogen's starting waitressing tomorrow. The student. But meet me when you've finished in the library, and we'll have a catch-up.' Lamorna was certainly happy now. 'That's if you can find time for your poor old mother.'

'I'll be there,' Morwenna said. She was smiling too.

'Good. It proper shook me up.'

'What did?'

'The incident in the corner shop.'

'What happened?'

'I'll tell you dreckly,' Lamorna said. 'There's an old film on the TV and it's starting now. I like Kirk Douglas. And Tony Curtis.'

'Are you watching *Spartacus*?'

'No. *The Vikings*. The one where Tony Curtis is the slave and he runs off with Janet Leigh and Kirk Douglas is the half-brother who gets his eye scratched out by the falcon.' Lamorna shuddered audibly. 'Oh, but he's handsome, Kirk, even with just the one eye.'

'I'll let you go and watch it, Mum.'

'I'll see you dreckly,' Lamorna replied, and the phone clicked.

Morwenna stretched her arms above her head. 'Right. I'll make myself a traybake. It's an early night for us, Brenda.' Morwenna frowned, thinking. This was going to be an interesting week, the week before Christmas. A lot of things needed sorting out. Starting with her mum. And Tamsin.

And Pawly Yelland.

MONDAY 15 DECEMBER

9

Monday morning in the library was usually slow going, but not today. From the minute Susan and Barb Grundy dashed in, wanting to know the latest murder update, Morwenna had been busy. A steady stream of people came in to discuss Pawly Yelland. Fascinated locals drifted in on the pretext of finding a good read, sure that Morwenna would have heard the latest report about who'd shoved Pawly down the steps.

Some people wanted to borrow Pawly's books on Cornwall, which Morwenna thought was sad. Had Pawly been alive, he'd have been delighted with the rush of interest. Other people wanted a thriller or a cosy crime. One older lady even asked, 'Have you got a book about a famous author getting pushed downstairs?'

By half past eleven, most of the Agatha Christie audiobooks had been lent out.

At ten to twelve, Morwenna handed Louise a cup of tea and a mince pie and noticed the dark rings around her eyes. She said, 'How's it going?'

'Not good,' Louise murmured. 'I'm not sleeping well.'

'What's on your mind?'

'Steve. I'm terrified the police will arrest him.'

'Why?'

'Every knock at the door, every time the phone goes, I think – this is it. Steve and Pawly, the fight in the library. Everybody saw it.'

'Steve reacted on impulse,' Morwenna said reassuringly. 'They shook hands afterwards. Nobody thinks it's Steve.'

'Don't they?' Louise shuddered. 'He'd been gone a long time at the party, just as Pawly was killed. He has no alibi. I can't say he was with me, because he wasn't...'

'He was in the loo.'

'For over half an hour.'

'He's a man, Louise. He was probably on his phone.'

'I keep imagining...'

'What?'

'What if Steve came out of the toilet and saw Pawly. What if he followed him to have another go at him. Steve can be a bit like a dog with a bone. What if they had an argument on the top step, and Steve got cross and pushed him?'

'Have you said this to Steve?'

'No, I can't. He just acts like nothing's happened. This morning, he asked me where his sandwich box was, gave me a peck on the cheek and was out the door without a thought. What if my Steve murdered Pawly?'

'He didn't.' Morwenna watched as Louise took a gulp of tea. Her hand was shaking.

'How can you be so sure?'

'When have you known Steve keep a secret?' Morwenna forced a laugh. 'On your last anniversary, how many times did he almost tell you he was taking you to The Marine Room?'

'It was lovely there.' Louise closed her eyes. 'Remember when you went with Barnaby? Have you heard from him recently?'

Morwenna was pleased the subject had changed, although she wasn't delighted with Louise's new choice. 'Barnaby's coming back for Christmas.'

'To Seal Bay?'

'Apparently.'

'Do you think you'll pick up where you left off?'

'I don't think so.' Morwenna chewed her lip.

'But you like him, don't you?'

'He's good company.' Morwenna sipped tea.

'And he's gorgeous.'

'I suppose so.' Morwenna wondered why Louise was being so persistent. She wasn't enjoying the conversation.

But Louise carried on. 'Is it because of Ruan? Do you still have feelings for him?'

'Ruan and I were together for years.'

'You should go back to him, Morwenna. Try again. It would be lovely, at Christmas, all that kissing under the mistletoe.' She stopped abruptly. Morwenna could see she'd remembered Pawly.

'It was bad when we split up. My temper. Ruan's stubbornness. I don't want to do that to either of us again.' Morwenna stopped. It was rare that she spoke about Ruan so openly. She pushed the mince pies under Louise's nose. 'Have another. The sugar will keep us going until lunch.'

'I probably should.' Louise took one and began nibbling just as the door creaked open. A man and woman made their way to the desk. Morwenna recognised them from the party, Peter Pan and Snow White, but without their costumes.

The man said, 'Can you recommend something?' He was smartly dressed, charming. 'My friend needs reading material to keep us going for a few days.'

The woman had a heavy accent. 'Perhaps you have something humorous. A love story. A murder mystery. In English is fine.'

'We have Agatha Christie's *The Murder at the Vicarage*,' Louise said. 'Or maybe *Gone with the Wind*? That's a love story, though not humorous, of course. Oh, I'll just get a selection.' She scuttled away. Morwenna wondered if the man had discovered his digital camera. She saw her opportunity to find out.

'I saw you up at the Pengellens'. Aren't you staying with them?'

'No,' the woman said simply. 'They are not my friends. I hate them all.'

The man took over. 'We came for the party. I'm a photographer and Fernanda's a model, so we thought we'd stay on for a photo shoot. The location's perfect.' He smiled. 'I need some fashion shots for a project.' He leaned against the desk casually. 'We're staying in The Blue Dolphin. Carole's very nice.'

'She is,' Morwenna agreed. 'So – I love photography. Can you recommend a good digital camera?'

'Any sort will do if you're an amateur. Mine's pretty expensive,' the man said.

'The Pengellens have a beautiful house.' Morwenna said, hoping to move the conversation to the party.

'I will not go there ever again,' Fernanda said curtly.

'Fernanda and Tristan are exes,' the man explained gently.

'Didn't Tristan invite you to the party?' Morwenna asked, hoping she wasn't coming across as too nosey. She recalled Ruan saying something about it.

'It doesn't matter who invited me.' Fernanda waved a hand dismissively. 'I wish I had not gone there.'

The man took over. 'Julian works in London. He and I know each other.'

Morwenna met Fernanda's eyes. 'You and Tristan must have been an item for a long time.'

'No. A short time. But he has another girlfriend now. A silly waitress from Seal Bay.' Fernanda sniffed as if being a waitress was the worst thing in the world. 'I pity her.'

'Oh?' Morwenna raised an eyebrow. She hoped she hadn't offended Fernanda but the information was useful. Louise was back with three books.

'I brought Jane Austen's *Northanger Abbey* too.' Louise laid the books on the counter.

The man flourished a library card. 'I'm a member of a library in London.'

'You'll have to get temporary membership here. You can do it now if you have ID.' He handed her his driving licence. Morwenna peered at his name. He was called Justin Kidd. She asked, 'Are you staying long?'

'I hope not.' Fernanda flashed dark eyes.

'We'll get some work done, with the sea as backdrop,' Justin said reassuringly. 'Then we'll be back in London for Christmas and put all this nasty business behind us.'

'Nasty business?' Morwenna wanted to know his thoughts.

Justin placed a protective arm around Fernanda, who looked away. 'The poor man who fell downstairs.' He turned to Morwenna. 'You knew him. Carole has told us all about you. You solve crimes with the police.'

Fernanda made a face. 'That is ridiculous.'

'Oh, I don't do much, really,' Morwenna said modestly as she handed him a library membership form.

'We like Carole. She's very friendly,' Justin said, taking a pen from his pocket.

'But there is too much breakfast,' Fernanda said sulkily. Morwenna couldn't imagine her and Tristan together. He was cheerful and upbeat, but she seemed sullen. Morwenna recalled Fernanda's dismissive words about his new relationship and she resolved to speak to Tamsin.

Justin filled in the form quickly, signed his name and picked up the books. 'Thank you. It'll definitely help pass the time. It rains so much here.'

'London is better. Here is too quiet,' Fernanda grumbled. Justin wrapped an arm around her, and they made for the door.

Louise spoke Morwenna's thoughts aloud. 'She doesn't seem Tristan's type.'

Morwenna shrugged. 'It takes all sorts.'

The door opened again and Donald scuttled in. Morwenna said, 'Is it that time already?'

'I'm a bit early for my shift but...' Donald's eyes glinted behind his glasses. '...I just had a thought I wanted to share.'

'Oh?' Morwenna knew what was coming.

'Lady Elizabeth,' Donald said reverently, as if she were listening.

'Our ghost?' Louise asked.

'Don't you remember what Pawly Yelland said last Friday?' Donald clapped his hands. It was as excited as he ever got.

'No, what did he say?' Louise was interested.

Morwenna remembered exactly what Pawly had said. But Donald was keen to tell the story.

'I mentioned Lady Elizabeth.' Donald's face was deadly serious. 'And I asked Pawly if he thought there was a curse, and he said...'

Morwenna took over. Donald could hardly bring himself to repeat the words. 'He said, "It's all hogwash. I'd like to see her curse me."'

'Do you think she did? Curse him?' Louise's voice trailed away.

'It looks that way.' Donald looked from Louise to Morwenna. 'Perhaps it was Lady Elizabeth's ghost who pushed Pawly downstairs?'

'Oh, what if it was?' Louise said, a touch too animatedly. Morwenna wondered if she was clutching at straws.

'We should wait for the post-mortem,' Morwenna said sensibly.

'But what if she pushed him invisibly?' Donald insisted.

It was time to go. Morwenna reached for her bag. 'Right. I'm off to the tearoom. I have some business to resolve.'

'Oh?' Louise picked up on Morwenna's determined tone, the set of her face. 'Is it to do with Pawly's murder? Are you seeing Jane?'

'Closer to home than that.' Morwenna grimaced. 'I need to sort some family business.'

'Right,' Louise said as Morwenna grabbed her duffel coat. As she hurried towards the door, she heard Louise say to Donald, 'If Pawly was cursed by the ghost, do you think we should tell the police? Or Bay Radio?'

'No.' Morwenna grabbed her bike and was on her way.

* * *

December was definitely the month for hot drinks, and the mug of chocolate Morwenna was holding was very comforting. She wiped a creamy brown moustache from her top lip and said, 'Go on, Mum.'

'Well, I was shopping for groceries.' Lamorna looked round. The tearoom was fairly full. Tamsin was serving at the counter. Imogen, the waitress, weaved between tables looking assured, her head of cropped brown hair bobbing up and down as she cleared tables.

'So, where was I? In the corner shop. I bought a few things, some pasta and fruit.' Lamorna lowered her voice. 'Then from out of nowhere, bang! It happened in a flash.'

'What happened?' Morwenna was concerned.

'Somebody pushed me from behind. I was in the cereal and breakfast aisle picking out some Weetabix. I fell against the display and boxes went everywhere. And my basket tipped over. Tomatoes rolling along the floor.'

'Oh, Mum.' Morwenna reached out a hand, grabbing Lamorna's ringed fingers.

'Eighty-three, and there I am sprawled on the floor with my red knickers for everyone to see.' Lamorna laughed. 'The young girl behind the till – Amy, she's called – helped me up and put my shopping in my bag for me. I hurt my knee. But it wasn't all bad. A gentleman came over and asked if he could carry my bag back home. Proper nice he was.'

'But who pushed you, Mum?'

'I don't know. He had a hoodie on. A teasy kid. I couldn't see his face.'

'Was it definitely a boy?'

'I've got no idea.' Lamorna shook her head. 'It could have been a girl. The person was slight. When they pushed me, it felt mean and nasty.'

'In what way?'

'It was a hard push. Not like an "excuse me" push but a "get out of the way, you old bag" shove. He meant business.'

'Were there any security cameras?'

'The kid's face was covered. Just a skinny kid, but he definitely had a hard push on him.'

'Mum.' Morwenna squeezed Lamorna's fingers. 'I'm going to report it to Jane. Can you give a description?'

'Black hoodie, jeans. Hood up. Could have been a teenager – maybe younger or older. Funny smell.'

'What funny smell?'

'I don't know. Perfume, the sort that makes you want to cough.'

Morwenna made a mental note. She told herself she might need the information for later. 'Were you hurt?'

'I've got a bruise on my knee. And I felt rufazrats for an hour or two afterwards,' Lamorna said. 'But Vernon was very kind. He walked me home.'

'Vernon?'

'Keep up, maid. The gentleman I met in the corner shop. Vernon. He got a good view of my bloomers, then he carried my basket back. I invited him in for a cuppa.'

'You didn't, Mum? You don't know him – you can't invite strangers into your home.'

'He was a nice man. Lovely accent, Welsh. And well dressed. He had one of those big overcoats, soft material, and a thick scarf.' Lamorna's face was dreamy. 'I hope I see him again.'

'How old was he?'

'How would I know? My age, I hope.'

Morwenna shook her head. 'But you're OK, Mum?'

'I'll live. I was jumping at the time though. The kid who shoved me was a thug.'

'And do you feel the attack was directed at you personally?' Morwenna asked worriedly.

'It was me who went flying through the air, so I'd say so.' Lamorna laughed.

'I mean, did you feel singled out?'

'No, it was just some silly tuss in a hurry.' Lamorna looked around the room and waved a hand. 'Imogen, you couldn't get me a refill? On the house?'

Imogen nodded. She had a placid face like a Madonna. She took Lamorna's cup and hurried towards the counter.

Morwenna was still anxious. 'Well, take care of yourself, Mum.'

'I'm hoping that lovely Vernon will take care of me. You should have seen the way he looked at me. All googly eyes. And he had a lovely moustache. Like fox fur.'

Morwenna pulled a face. She couldn't imagine that being appealing. But she was still filled with concern. 'If you see the kid in the hoodie again, make sure you get a good look at his face. And we'll report him.'

'Ah, it's done now. But I do hope I see Vernon again. I might just get the two-thirty bus home and see if he's called round on the off chance.' Lamorna reached for her bag. 'What are you doing later?'

'The school run, then I'm staying on for a bite with Tam and Elowen. Afterwards, I'll go home and put my feet up. I want to catch up with Jane.'

'Right. That's good.' Lamorna was probably not listening. 'Oh, I forgot I asked Imogen for a refill. You can have it. The bus will be along soon. I'll get off.' She stood up and gave a sly wink. 'I wonder what it's like to kiss a man with a moustache like a fox's tail. I bet it tickles...'

10

In the flat above the Proper Ansom Tearoom, Morwenna was washing up. Tamsin was drying plates distractedly, looking across at Elowen, who was hunched over a piece of paper writing slowly, moving her lips with each word. Without looking up, she grumbled, 'I hate Ms Stark.'

Tamsin made a face that meant it was best to say nothing, and Morwenna said, 'You know about the way of peace, Elowen. It's wrong to kick people.'

'It was only Billy Crocker.' Elowen sniffed. 'He was showing off about having two dads.'

Tamsin and Morwenna exchanged looks.

'It was just a little kick. I told Ms Stark it was just like taking a free kick in football. I'm good at free kicks.'

'You mustn't kick other children,' Tamsin said. 'While you're writing, Elowen, think about being nice to Billy.'

'Three bleddy sentences about kindness,' Elowen blurted.

Tamsin said, 'Elowen,' in exactly the same warning voice that Morwenna had used to her own daughter years ago.

Morwenna said, 'Finish off and have a bath. Oggy Two's in the bed already.'

'Oggy Two needs a bath. He smells,' Elowen whined without looking up. 'I dropped him in the sand. Anyway, I'm too old for Oggy Two. He's for babies. I need a puppy. I'm grown up now. I don't need him.'

'Oh?' Tamsin replied. 'So Oggy Two can go in the toy cupboard if you're bored with him.'

'Like you put my real daddy in the toy cupboard when you got bored with him?' Elowen asked, pen in hand. 'Now you've got another boyfriend. Will he be my daddy next?'

Tamsin exhaled slowly. 'Tristan's not my boyfriend.'

'Why does he keep sending you texts? Why have you got that funny look on your face when you talk to Becca about him?' Elowen didn't miss a trick.

Tamsin gave Morwenna a quick glance. 'It's time for bed, Elowen.'

'I haven't finished these sentences.' Elowen looked up and gave Morwenna a heart-melting look. 'I don't want Mummy to have a boyfriend.'

Morwenna thought again about Jack Greenwood. That was three times in as many days. He didn't deserve a place in her thoughts. She went over to Elowen and read what she'd written.

I must not kik people its not kind kindness is haveing a daddy whos nice but I only have a grandad to take me to futbal but my mummy sez

'You've almost finished. Come on, let's have some wind-down time. Bath first, and snuggle in bed for a story.'

'Can I have *The Great Reindeer Rescue* and *The Christmas Pig*?'

'One of them. You choose which.' Morwenna turned to Tamsin, who was already on her phone texting, a smile on her face. 'I'll sort Elowen out, then you and I'll have some mum-and-daughter time.' She gave her a meaningful look, held out a hand and led Elowen towards the bathroom.

* * *

It was well past eight o'clock when Elowen finally fell asleep and Morwenna emerged from the bedroom. Tamsin was lounging on the sofa, her feet up, still texting. She looked up. 'Do you want a glass of wine, Mum?'

'On a Monday?'

Tamsin nodded. 'I might need it. I know what's coming.'

'Oh?'

Tamsin moved to the table and picked up a bottle of red, already open, pouring wine into two glasses. 'I think I need a drink.' She gave one to Morwenna and they settled themselves on the sofa. 'I can feel twenty questions coming on.' Tamsin bit her lip. 'Where do you want to start?'

'Shall we start with Tristan? Is he your boyfriend? I don't want to pry, Tam.'

'It's not prying.' Tamsin exhaled slowly. 'At first, I thought he was privileged and superficial. But there are things I really like about him.'

Morwenna hoped it wasn't his money and the fact that he was handsome. But that wasn't fair. She said, 'He seems nice. He works in London, doesn't he?'

'He does. In finance.' Tamsin took a gulp of wine, Dutch courage. 'We hooked up in the summer. He and Seb and me and Becca. We all went out a few times as a foursome. I knew Tristan liked me. I wasn't really bothered about him though. Becca liked both of them. But Tristan gave me space to think about what I wanted.'

'I see.' Morwenna wondered if Tristan was made from the same mould as Ruan. Kind. Considerate. The keeper type. Like mother, like daughter.

'He came home for Christmas and we all met up at their party. Tristan gave me a tour of the house and we drank champagne on the top floor. Becca went off with Seb.'

Morwenna was listening intently.

'Tristan and I went to the solar. Tristan said no one goes there and it would be quiet. It's a sweet little room at the other end of the house. We just talked and talked for ages. He told me about his job, his past, and how he's made mistakes, and I said, "haven't we all?"'

'We have.' Morwenna was speaking for herself too. She met Tamsin's gaze levelly. 'So he's a good guy, Tristan?'

'He's asked me to go out with him tomorrow, just me and him. A first proper date. I want to go.'

'Well, you should have a life, Tam. It's good to go out occasionally.'

'Imogen said she'd sit with Elowen. Tristan and I are going for a meal.'

'Take it day by day, see how it goes.'

'But it's Elowen I'm worried about, Mum. You saw how she was earlier. Being aggressive again. Kicking another child. I thought she'd settled recently because it's been just her and me. I've avoided relationships for her sake – she's my priority, I promise you. I made a huge mistake with—' Tamsin couldn't bring herself to say his name.

'Jack Greenwood,' Morwenna whispered. It still sounded like a curse.

'I didn't trust myself after that. My last two relationships were bad choices.' Tamsin took a breath. 'Tristan knows about Elowen, and how she comes first. But he still wants us to be together.'

'Early days,' Morwenna said again, trying to be rational.

'I think I know how it's going to go,' Tamsin said slowly. 'We really get on. We've both noticed it. It could be really special.'

'For Christmas? Until he goes back to London?'

'I think it's more than that, Mum.'

Morwenna frowned: her daughter was leaping in at the deep end again, not knowing what sharks swam in the water below. She said, 'Take it day by day.'

'I will.'

'And what about Elowen? How will you break the news to her?'

'I'll see how things go with Tristan. Maybe she can come out with us both and get used to him being around.' Tamsin looked sad and Morwenna's heart went out to her. 'Elowen's desperate for a dad. And I'd love to have the right man in my life.'

'You both need a good one or none at all.'

'I know that, Mum.' Tamsin sighed. 'Grandma says we Mutton maids are cursed with our relationships.'

'You're a Pascoe as well, Tam.' Morwenna took her first swig of wine. 'And your dad's there for you and Elowen.'

'He's brilliant. I ought to introduce him to Tristan. I'm sure they'd get on.'

'In good time.' Morwenna edged towards the next question. 'You know Elowen's been asking everybody about her real dad?'

'Yes, you said. I've been worrying about it. She had to, at some point. I don't know what to tell her, Mum. Other than he was a mistake.'

'A mistake with no name,' Morwenna said. 'From the Caribbean.'

'He was called Junior. I didn't even know his real name. His friends called him that. Junior Bailey. He came from Negril. I met him on Seven Beach. He was selling things – you know, wood carvings. We hit it off.'

'Where were the other girls you went on holiday with?'

'They left me. There was a rum bar across the road playing music. I sat with Junior all afternoon, talking, and he invited me back to his tiny room for coffee.'

'You were young, Tam. Your defences were down.'

'I was stupid.' Tamsin drained her glass. 'He was so nice. That was the strange thing. He treated me like I was special.'

'Some men are like that.'

'He was full of compliments. We drank coffee, then rum. He called me honey and baby, said I was pretty, and before I knew it, I was in his arms and...'

'I can imagine,' Morwenna said, trying not to.

'The next day, I thought we'd be together for the whole holiday and beyond. He'd said that we meant something to each other. He kissed me goodbye first thing and we made plans to meet for lunch. I never saw him again.'

Morwenna wrapped an arm around her. 'That must have been tough, Tam.'

'I came home and pretended I'd had a lovely holiday, but I felt rubbish all week. Like I was an idiot. A few weeks later, I found out I was pregnant. You and Dad were arguing a lot, and I didn't know how to tell you. Then I had to. I was embarrassed.'

'I'm sorry I let you down,' Morwenna said.

'You didn't. I was naïve and stupid. I had Elowen, and she was the best thing ever, and I promised her when I held her in my arms for the first time that it would just be her and me forever. Five years later, I was a bit vulnerable. I met that awful Jack, and I hoped against all odds that he was the one...'

Tears came. Tamsin's face was wet and Morwenna gathered her in her arms, her own eyes brimming. She whispered into her hair, 'We're family, Tam. We're all here for you.'

'I know.' Tamsin sniffed, wiping her face with her hand. 'You and Dad are the best. I don't deserve you.'

'You deserve to be happy. We all do.' Morwenna let out a deep breath. 'So, let's focus on Tristan. Take it slowly.'

'You think I'll make the same mistake?' Tamsin asked.

'Not at all. Tristan may be the best person in the world.' Morwenna wiped a tear from Tamsin's cheek. 'Go on your date. Enjoy yourself. See what happens.'

'But don't throw myself in, I know.' Tamsin forced a laugh. 'Thanks, Mum.'

'You have a family of babysitters too,' Morwenna said kindly. 'Your dad and I—'

'At the same time? That's a great idea,' Tamsin said mischievously. 'I mean, Christmas is a time for romance.'

'I think your father and I have gone beyond that.'

'I don't agree,' Tamsin said softly. 'Dad still loves you. He told me.'

'It's time to go home.' Morwenna stood up, ignoring the last comment. 'I've got other things on my mind.'

'Barnaby?' Tamsin asked, her expression incredulous.

'Pawly. I need to work out what happened.'

Tamsin poured herself another glass of wine. 'You're amazing, Mum.'

'I do my best,' Morwenna said. 'Right. I'll pop round soon. Just try to keep Elowen under control. Christmas makes kids overexcited.'

'I've always worried about her being a tearaway. Because she's got no dad. It's my fault.' Tamsin welled up again, more shiny tears.

'No, it isn't,' Morwenna said firmly. 'I was just the same at her age. It's genetic.' She opened her arms for a hug and breathed her daughter's scent deeply. 'Sleep well, Tam. Maybe this will be the best Christmas ever and Tristan will be the one.'

'I hope so,' Tamsin said; Morwenna was worried Tamsin had given her heart away already and felt she should offer more wise words. Instead, she said, 'I'll see you dreckly,' and made her way towards the door. It would be a long slog home in the cold sea air.

* * *

Morwenna walked a few yards along the road, her head full of what Tamsin had told her about Tristan and Junior and Elowen. Shivering, she increased her pace to reach the hill sooner and get home quicker. She was conscious of a rumbling noise next to her. Pawly's death had made her jumpy. She turned to see a police car moving slowly. It was Jane Choy, in uniform. Morwenna stopped and Jane opened the door.

'Hop in. I'll give you a lift.'

Morwenna clambered gratefully in the passenger seat, immediately warmed by the heater that was blasting out hot air. 'Thanks, Jane. Is this part of the Seal Bay service for seeing old people safely home?'

'Maybe. But I need to talk something over.'

'Oh? Personal or professional?'

'Both,' Jane said enigmatically. 'My private life has taken an interesting twist.'

'Tell me more.' Morwenna watched Jane driving along, her uniform pristine, her eyes on the road, and decided it was about time she had a bit of romance.

'Another time.' Jane turned the car around a corner and up the long drag that led to Harbour Cottages. 'I need you on board.'

'With what?'

'Can I pick your brain about Pawly Yelland?'

'Of course. Why?'

'The results came back from the post-mortem today.' Jane took a breath. 'Pawly died from a fall. That's clear. So the case will now go to the coroner's court on Tuesday and all the evidence will be looked at.' They had reached number four, and the engine idled. Jane turned to Morwenna. 'We'll wait for the outcome. But if someone did push him then the person we're looking for was at the party. That would make them someone we know.'

'You think he was murdered?'

'I'm keeping an open mind, but my instincts tell me something's not right. Off the record, I'd appreciate it if you kept your ear to the ground.'

'Oh, right.' Morwenna was taking in the information slowly.

'As far as Seal Bay is concerned, Pawly tumbled downstairs because he had a few drinks,' Jane said crisply. 'But we both know there's another possible scenario, don't we? Several local people are in the frame, people who had a grudge.'

'There's a long list.'

'Who's on it, Morwenna? In your opinion?'

'The Pengellens, obviously. Julian and Pippa.'

'Tristan?'

'Probably not.' Morwenna shook her head. 'A few people were angry with Pawly though.'

'Damien Woon. His ex, Faye Bryce.' Jane focused on the road. 'Anyone else?'

Morwenna thought about Steve Piper. She wouldn't mention him. 'Anyone who was there. We were all in fancy dress. Someone could have sneaked in from outside. But there was definitely another person on the stairs. After the bump, I heard footsteps.'

'Are you sure?'

'I'm positive.'

'Then we have to find who it was,' Jane said softly, turning up the hill to Harbour Cottages. 'Between you and me, it looks like Pawly didn't fall at all. He was pushed.'

TUESDAY 16 DECEMBER

11

Morwenna slept badly. She woke up, yawned and stared at Brenda, who'd leaped onto the bed with an expression that said, *Feed me*. Morwenna struggled into her dressing gown. It was pitch dark outside. Not yet seven.

She rubbed bleary eyes and her worries came back like an icy flood. Tamsin. Elowen. Her mother. Pawly.

Pawly was probably pushed downstairs by someone who crept up on him. Her mother had been shoved from behind in the corner shop.

Could it have been the same person?

She was being silly. Her mum had probably been the victim of an impatient kid with too much testosterone. Pawly had either tumbled or been targeted. Morwenna reminded herself to stop trying to be a sleuth. She ought to concentrate on being a daughter. A mother.

In the kitchen, she fed Brenda dried food. The packet said salmon flavour, but it smelled musty. Her laptop was still open on the table. She ought to go through Justin Kidd's photos again. She sat down for a moment and typed his name into a search engine.

Justin Kidd, fashion photographer.

There he was, his website. So many photos of models, mostly women, a few elegant men in suits, many taken on location, beaches, palm trees, woodlands. A woman glared into the lens, dressed in a purple frothy dress that looked as if it was made of flowerheads.

A woman in a man's jacket and little else stood on a stretch of burnished sand. There she was again, Fernanda: pouting in a floaty headscarf, sitting in a wicker chair, peering over her shoulder, or smouldering in a long silk kimono. She was professional, poised.

Morwenna clicked the mouse again. He had different pages on his website:

Commercial fashion, portraits, moving images, contact me.

She clicked on the last one. There was an email address, a mobile phone number and the words:

I work with my small team in south London to create shoots for everything from large global brands to small independent labels. I shoot both stills and moving images.

Nothing out of the ordinary. Morwenna was wondering where to go with her research next. She heard the letterbox click.

Hugging her dressing gown, she scurried to the front door and picked up the letters on the mat. There was an advertisement for bargain wine from the local supermarket, a brown envelope, a letter from the doctors' surgery – a flu jab reminder. And a Christmas card. Her first one this year. The writing was unfamiliar, a round hand like a schoolkid's scrawl. She opened the envelope with eager fingers.

A huge red Santa Claus with cherry cheeks ho-ho-hoed on the front, his frothy white beard covering most of his face. An arm was raised in salutation, holding a mince pie. At the top, she saw the blood-red heading: 'MERRY CHRISTMAS'.

Inside the card were the gold-printed words, 'Wishing you a Christmas that is merry and bright.' Someone had put a large X through the greeting, crossing it out, filling the whole page completely. A huge black mark, like a kiss of death.

Morwenna shuddered. Who would have sent such a nasty thing?

She was staring at the card, lost in thought, when someone rapped at the door. Her heart leaped in alarm before her brain recognised the knock. She opened the door to see Ruan in his fisherman's oilskins. He was holding up a card with a Santa on the front. He noticed the identical one.

'Did you get one too?'

'I did. Come in, Ruan.' Morwenna stepped back. 'Do you have time for a cup of tea before you go down the harbour?'

'A quick one,' Ruan said. She watched him close the door behind him against the dark morning sky. He'd always looked lovely in oilskins.

In the kitchen, she poured water onto teabags. 'Is the greeting crossed out on your card?'

'Yes. Like someone really meant it,' Ruan said.

'What do you make of it?'

'I don't know. It's a Santa Claus on the front,' Ruan said simply. 'Like Pawly. Is that a connection?'

'It could be. Off the record, Pawly's case has gone to the coroner's court,' Morwenna said, handing Ruan a mug.

'I heard in The Smugglers last night that the police think it was an accident. I had a drink with Damien.'

'News travels fast.' Morwenna had a thought. 'But what about these cards? I wonder who else has got one.'

'What are you thinking?'

'A packet contains more than two. Have other people at the Pengellens' party got one?' Morwenna frowned. 'Is it a message? A threat?' She met Ruan's eyes. 'I'll phone Jane.'

'Why would someone send a card like that?' Ruan asked thoughtfully.

'I've no idea,' Morwenna said. 'Mum was pushed over in the corner shop by a kid in a hoodie.'

'You think it's connected with Pawly?' Ruan asked.

'It could be.' Morwenna changed the subject. 'Tam has a date tonight with Tristan Pengellen.'

'She told me,' Ruan said. Morwenna wondered if she was the last to hear about their romance. 'He seems a nice lad.'

'Not like Elowen's father, Junior,' Morwenna said.

'I don't know anything about him.' Ruan's eyes shone. 'We should catch up at some point and share notes.'

'We should.' Morwenna held his gaze.

Ruan finished his tea in two gulps. 'I have to go.'

'Right.' Morwenna followed him to the front door, opening it and letting in an icy blast. 'Safe fishing,' she called after him.

She'd always said that when they were together. For a moment, she felt sad. Those times had been good. With a heavy sigh, she made her way back to the kitchen.

The open laptop caught her eye, and she sat down, fingers poised. Brenda perched on the chair next to her, watching. Morwenna thought for a moment. 'What about Pawly's girlfriend? Faye? I need to know more about her.'

She brought up the Peter Pan photos and examined the one of Faye and Pippa dancing, with Pawly cavorting in the middle, trying to catch their attention. Morwenna looked closer. Pawly's eyes were on Faye; he was besotted. She assumed he was drunk. Pippa's expression was one of concern for Faye. She was clearly a loyal friend.

Morwenna made a mental note to talk to Pippa. Interestingly, despite Pawly's proximity to her, Faye was looking away, as if he were a nasty smell. Morwenna noticed her hand, raised in a nifty dance movement. She was wearing a wedding band and a sparkling eternity ring.

'Now what did Pawly say?' Morwenna tried to remember. 'She and Pawly hooked up at the end of the summer. They had great sex. He told her he loved her, and she told him that she loved him back, but not in *that* way.' She reached out an arm to stroke Brenda.

Again, she noticed the photo of Pawly, his arms around Damien and Beverley. Damien was furious. There was a murderous glint in his eyes.

Morwenna recalled what Pawly had said at the library talk. 'Woon's boatyard, for instance. There are a few tales I could tell about that place.' She looked closer at Damien's expression. He was moody, brooding. What had Pawly meant by a few tales? Morwenna needed to find out.

Motives were coming out of the woodwork, thick and fast.

But right now, Morwenna had her morning shift in the library to think of. Another mug of tea, then she'd be on her way, out into the December cold.

* * *

Morwenna left the library shortly after twelve-thirty and rode down to the seafront. The tide was out, the waves choppy, like corrugated metal, the line between water and sky indistinct. The wind was flinging seagulls upwards and their cries split the air.

On the horizon, she could see a trawler, tiny against the vast grey of the ocean. She imagined Ruan at work and a cold gust of wind made her shudder.

There was no one about the beach except for a lone jogger with a pale dog. In the summer, the place would be heaving with families, fast food, ice-cream sellers. Now it was desolate.

A light voice pulled her from her thoughts. 'Eh up, long time no see.'

She turned round, still leaning on her bike. 'Sheppy, how are you?'

'Can't complain.' Sheppy gave his usual mischievous grin. Morwenna noticed he was wearing a heavy coat that looked quite new.

'So, what are you up to? There can't be much call for a beach entertainer right now.'

'Oh, I'm raking it in.' Sheppy's flossy brown curls had grown almost to his shoulders, sticking out beneath a beanie. 'I'm doing kiddies' birthday parties, and the landlord in The Smugglers gets me in there at weekends to do magic tricks for the customers. I get to keep whatever tips I make – the landlord thinks it makes the punters thirsty if they're watching a bit of magic. And guess what else?'

Morwenna was glad to see Sheppy blossoming. Months ago, he'd been living in a battered old caravan on a down-at-heel site. 'Tell me.'

'I'm Santa Claus.'

'What?' Morwenna shivered. She'd had enough of Santas this Christmas.

'The Quilkin Emporium, with the green spotted frog over the door, wanted a Santa Claus. I get four days a week as Santa, chatting to the kiddies, listening to them mither on about what they want for Christmas. So I'm raking it in.'

'That's good.'

'And guess what else? I might have a girlfriend.'

'You *might* have?' Morwenna asked. 'Does she know yet?'

'Not exactly. But you know where I live, on Camp Dynamo? Well, it's right quiet there now all the surfers have gone, but this new girl's moved into the caravan opposite me and she's well fit.'

'But she's not your girlfriend yet?'

'No, but she will be.'

'Why don't you bring her down to the tearoom?' Morwenna said.

'I just might,' Sheppy said. 'Hey, I hear you're sleuthing again. That fella on the radio was banging on about it.'

'Mike Sheridan? What's he saying?'

'That the writer was shoved down the stairs and Dibble don't know nowt about owt.'

'Dibble?'

'The coppers. But he says you're on the case and you're sound. If anyone can find who killed him, you can.'

'Really?' Morwenna didn't like the sound of that.

'I'm not being funny, but it must have been someone at that posh party,' Sheppy said, kicking a pebble. 'Can't they just interview them all? Someone's bound to crack under pressure.'

'Who knows?'

'You'll sort it all out for Dibble.' Sheppy turned to go. 'Oh, and if you need an accomplice, like – I'm mad for it. We could be Sherlock Holmes and Dr What'sisname.'

'That's not the worst idea.' Morwenna leaned forward. 'Sheppy, when you're in The Smugglers doing card tricks, keep your ear to the ground. Let me know anything of interest.'

'Sound. I will. See you around, Miss Marple,' Sheppy said with a wink, and strolled away.

Morwenna clambered on her bike and set off for the tearoom.

Talk of a cuppa had made her realise that the cold had set in her bones. She needed warming up.

Ten minutes later, she secured her bike outside the Proper Ansom Tearoom and hurried into the warmth. Tamsin seemed in a good mood as she took Morwenna's order. Her eyes sparkled and she looked full of energy. Morwenna remembered that she had a date with Tristan.

'Tea and a mince pie coming up, Mum. Imogen will bring it over.'

'Thanks, Tam.' Morwenna hung back. 'Did you get any Christmas cards this morning?'

'A couple, old mates from school. Why?'

'No reason.' Morwenna didn't want to say. 'Have you seen Mum today?'

'She rang a few minutes ago. She said she'd pick Elowen up from school.'

'She didn't mention anything about Christmas cards?'

'No, why? What's going on?'

'Oh, I had an anonymous one.' Morwenna tried to make light of it.

'An admirer?'

'I doubt it.' Morwenna decided that romance was all Tamsin could think about right now. Fair play. 'I'll have a seat.'

'I can't chat.' Tamsin indicated the customers. Almost every table was full. 'We're doing a big deal on turkey soup today. Zach's in the kitchen, melting under the pressure. I'd better check.'

'Right.' Morwenna sat down and took out her phone. She thumbed a message to Lamorna.

MORWENNA

All right Mum.

The reply came back almost immediately.

LAMORNA

> Can't talk now. Have a visitor.

And a heart emoji.

Morwenna wondered if Vernon had called round. Love was everywhere.

A light voice came from behind her. 'Here's your tea and mince pie.' Imogen placed the tray on the table.

Morwenna took in her cropped brown hair. It had been dyed in the pattern and colours of a leopard. She said, 'Your hair looks great.'

'Thanks.' Imogen ran her fingers through it. 'Faye did it for me.'

Morwenna sat up and paid attention. 'Faye?'

'Faye Bryce from Mane Attraction. It's a great hairdressing salon, not far from The Quilkin Emporium.'

'Is Faye tall with smooth dark hair?' Morwenna fingered her own silver locks.

'She was until yesterday. She's gone blonde crop for Christmas. She needed to cheer herself up.'

'She's a friend of Pippa Pengellen's?'

'I've seen Pippa in there.'

'I wonder if she has any spare appointments. Does she do walk-ins?' Morwenna asked.

'On Tuesdays and Wednesdays – and it's Tuesday today,' Imogen said. 'Enjoy your mince pie.'

12

As soon as she opened the door, Morwenna could smell the sharp odour of ammonia and baked hair. It had been years since she'd been to the hairdresser's. She wasn't really sure what to say when a young woman with a French plait sidled over and asked, 'How can I help you?'

Morwenna sized the young woman up. Eighteen, most likely. Local. Friendly. She wouldn't be difficult to get on side. Over her shoulder, she noticed a newly blonde Faye and another woman with long red hair attending to two customers facing tall mirrors.

Morwenna gave a beaming smile. 'Oh, I do hope you can help me out. I've got an invitation to dinner. A romantic evening. With a man. Think George Clooney cloned – and, well, I need to look my best.' She tugged at her hair and made a face. 'Split ends. Not great.'

The young woman was all sympathy. Her name badge said she was called Chloe. 'I see what you mean. Did you want to book?'

'Can I see someone now?' Morwenna looked horrified. 'My date's tonight and I so want to impress… Bear. That's my date's name.' She rolled her eyes and said, 'Grrr,' just to emphasise her point.

Chloe understood completely. 'Right, we can't let you go looking like this, can we?' She went over to the desk and examined the screen. 'Michelle can see you in ten minutes for a quick trim. She's got another customer booked in for three or, if you're happy to wait, Faye can do you a refresh and style. She'll be available in twenty minutes.'

'A refresh and style sounds perfect.' Morwenna had no idea what she was booking. 'I'll wait for Faye.'

'Good plan. What name is it?'

'Freda Lovejoy.' Morwenna said the first name that came into her head.

'Right, Freda. Take a seat. Can I get you a coffee and a magazine?' Chloe asked.

'Thanks.' Morwenna dropped down on the squashy sofa.

For the next twenty-five minutes, she was staring round the salon holding a copy of *Hello!* magazine in front of her face like a spy, listening in to conversations.

The red-haired woman, Michelle, was finishing a cut on a middle-aged woman with short, neat hair. Her customer complained about how she was the only person responsible for her demanding mother, and how her useless brother did nothing at all. Morwenna blocked the conversation out and tuned into Faye, who was cutting a woman's hair, flourishing scissors, speaking in a light tone. 'Oh, I'm not ready for Christmas.'

'We have family coming. My mum brings the turkey already cooked,' the customer said to the mirror. 'What are you doing?'

Faye shrugged. 'We'll stay home. My husband works in construction, so he's often away, but he's back on Christmas Eve. It'll just be the two of us.'

'That's nice,' the client said. Morwenna leaned forward to hear better.

Faye continued chatting. 'Craig's away a lot. It can be hard on my own.'

'Darren and I never go out together now we have little ones. Do you have children?'

'No.' Faye snipped away efficiently. 'I get bored though, by myself. I often think I should have a bit of a fling, you know, to keep myself occupied. What do you think?'

'Why not?' The client's laugher tinkled. 'Oh, I love a bit of juicy gossip. Wouldn't your husband be angry?'

'He wouldn't know,' Faye said confidentially. 'I wouldn't tell him.'

The two women laughed together for a moment. The client started to talk about recipes for Christmas desserts. Michelle finished with her customer and they were bustling at the desk with Chloe, making the next appointment. The customer left and Michelle disappeared into a back room. Faye peered over her shoulder and called, 'I'll be with you soon.'

'No worries,' Morwenna said, wondering if Faye recognised her from Pippa's party. She didn't appear to.

Fifteen minutes later, she was sitting in front of the mirror, her hair being brushed vigorously. Faye said, 'What sort of cut did you want?'

'Cut?' Morwenna hadn't expected to have her hair cut.

'A great cut with lots of texture would suit you. A short-layered bob. Your hair's a bit coarse and dry. I could put highlights through to make it shine.' Faye raised her scissors professionally.

Morwenna felt herself cringe and sink lower in the seat. She took a deep breath for courage. 'Can you just trim the ends? My...' She lowered her voice. 'My secret lover likes it long.'

'Highlights?' Faye asked optimistically.

'Just a few, then,' Morwenna said nervously.

'Your man will love what I'm going to do.' Faye was firing on all cylinders. 'We'll make it glossy, cascading waves. Is it for a special occasion?'

'Yes.' Morwenna made her tone sound confiding. 'My husband thinks I'm at the WI Christmas dinner.' Faye flounced off and returned with a tray full of bottles. Strands of her hair were painted with something purple that Morwenna hoped wouldn't resemble the final colour. Half an hour later, she was ushered to a sink, her hair was washed and she was led back to her seat in front of the mirror, where Faye busied herself cutting her hair at strange angles.

'I hope Bear will like this,' Morwenna said, encouraging conversation.

'So, tell me about this mystery man,' Faye said.

'Bear and I meet when we can.' Morwenna was improvising. 'He picks me up on the seafront – I pretend I'm getting the bus – and we drive somewhere quiet.' She gave Faye a trusting look. 'You've no idea how hard it is to keep an affair secret with a jealous husband.'

'Oh, I'm sure I do.'

'All the secrets and lies. It's exhausting,' Morwenna said anxiously.

'It is,' Faye agreed.

'And the times we've nearly been discovered,' Morwenna breathed out as if she were in a horror film.

'Why don't you leave your husband?' Faye asked, her eyes meeting Morwenna's in the mirror.

'Habit. Routine. And I love him, I suppose.' Morwenna gave a weary sigh. 'Although' – this was her killer attempt at getting Faye to confide in her – 'I don't love him in *that* way any more.'

'Mmm.' Faye made a sound that meant she understood. 'That's the thing, isn't it? I fell out of love with my husband and had a torrid affair.'

'Oh? I love the feeling of doing something you shouldn't. It's like a drug, it's thrilling.' Morwenna was lying through her teeth.

'I know what you mean.' Faye seemed suddenly sad.

'So – if you don't mind me asking – did your secret lover make you feel like I do with my Bear?' Morwenna whispered. 'All tingly?'

'It went badly wrong.' Faye produced a curling iron and set to twisting it in Morwenna's hair. 'We split up.'

'Did you break his heart?' Morwenna asked as tragically as she could.

'He became clingy.'

'How awful.' Morwenna put a hand to her mouth. 'What did he do?'

'He followed me around, drank too much. He was really besotted.'

'No!' Morwenna was exaggeratedly shocked. 'So where is he now?'

'Gone. And good riddance.' There was a moment's pause, longer than it should have been. 'He won't bother me again. I'm back with my husband.' Faye took a deep breath, stood back and surveyed her handiwork. 'Whereas you look a million dollars. Bear's going to love you.'

'He will.' Morwenna gazed at her reflection, silver hair shining, waves highlighted silver with an almost light bluish tinge. 'Thanks, this is great.' She meant it.

Faye took the towel from her neck. 'Would you like to make another appointment, Freda?'

Morwenna had almost forgotten that was her name. 'Yes. But can I have a business card and call when I've checked my diary?' She gave Faye a look that said they understood each other. 'You know how it is, trying to organise a double life.' She flourished her card to pay, taking care to keep her name covered. 'Thanks, you've been really helpful. I couldn't be more delighted.'

* * *

Morwenna sat at the kitchen table thinking about Faye's words about Pawly. '*Gone... He won't bother me again.*'

Despite the wind blowing her hair all over the place on the cycle ride home, it still looked good. But she wouldn't be able to go back to Mane Attraction again, certainly not as her own self. It was unlikely she'd bump into Faye, unless it was through Pippa.

The Pengellens. Morwenna's fingers tapped the keyboard. She wanted to check Justin Kidd's photographs again to check Julian's and Pippa's movements at the party. There were a couple of photos of Pippa dancing in her flouncy dress, another of her with Faye guzzling champagne, and one in which she was speaking to Julian in the corner near the mistletoe. They didn't look as if they were about to kiss. In fact, Julian had a finger raised and Pippa looked distinctly annoyed.

There were no other pictures of Julian. She wondered where he'd gone. She leaned her head on her hands and thought about who might have killed Pawly, if that was what had happened. There were certainly plenty of suspects.

Morwenna made a list in her head of people she wanted to talk to, all those with motives. It had been useful meeting Faye. There was certainly no love lost between her and Pawly. She had said, 'Good riddance.' And changed her hair colour. Clearly, she intended to put bad memories behind her.

It was past six. She ought to cook something.

She felt Brenda clamber on her knee, digging in sharp claws. Her phone rang and she picked it up. 'Mum?'

'Hello, maid. I was talking to Tam when I brought Elowen back from school. She said you'd been asking if I got a Christmas card this morning.'

'That's right.'

'How did you guess?'

Morwenna caught her breath. 'Did you get that Santa card, Mum?'

'Santa card? No. Mine was a big one with hearts and roses and a teddy bear skating on ice.'

'Oh?' Morwenna breathed out in relief.

'It was from Vernon. He took me out for lunch. Afterwards, we came back here and talked and talked all afternoon.' There was a sound that might have been a full-blown sigh. 'He's lovely. Oh, and that 'tache is so sexy.'

'Tell me about him, Mum.'

'He's called Vernon Lewis. He's seventy-nine, a bit younger than me, but not that you'd notice. He's from Swansea. He used to be a stockbroker. He drives a BMW saloon, a black one. He's going to take me out again.'

'When?'

'He'll call round.'

'Where does he live?'

'He's staying in The Fisherman's Knot Hotel, on the edge of town. He drinks in The Lugger Bar there. It's posh.'

'How long is he in Seal Bay?' Morwenna was suspicious.

'Just for Christmas. He's a widower. He hates being on his own at this time of year.'

'Right.' Morwenna wasn't convinced.

'A Christmas romance. And Tam's going out with the

Pengellen boy tonight. That's grandmother and granddaughter done. There's only you left to sort.'

'I don't need sorting,' Morwenna said quickly. She heard two raps at the front door, a familiar knock. 'Mum, just take it a day at a time, promise me.'

'You're always the same,' Lamorna laughed. 'You just can't throw yourself into a relationship with glorious abandon, can you?' She cackled even louder. 'We'll catch up dreckly.'

'We will.' Morwenna put the phone down and heard Ruan's spare key turning in the door. His footsteps sounded in the hall as he called, 'It's only me.'

He appeared in the doorway in a dark jacket and jeans, carrying a brown paper bag. For a moment he stared. 'You look nice.'

Morwenna wasn't sure what to say. She fluffed her hair, feeling awkward. The compliment had made her heart thump. 'Thanks.'

'Are you going out?'

'No, I got it done in the hairdresser's. It cost me a bomb. I only wanted to speak to the hairdresser, Faye Bryce, but I stayed for the whole hairdo. She's Pawly's ex. I needed to check out if she could have pushed him.'

'And did she?'

'She might have.' Morwenna noticed the bag. 'What have you got there?'

'Steamed rice, crab and sweetcorn soup, Szechuan prawns, vegetable stir-fry,' Ruan said. 'I hope you haven't eaten.'

'I haven't,' Morwenna said. 'When have you known me have food on the table by half six?'

Ruan put the bag down. 'We have a lot to talk about. Tam, Pawly.'

'And Mum. She's got a new man. I just hope she's not going to get hurt.'

'She's all grown up,' Ruan said kindly.

'Oh, and Jane messaged me earlier. She's asked me to go into Bay Radio with her tomorrow. She wants us to make a public statement on Mike Sheridan's show, to calm things down.'

'No clues about Pawly, then?'

'I've got a few irons in the fire, Ruan.'

'I'd like to help.'

'Right. Well, when we've eaten all this food, how about I show you some photographs of the party?'

'Photographs?' Ruan met her eyes. 'Where did you get them?'

'That would be telling.' Morwenna tapped her nose. 'But they'll be useful. We might come up with a few theories.'

She almost added 'as friends' and thought better of it. It didn't need saying. She was about to open a bottle of wine, fill two glasses, and she checked herself again.

It was probably better to stay sober if she was trying to solve a crime.

And drinking wine with Ruan into the late hours wasn't the wisest idea.

WEDNESDAY 17 DECEMBER

13

Jane drove Morwenna down a narrow side street and came to a halt. The radio station frontage looked the same, despite being under new ownership. There was a neon sign that said 'Bay Radio' with the logo of a palm tree with green leaves like the top of a pineapple. Morwenna climbed from the police car and pulled up the hood of her duffel. It was raining hard, stair rods, splashing into puddles on the pavement, the sky overhead thunderously dark.

Morwenna made a dash for it, Jane at her heels. She pressed the buzzer on the keypad and an uninterested voice crackled, 'Hello – do you have an appointment?'

'It's Morwenna, Trudi.'

Jane took over. 'Open up, please. It's the police.'

There was a click; the electronic door buzzed, and they stepped inside, shaking raindrops. Morwenna's hair had lost all the curl now. Most of it was damp. Jane removed her hat briskly as a young woman with a blonde ponytail, false eyelashes and a silver lanyard arrived carrying a clipboard.

'Good morning, Trudi,' Jane said. 'We're here for the Mike

Sheridan show.' She looks around. 'Who owns Bay Radio now that it's parted company with Tom Fox?'

'An artist from Truro bought it. He never comes down. Most of the organisation is left to the DJs and me.' Trudi seemed unimpressed with the new arrangement. 'This way, please. Mike's ready for you.'

Trudi slipped a magic card into a magic lock and another door sprang open. She indicated a seat in a row of five green plastic chairs, all vacant.

'Take a seat please.' She waved her clipboard, hurrying away on high heels. Mike Sheridan's voice came from speakers on the wall.

'So that was "I Fought the Law" by The Clash. And talking of the law, we have an imminent visit from WPC Jane Choy and Morwenna Mutton, the Seal Bay sleuth. I'll be asking questions about the recent horrific death of local writer Pawly Yelland on Pettarock Head and attempting to discover if it was foul play. Folks, do we have someone running round on the loose in Seal Bay right now who is a danger to the public? With Christmas just around the corner, the people of Seal Bay have a right to know. And on that troubling note, here's "Killer on the Loose" by Thin Lizzy.'

The sound of a rocking guitar belted from the speakers. Jane looked cross. 'He's a loose cannon.'

'He is,' Morwenna said.

'I'll take him down the nick if he's not careful,' Jane whispered.

Trudi reappeared, clipboard held like a shield. 'We're ready for you.'

Morwenna and Jane followed her through a glass-fronted room where several people sat working at laptops. Mike's studio was directly in front of them. Jane pushed the door open and walked in, Morwenna at her heels. Mike waved a cheery 'Hi' and put a finger on his lips to indicate that they should be silent. Jane exchanged a look with Morwenna that meant she had no intention of being shushed. They both took seats in front of a microphone as the song ended.

'That was "Killer on the Loose",' Mike said emphatically. 'So – welcome, WPC Jane Choy.'

'It's just PC nowadays, since 1999. Keep up, Mike,' Jane said humourlessly.

Mike ignored her. 'And Morwenna Mutton, who's been behind several crime-busting escapades, solving problems that our police force couldn't—'

'That's not exactly true,' Morwenna began.

'But it has to be said, Morwenna,' Mike continued, 'they've depended on your initiative in the past when they've drawn a blank. Our own DJ, Irina Bacheva, for instance, last summer.'

'I'd rather we kept to the subject in hand,' Jane said firmly.

'Let's talk about Pawly Yelland, then. A talented writer, a local celebrity, no less, in his fifties, currently working on a new project to do with Seal Bay. Who apparently, at a local library talk just a day before his death, uncovered all sorts of information about people in Seal Bay that might incriminate them—'

'That's not accurate, Mike,' Jane said smoothly. 'Unless you have any information you'd like to share with the police.'

'He was found at the bottom of the stairs in Pengellen Manor the following day, dressed as Santa Claus, with his neck broken. He had a bottle of bubbly in one hand and a mince pie in the other.' Mike was on a roll. 'It was no accident, PC Choy. True or false?'

'We believe that Mr Yelland's death was accidental.'

'But how can you be sure?' Mike sat back in his seat

triumphantly. 'PC Choy, do we have a murderer in our midst? The people of the bay need to know.'

'As I said, Mr Yelland's death was ruled misadventure by the coroner yesterday afternoon. I can reassure the public that they're safe. You mustn't whip up hysteria when there's absolutely nothing to worry abou—'

'Morwenna.' Mike cut Jane short. 'Who do you think's responsible? And if there's a killer on the loose, will you catch him before Christmas?'

'Him?' Morwenna's eyes shone.

'Pawly was quite a big man. It would take some effort to push him down the stairs.'

Morwenna said slowly, 'We need to trust the police and not pass on false information.'

'Mike, I'm here to tell your listeners what the police position is,' Jane said clearly. She exchanged a glance with Morwenna. 'We need an atmosphere of calm in order to do our jobs.'

'Morwenna.' Mike turned to Morwenna. He'd had enough of Jane's official line. 'Do you have any leads?'

'No,' Morwenna said. 'There's no case. Pawly was a friend, and I'd be glad if we could just put his unfortunate death behind us.' She thought of the cards, the greeting crossed out emphatically, and decided that the radio show gave her an opportunity. She moved closer to the microphone. 'Hypothetically, though, if there were a murderer, they'd be behind bars before Christmas.'

Jane raised a finger, a signal to stop. 'Morwenna means that the matter's in hand. Thank you, Mike, for allowing us to speak to your listeners. Seal Bay police officers wish them a wonderful and worry-free festive period.'

'I hope so, Jane. That was PC Jane Choy,' Mike said, his tone sarcastic. 'And now for some music. We may have had murder in the manor house. Here's "Murder on the Dancefloor" by Sophie

Ellis-Bextor. And let's all hope it doesn't come to that this Christmas.'

The music began gently, a woman's voice, and Mike flicked a switch. 'Thanks for coming in.' He gave Jane a false smile. 'The people of Seal Bay need updating.'

'They don't need scaring, Mike,' Jane said. 'I'd like you to take that to heart.'

'Is that a threat?' Mike scoffed.

'I'm asking you not to be a scaremonger,' Jane replied. 'No speculation, no hysteria. Understand?'

Mike turned to Morwenna. 'It's good that you're representing the local people, Morwenna, getting involved.'

'We have police officers to do police work. Morwenna takes a back seat,' Jane said emphatically.

'Jane knows what she's doing,' Morwenna said, standing up and following Jane to the door.

They hurried outside, pushing the buttons for the electric doors. The skies were ominously dark, with low brooding clouds, and the rain was bucketing down. In the shelter of the police car, Jane said, 'I could swing for that man.'

'He's all hot air.'

'Rick wants the case closed.' Jane spoke confidentially. 'But I could tell by what you were saying in there that you think it shouldn't be.'

'Just instinct,' Morwenna said.

'I'm with you on that one.' Jane met Morwenna's eyes. 'So what evidence have you got?'

'Well...' Morwenna lowered her voice although no one was listening '...I'm late for my library shift. But can you come round later? I've got something I need to show you.'

'I'll bring Blessed,' Jane said. Her phone buzzed and she rolled her eyes. 'It's a message from Rick. He's heard the interview with Mike and he's not happy.' She took a breath. 'This isn't going to be easy.'

'Can I help?'

'Rick's going to invite a few people who were at the party in for a chat, just so he can put the record straight, close the case and announce to the public that Pawly's case is closed.'

'But I'll keep my ear close to the ground, right?'

'Just keep a low profile. As far as the public are concerned, there's no investigation. Now I need to talk to my boss and calm him down.'

'Right. Can you give me a lift to the library? I'll be a drowned rat if I walk.'

* * *

Morwenna was drying out and warming up. The old heating system in the library belted out hot air. It was a quiet morning, Louise putting books away distractedly, as if her thoughts were elsewhere. Morwenna was selecting new stock, reading online book reviews, publishers' announcements and catalogues. She checked the clock. It was past eleven-thirty and they hadn't stopped for a tea break yet. She was about to fill the kettle when the door crashed open and an anxious figure in a damp mackintosh rushed in, lowering an umbrella. It was Pippa Pengellen. She was breathless as she reached the counter.

'Morwenna. I'm so glad you're here.'

Morwenna smiled in welcome. 'Where else would I be?'

'I heard you on the radio.'

'I popped in with Jane first thing,' Morwenna said.

'I need to talk to you.'

'Of course.' Morwenna tried a little joke to calm the situation down – Pippa looked anxious. 'I mean, we're practically in-laws.'

'What? Oh, did Tristan have a date with your daughter?' Pippa seemed uninterested. 'He goes through girlfriends like they're going out of fashion. That last one who turned up to the party, the Mexican model – horrendous. I don't know who invited her. Julian, I think – ah, that's why I'm here. The police have just come for him. The DCI from London, Barnarde, she came to the house and took him away in her car.'

'They just need a few more questions about the party, Pippa.'

'Yes, but I'm worried that she'll want to talk to me next after that dreadful talk by Pawly—' Pippa looked around. 'Is there somewhere we can talk? Privately?'

'Here,' Morwenna suggested. There was no one around except for a young man in tortoiseshell glasses in the far corner, who was pretending to read a book on nuclear physics – though Morwenna suspected he'd just come in to stay out of the rain. Louise was over in the reference section, putting dictionaries in order.

'The thing is, about Pawly... I really can't forgive him.'

'Oh?' Morwenna leaned forward. 'He did a lot of research at your place.'

'Julian and I welcomed him into our home and he found things out. Then when Faye finished their relationship—'

'Faye?' Morwenna pretended not to know.

'My friend, Faye Bryce. We've known each other for years. She has a dreadful marriage. Her husband, Craig, is the most terrible womaniser. He's always away from home. Goodness knows what he gets up to. Faye's lonely, and vulnerable. She had a romance with Pawly last summer. I don't blame her – he could be charming. But it was just a distraction. Pawly was obsessed though. Truly awful. She brought him to dinner at the manor a couple of times, and all he could do was talk about how he wanted her to leave Craig. When they broke up, he was a nuisance, and I had to tell him to stop pestering her. I had to be really firm.'

'A tangled web.'

'Well, you know Julian works in London. In finance. He did some work years ago for an oligarch from Moscow. It's not fashionable to talk about these things now, but the Russian turned out to be a bit of a dirty dealer with fingers in all the wrong pies and after the transaction went through, it didn't look good for Julian.'

'Was it illegal?' Morwenna asked.

'Not so much illegal, but let's say it wouldn't do Julian's reputation any favours. Or mine. And all that awful stuff Pawly was saying about my family, the Lamberts, being mixed up with the slave trade. If people knew—'

'It's terrible, Pippa, but it wasn't you, it was your ancestors—'

'Mud sticks, doesn't it? I mean, I'm up for an MBE for my charity work, things like the Cornish Consortium for Equality, but if the gutter press choose to make a big thing of it then that's a huge chunk of public opinion turned against me, and these things matter. They'd never give an MBE to someone who'd been publicly smeared, and that's what would've happened if Pawly had put all that in his book. Pawly was a loose cannon. He was dangerous.'

'I see.' Morwenna nodded. 'Have you told this to the police?'

'No.' Pippa was appalled. 'And I don't intend to. Julian's with them now. He certainly won't mention his deal with Boris Sokolov. But this has nothing to do with Pawly falling downstairs – that was an accident, wasn't it?' She clutched Morwenna's arm. 'There are some things one just doesn't need others to hear. I'm sure you understand.'

'So why are you telling me?' Morwenna wanted to know.

'You're friends with the police. Just ask them to lay off me and

Julian. I mean, clearly neither of us harmed Pawly. Why would we?'

'I've no idea,' Morwenna said, although Pippa had just given her two good reasons.

'The thing is' – Pippa looked terrified – 'it all happened at our party. Imagine how bad that looks.'

'I suppose so,' Morwenna agreed.

'Julian can give the police a list of everyone we invited to the party. He was busy all evening serving drinks. I hardly saw him except for the blazing argument we had.'

'Argument?'

'Julian was being irritating. He wants us to get away for Christmas Day. He's organised a spa hotel with some friends of his, and I was so cross with him.'

'Why?' Morwenna covered a laugh. 'I mean, a spa hotel.'

'They're Julian's friends, not mine. Some of the wives are hard work. I'd rather spend Christmas here in Seal Bay. At times, Julian gets my goat.' Pippa paused as if she had said too much. 'Morwenna, can I count on you?'

'What can I do?'

'My reputation's at stake. Tell the police that Julian and I couldn't possibly have had anything to do with Pawly falling down stairs. I mean, it was our house, but that's where it ends. You will tell them, won't you?'

'I don't think you're suspects. What makes you think it was murder? The case is closed.'

Pippa looked flustered. 'But it happened at our house.'

'Even if the police were looking for someone, which they're not, there'd be other people higher on their list.'

'Who?' Pippa's eyebrows shot up.

Morwenna asked herself the same question. There was a bloodcurdling scream from the research section and Louise came rushing over, holding out her phone as if it had scorched her hand, yelling 'No – oh, no. I don't believe it.'

Morwenna held out an arm for comfort and Louise rushed into the embrace. Her face was already covered in tears. She ignored Pippa as she gasped, 'It's Steve. One of his workmates just messaged me.'

'Is he all right?' Morwenna asked gently.

'No, he's not,' Louise shrieked. 'The police have just turned up at the depot. Jim Hobbs has taken him in for questioning. Morwenna, you don't think he murdered Pawly?'

14

Morwenna stayed on in the library for two hours after her shift ended. While Donald looked after the desk, she sat in the storeroom with Louise, sharing a cup of tea, telling her that Steve was just helping the police tie up a few loose ends. He'd be back home in no time.

Louise couldn't help blubbing, 'He was in the toilet all the time.' Morwenna understood her worries. Steve had been angry with Pawly.

By a quarter to three, Louise was feeling better. She was determined to finish tidying books: it would take her mind off things. Morwenna pulled on her duffel coat and stepped out into the rain.

She was glad she hadn't brought the bike. It was drizzling still, soaking into her clothes and drenching her hood. It wasn't too much of a detour to pop in to see Tamsin. She was hungry and, besides, she wanted to hear about the date with Tristan.

The door pinged as she went into the tearoom. There were a few customers. Morwenna recognised Sheppy, with his feet up on a chair, forking cake into his mouth. The photographer and the model were at a table in a corner, whispering together. Morwenna went up to the counter. 'Any soup left?'

'Spicy parsnip. Zach's gran's recipe,' Tamsin said and Morwenna tried to work out from her expression if the date had been a success. Did she look disappointed, besotted? It was hard to tell.

Morwenna thought she might as well ask the question directly. 'How did the date go?'

Tamsin nodded as if that in itself was an answer. 'Well...' she lowered her voice '...that's his ex over there. I won't say anything yet.'

'Right,' Morwenna said. 'I'll sit down. Imogen can bring the soup.'

Tamsin turned to the two women in heavy coats who had just come into the tearoom. 'Can I help you?'

'Do you have toasted teacakes?' one of the women asked.

Morwenna went over to Sheppy and sat next to him. He said, 'How do?' and leaned forward. 'I'm doing a bit of sleuthing for you, Miss Marple.'

'Oh?' Morwenna leaned forward too. 'What have you found out?'

'The couple in the corner were talking about the party where the author was pushed down the stairs.'

'What were they saying?'

'She was mithering on about it upset her and she wants to go home to London. But he needs to take some photos on the cliff top of her in nowt but a skimpy dress.'

'In the rain?'

'No, when it's dry. She's a professional though. She doesn't care about the cold.'

'How does that help with the inquiry?'

'It doesn't. But she was crying just before, and the bloke told her not to keep banging on about it because it was upsetting her.'

'What was? Pawly's death?'

'No, she still has a thing for the son. She said he'd broken her heart. That's why she came here. Apparently, he's dating a waitress now. By my deduction as Dr What'sisname, I reckon it's either the fit waitress here who's on holiday from uni, or your Tam.'

'It's Tam,' Morwenna whispered. Imogen arrived with a bowl of soup and Morwenna changed the subject.

'So, how's romance, Sheppy?'

'Ticking over. Slow, like. She's called Courtenay Lamb. She's living in the caravan across from me. I was chatting to her yesterday. She's well nice. I'm going to ask her out.'

'Where will you take her?' Morwenna looked over her shoulder as Imogen walked away, and called, 'Thanks.'

'Here, of course,' Sheppy said. He turned to look over his shoulder, a movement that was pure James Bond. 'Eh up. They're leaving.'

Morwenna watched Justin and Fernanda approach the counter. Tamsin said, 'I hope you enjoyed your lunch.'

'There was too much—' Fernanda began but Justin held out his card to pay.

'It was absolutely fine.'

Fernanda fingered an earring. It was a dangly one, tiny diamonds glittering around a ruby stone. 'I have something I want to say to you.' Her voice rose and cracked a little as she faced Tamsin.

'Eh up.' Sheppy held a finger to his lips, listening. Morwenna was all ears too.

'You are with Tristan? You are his girlfriend now?' There was a definite wobble in Fernanda's voice.

Morwenna was proud of Tamsin, who spoke kindly. 'We've only just met.'

'But you had a date with him?'

'I know he was your boyfriend,' Tamsin said quietly.

'Not for long.' Fernanda appeared to be struggling to hold it together. She paused and swallowed a sob. Justin wrapped an arm around her. 'He will break your heart as he broke mine.'

'We should go back to the boarding house,' Justin said gently.

'I just have to tell her this.' Fernanda wanted to say her piece. 'He did not love me. He will not love you. He has a cold heart.'

'I see,' Tamsin said.

'We should go,' Justin said.

'He will hurt you like he hurt me.' Fernanda's voice rose. 'I hate Tristan. I hate him so much. *Ojalá el cabrón estuviera muerto.*'

Morwenna widened her eyes. She understood some of the words. The ones that said Fernanda wished Tristan were dead.

'Come on,' Justin said, his voice a whisper. Fernanda was crying now. He led her gently out into the rain.

'I don't speak Spanish.' Sheppy burst out laughing. 'What was that about?'

Morwenna shook her head. '"Cupid is a knavish lad."'

'Is that Shakespeare?' Sheppy guessed.

'Definitely. Do you think the photographer's her new boyfriend?'

'No.' Sheppy shrugged. 'He's gay.'

'How do you know?'

'I was listening in to what they were saying before you came. He was talking about his partner. He's a banker called Harvey.'

Morwenna said, 'You're a great sleuthing assistant.'

'I know, right?' Sheppy swallowed the last of his tea. 'I'm not being funny, but I can't hang around. I'd better get back. I've got some serious chatting up to do.'

'Oh?'

'I'm going to iron my best kecks and shirt and get over to see Courtenay. Who knows? She might just fancy a beer with me.'

'Good luck,' Morwenna said, watching him shuffle towards the door. It clanged as he stepped out into the rain.

Tamsin took his place almost immediately. She reached for Morwenna's hand. 'Well, that was weird.'

'What was?'

'Tristan's ex. He doesn't even know why she came down here.'

'I wouldn't pay much attention. They'll be gone soon.'

'I hope so. But I want to tell you about the date last night. It was wonderful.' Tamsin's expression changed to one of bliss and, for a moment, Morwenna was reminded of Lamorna. They were both suckers for romance. It must be genetic. 'Except for one thing.'

'Oh?' Morwenna was interested. 'Except for what?'

'We went to The Lugger Bar. They do great cocktails. And gastro food.'

'Don't tell me the Spanish ex was there too?'

'Furious Fernanda? No, she wasn't. We had a great time.'

'What about Seb and Becca? Did you double date?'

'No, Seb's round Becca's flat every night. He's got no money. Tristan usually bails him out when he needs it.' Tamsin rolled her eyes, as if Tristan were a hero. 'Tristan and I really get on. We both said how nice it was to be with someone who really gets us.'

'Tam—'

'Tristan told me he'd never met anyone he'd clicked with so quickly.'

'Don't throw yourself in.'

'I won't, but – I'm seeing him on Friday.'

'What about Elowen?'

'We're going to get her used to the idea of us being together slowly. I'll make sure she doesn't feel left out.'

'So – what's the *but*?'

'The *but*? Oh, I nearly forgot. At the end of the date, Tristan asked for the bill and the waiter said someone had left him something, and he gave him a card.'

'What sort of card?'

'A Christmas card. It was really odd. It wasn't signed. Just a big X scrawled through the greeting inside.'

'Ah.' Morwenna took a slow breath. 'Was there a laughing Santa with a mince pie on the front?'

'Yes.'

'I got one. Your father did too.'

'You did?' Tamsin's eyebrows knotted. 'Tristan had no idea who'd do that.'

'That's three of us. I'll let Jane know.'

'What did it mean though?'

'I can only assume it's to do with Pawly. The Santa on the front.'

'But Pawly's death was an accident. And why you and Dad? Why Tristan?'

'Who knows? Tristan's a Pengellen. Pawly died at his parents' house. And my name's been all over Bay Radio. Mike's saying I'm involved in finding out about Pawly.'

'Do you think it was an accident, Mum?'

'I'm not sure.'

'And why would Dad get a card?'

'It makes no sense.'

'Is it a warning?'

'It could be a prank, but it doesn't feel that way.'

'What shall I tell Tristan?'

'It might be an idea if he shows it to Jane.'

'Do you think someone was warning him?' Tamsin asked.

'I don't know yet.' Morwenna chewed her lip thoughtfully. 'It will come to me in time.' She realised that she hadn't touched her soup. She spooned spicy parsnip into her mouth and said, 'Mmm. Tell Zach his gran's recipe is lovely.'

* * *

Much later, Jane and Blessed, wearing civvies, were sitting around the fire in Morwenna's house as she showed them the Santa card. All three of them looked puzzled.

'We have to see this as a threat,' Blessed said crisply. 'Do you mind if I take it in and have it looked at? The envelope too?'

'Of course,' Morwenna sighed. 'It'll have my fingerprints all over it.'

'I'll try to find a pointer,' Blessed replied.

'How are investigations going?' Morwenna stared into the fire. It had been cold and damp today. She was feeling tired.

Jane met Blessed's gaze. 'We've got suspects. Steve Piper was in the toilet for ages and that means there's no one to confirm or deny if he was with Pawly at that time. Julian Pengellen was in the drawing room serving drinks. Pippa was mingling.'

'No, he wasn't,' Morwenna said.

'No, who wasn't?' Blessed asked sharply.

'Julian – he wasn't in the drawing room all night. Ruan and I were getting fruit punch, and he was definitely not there.'

'When was that?' Jane asked.

'About ten minutes before I found Pawly.' Morwenna took a deep breath. 'I've got something else to show you.'

'What?' Blessed gave her a look that suggested she might not like what was coming.

'Photos. Come and see. My laptop's open.' Morwenna led

them into the kitchen. Brenda was asleep in her basket in the corner.

Blessed sat down and Jane peered over her shoulder.

'These are pictures of people at the party, with timings.' Blessed didn't miss a beat. 'Where did you get them?'

'The photographer was taking pictures all night. Justin Kidd.'

'I asked, how did you get them?' Blessed made her eyes piercing.

'I borrowed his digital camera and returned it.'

'With his permission?' Jane asked.

'Not exactly.'

Blessed was busy scrutinising each picture. She appeared not to care at all where they had come from. She said, 'There are videos here too. That's useful. Perhaps they'll give us a lead.'

'You're something else, Morwenna.' Jane winked.

'I'll have to take this.' Blessed meant the laptop.

'My laptop? Can't you just copy the photos?' Morwenna was disappointed. 'I need them.'

'What for?' Blessed asked.

'So I can do what you're doing,' Morwenna answered without thinking. 'Work out what happened to Pawly.'

'I'm here to tell you not to,' Blessed said firmly. 'This is police business.'

'It's my laptop.' Morwenna retorted. 'And I need the Internet for all sorts of things. You can't confiscate it. I'm not a suspect, am I?'

'No, but, strictly speaking, these are Justin Kidd's photos. And now they're police evidence,' Blessed said. 'I want everyone down the nick to see this. I'm not going to reprimand you for stealing.'

'Borrowing,' Morwenna shot back.

'We'll let that one go, just this once, but you're not to take anything again, do you understand? These photos might be really useful. We'll copy them and bring the laptop straight back, all right?' Blessed said. 'I'll tell Rick we're thinking of reopening the Yelland case. The Santa cards are worrying me.'

'OK.' Morwenna was pleased her laptop would come back quickly.

'Jane.' Blessed stood up. 'We should get going. We'll be spending the whole evening looking through photos. If there's anything on here that's useful, I'll ask for Justin Kidd's camera, and pretend we know nothing about you taking it. That gets you out of the frame, Morwenna. It must be the last time you take something, though. I mean it.'

'Thanks, though, Morwenna,' Jane whispered as she followed Blessed to the door. 'Off the record, that's really smart of you. It'll help tons.'

'We'll let ourselves out,' Blessed called from the hall. 'I won't be long with your laptop.'

'I'll be in touch,' Jane shouted. The door clicked.

'Right.' Morwenna folded her arms like a schoolgirl who'd just had a telling-off. 'There's nothing I like more than a challenge. I'll find out who killed Pawly. Just see if I don't.'

**THURSDAY 18 DECEMBER**

15

After her library shift, Morwenna rode her bike through Seal Bay, aware of the gaping potholes in the road, being splashed by cars and buses and a large Korrik Clay lorry. The rain was holding off, which was just as well. There were things she needed to do, to do with Pawly and sleuthing. Pedalling fast, she took the harbour road, cycling slowly down a narrow, twisting road, past straggling fishermen's cottages. She passed beneath the tall gates, below a sign that read 'D. WOON, BOATS'.

Her tyres scrunched across gravel and she came to a halt. There was a large boat shed where all sorts of craft were repaired and rebuilt, and, next to it, Damien Woon's small business office. Woon's boatyard always gave her the shivers nowadays. But there were things she needed to hear from Damien about Pawly.

She clambered off and looked around. The smell of diesel fuel from the boats hung lightly on the air. She hated that smell now. It reminded her of Tamsin's ex. Not far away, little sailing boats bobbed and dipped, a row of masts. Morwenna felt the bite of the cold air through her duffel coat. Despite the woollen hat that covered her ears, and her scarf, thick mittens and warm socks, she trembled.

Several cars were parked in a row, including Damien's truck and Beverley's Fiat. Morwenna recognised two more of them. One was a large Range Rover; she'd seen it several times up at Mirador, the Truscotts' house. The other was a familiar white van.

She was dragged from her thoughts by footsteps on the gravel – a broad-shouldered man with a beard was walking briskly towards her. Morwenna called out a greeting. 'Hello, Damien.'

Damien Woon didn't look pleased to see her, but then he could be quite abrupt and irritable. He wasn't smiling now. 'What are you after, maid?' His lip curled. 'Trouble usually follows you, I seem to remember.'

'I wanted to ask you something.' Morwenna decided that it was best to be honest with Damien. She said, 'When Pawly Yelland made that comment about the boatyard, what did he mean?'

'What comment?'

Morwenna was ready with the answer. 'At the library talk, he said, "There are a few tales I could tell about that place." What did he mean?'

Damien looked unimpressed. 'Pawly was an irritating little tuss who didn't pay his bills.' He folded his arms. 'He was always down here, pestering me to let him buy a motorboat.'

'That's not a bad thing.' Morwenna was ready to take him on. 'You run a boatyard. You buy and sell boats and do them up.'

'Not for charity, I don't,' Damien grunted.

'What do you mean?'

'Yelland wanted to buy a fast boat to impress some woman he was knocking around with. He gave me a deposit and when I asked for the rest, he couldn't pay. Yet he thought the boat was his to take away. I had to remind him that he owed me.'

'Oh, how did you do that?'

'I was bigger than he was.' Damien shook his head slowly. 'I got my deposit back. The boat's in the yard now, up for sale. I've got a buyer in mind.'

'And that was all?' Morwenna asked. 'A disagreement between you and Pawly?'

'Not at all. He had a grudge against me – you heard what he said at the library. And he was rude to Bev.'

'How rude?'

'Ruder than I'm prepared to take off a man with a big mouth.' Damien glowered. 'Have you heard enough? You can go back to your cottage and talk to your policewoman friend and find someone else to pester. I've got customers.' He pointed to a blue boat, the *Pammy*. 'Ones that don't waste my time.'

'Is Pam Truscott here?' Morwenna asked.

'She is.' Damien laughed, the sort of chuckle that wasn't friendly. 'She's got a few jobs on her boat that need doing. She's asked for a bit of help.'

On cue, Pam emerged from below deck, followed by a man in a dark jacket and jeans. It was Ruan. Morwenna had recognised his van. She felt suddenly awkward. Worse than awkward. A feeling she didn't like filled her chest and made it difficult to breathe.

'Morwenna. Nice to see you.' Pam was brisk and friendly as she walked over. 'What are you doing here?'

Damien threw Ruan a look that said he would be polite to Morwenna because they were friends. He said, 'You know this maid's always got her nose in something she shouldn't.'

'Hi.' Ruan clambered from the boat. 'Did Damien tell you he got a card this morning?'

'A card?' Pam was all interest.

'Some silly tuss sent me a Christmas card with the inside words crossed out. A big X.' Damien snorted. 'It's nothing.'

'Was the card sent just to you, or to you and Bev?' Morwenna asked.

'Just me. Why does it matter?' Damien said.

Morwenna shrugged. 'It might.'

'It sounds horrible,' Pam said. 'But on a nicer note, I have to say, Morwenna, Ruan's a treasure. I brought the *Pammy* up here for a service. Damien changed the oil in the motor and Ruan's been looking at the loose tiles and the leaky tap in the galley kitchen. I was hoping to take her out when the weather's OK.'

Ruan looked unconcerned. 'I'm happy to help out.'

'Oh, you must let me pay you,' Pam said.

'No need,' Ruan replied kindly.

Pam's laughter tinkled. 'I'm sure I can think of something.'

Morwenna met his eyes. 'Aren't you on the trawlers today?'

'The weather's bad for fishing,' Ruan said.

Damien wanted to talk business. 'What did you think of *The Swordfish*?'

'Nice little motorboat,' Ruan said. 'Just the sort of thing I'm looking for.'

'I can do you a good deal,' Damien offered. 'Mate's rates.'

Ruan looked interested. 'I'm thinking a boat might be nice for when I retire.'

'You'll be a better customer than the last bloke I tried to sell it to.' Damien guffawed. 'He could hardly afford the deposit.'

'Was that the one Pawly wanted to buy?' Morwenna asked.

'It was. He wanted to change the name to *The Lady Killer*.' Damien snorted. 'I didn't take to the bloke.'

'It was a shame though, what happened to him,' Pam began.

'Oh, Morwenna, did I tell you that Barnaby's home at the weekend? He asked me to pass on his love.'

'Thanks,' Morwenna said, feeling even more uncomfortable. She noticed that Ruan was looking at her steadily.

It started to rain, thick heavy drops. Damien said, 'Bev's in the house cooking tea. I'm not stopping out here. Let me know what you think of *The Swordfish*, Ruan.'

'I'll certainly think it over,' Ruan said.

'And you must come up for that coffee soon, Ruan,' Pam said. 'You promised.'

'I did.' Ruan turned to Morwenna. 'I'll give you a lift. We can fit your bike in the back of the van.'

'Thanks, Ruan,' Morwenna said gratefully. She was always happy to leave the boatyard and its awful memories. And some time with Ruan might help her understand exactly why her emotions were so confused.

* * *

She didn't say much on the way home. It was easier to watch the rain drip down the window, running in rivulets. The sky was darkening as they chugged up the hill towards Harbour Cottages.

Ruan said, 'Do you want to come in for a drink?'

Morwenna shook her head. 'No, I've got things to do. Thanks for the lift.'

Ruan watched her as she scrambled out of the van and tugged her bike from the back. 'I'll be seeing you.'

She pushed it up the path and into the house, breathing deeply, wondering if Ruan and Pam were attracted to each other. The idea disturbed her. But that wasn't fair – she'd been out with Pam's brother a few times, so why shouldn't Ruan go out with his sister? Cornwall was a close-knit community. She laughed out loud, one cynical snort, but it didn't help the tightening around her heart. The thought that Ruan and Pam might become a couple gnawed at her more than a little.

She closed the curtains, switched on the amber lamp in the corner and lit the log fire. The room felt cosy as the cold air warmed. Brenda rubbed against her legs; she pushed thoughts of Ruan from her mind. 'Supper for you, Bren. Me too. Afterwards, we'll have a bit of time thinking, shall we? I need to put my thoughts in order. The suspects too. And there's someone else I need to have a chat with.'

Three hours later Morwenna, her socked feet stretched out towards the fire, lay on a rug hugging a mug of tea, Brenda curled against her body, purring contentedly. Morwenna frowned. 'I need my laptop. I need to see the big picture, Bren. I'm missing something really important.' She exhaled, frustrated. 'Someone pushes Pawly downstairs in Pengellen Manor. At the party. Why? Because the opportunity was there? I wonder – what was the relationship between Pawly and the person who pushed him?'

Brenda rolled onto her back and stuck four paws in the air. It was a cute way of begging for treats. Morwenna trailed her fingertips across the delicate fur.

'If it was just a simple murder, a one-off, it might be a grudge or an argument. But where do the Santa cards fit in? I've got one, and so have Ruan, Tristan, Damien. But not Bev. Or the Pengellens. What links us with Pawly?'

Brenda rolled over and stood up, suddenly alert. Her ears twitched.

'What is it, Bren?' Morwenna watched as the cat shifted position, staring towards the window that would have looked onto the tiny back garden had the curtains not been closed. Brenda's fur seemed to stand on end as she took several timid steps backwards.

Morwenna whispered, 'What can you hear?'

She heard it. A soft sound against the windowpane, not unlike fingers rubbing against glass. The dull squeak became a soft knock. There was a pause. There was a loud rap, and silence again.

Morwenna called out, 'Ruan?' Why would he go round to the back of the house and knock at the window? He wouldn't.

It came again: tap, tap-tap. It must be a bird. Morwenna had a sudden image of fluttering wings against the glass, or a sharp beak. But it was inky dark outside. Birds would be roosting by now.

Morwenna approached the window slowly and held her breath. The sound had gone. Whatever small creature was there had moved away. But she wanted to make sure. Grabbing the curtains, she drew them back with a sharp movement.

And gasped in horror.

A Santa face was looking at her, right at her. It was a leering plastic mask with a gaping mouth, huge staring eyes. The Santa was wearing a red hat trimmed with white fur, and below it she could see part of a red suit.

Morwenna was too stunned to move. As if in slow motion, the Santa raised a flat hand to his neck and made a sawing motion. A threat, slicing his hand back and forth, across his throat. Morwenna knew exactly what he was suggesting. She snapped the curtains closed and recoiled in fear.

Her first movement was to hurry to the kitchen and grab a bread knife and a frying pan. Weapons, just in case. She locked the back door, turning the large key, peering briefly through the kitchen window. Darkness seemed to swim outside like the ocean. She hurried to the front door and tugged the bolts across, top and bottom, then she was back in the living room. Despite the fire blazing, she was cold and trembling. She whisked Brenda into her arms and sat on the sofa, huddled as if for protection, reaching for her phone. There was one person she needed to talk to. She heard Jane pick up almost immediately.

'Morwenna?'

'Jane. There's someone in my garden.'

'Someone?'

'A person. In a Santa mask. And suit. Banging on my window. It was a threat – they made a sign of cutting their throat.'

'I'm not at work right now. I'm out – having dinner. A date. But I can come straight round.'

'Oh no, don't. I'll be fine.'

'I'll ring Jim Hobbs. He's on duty. He'll call in and check the place.'

'I'm sure it's nothing.'

'And if it is something?' Jane asked anxiously. 'You've been on Bay Radio, talking about Pawly. It's quite likely someone wants to tell you not to get involved. Best to be safe, not sorry.'

'Right.' Morwenna exhaled slowly and glanced towards the window again. The curtains were closed, but she was still trembling.

'It's probably kids messing about,' Jane said reassuringly, but her voice told Morwenna that she didn't really believe it was. 'I'd like Jim to call anyway.'

'Good.' Morwenna tried to relax. She was relieved that Jim was calling round. Her instincts warned her that something was very wrong. Her blood was pumping fast.

'I'll ask him to make it a priority,' Jane said. 'We'll catch up tomorrow.'

'Thanks, Jane.' Morwenna remembered where she'd said she was. 'Enjoy your date.'

'I will.' The phone clicked. Morwenna wondered who Jane was out with. She was glad she had a bit of happiness in her life.

Her hand was still shaking. Morwenna pressed a number on her phone. There was someone she had to check on. 'Mum. Are you all right?'

She heard Lamorna laugh. 'Of course I am, my bewty. What kind of question is that?'

Morwenna made her voice light. 'Just checking you're not lonely.'

'Oh, I'm not. I had a visitor.'

'Oh?' She pushed the phone right against her ear.

'Vernon just popped in to ask me out tomorrow night.'

'That's nice.'

'We're going somewhere nice. It's a surprise.'

Morwenna was concerned. 'Mum, I need to know where you're going.'

'I'll be with Vernon.'

'But where?'

'Somewhere romantic, I don't know.' Lamorna laughed.

'I just want to know. We hardly know the man and...' Morwenna was conscious that she sounded like Lamorna's mother. 'Where is he now?'

'He left backalong. He stayed for a coffee and a biscuit. He's partial to Jaffa Cakes.' Lamorna sounded happy.

'Can I meet him?'

'Oh, that's sweet of you,' Lamorna said. 'Yes – let me set something up and I'll call you. I'll bring him down the tearoom or we can meet here...'

'Thanks, Mum.' Morwenna kept her tone light. 'I'm glad you're having fun.'

'Oh, I am. He could be the one, Morwenna. He treats me so well, a proper gentleman. He's a lovely man.'

'Right. I'm looking forward to meeting him. Mum?'

'What is it?'

Morwenna tried her best not to alarm her mother. 'I'm a bit worried about – you know – about what's happened in the bay. Keep your doors locked. Just in case.'

'I will. And I'll put a bleddy gurt frying pan under the bed.'

'I'll tell Tam to do the same. And Ruan. Night, Mum.'

'Night.'

Morwenna clutched the phone. She didn't want to frighten her mother. Her own heart hadn't stopped thudding yet. And now there was another reason to worry: the new romance with Vernon. Lamorna gave her heart away so readily with every man she met. She'd be making mental plans to move him in and choose names for their pet puppy before Christmas was over. A smile played on Morwenna's lips – her mother would never change.

A sharp knock on the door made her heart leap. She grabbed the frying pan and bread knife. Just in case. She hurried through the hall and called, 'Who is it?'

'PC Hobbs,' the voice came back and Morwenna recognised his warm tone. She tugged the door open gratefully. An icy blast came in with Jim, who removed his hat, his face concerned.

'Are you all right, Morwenna?'

'I am now, thanks,' Morwenna said.

'I've had a look round your garden. Everything's quiet.'

'I'll make you a cuppa, Jim, and tell you what happened.'

'Thanks,' Jim said, making himself comfortable on the sofa by the fire, reaching out to stroke Brenda, who was snoozing. The frying pan and the bread knife that Morwenna had picked up to defend herself with were back on the low table.

Morwenna was beginning to feel calmer. She was all right. No one had visited her mum. She'd been terrified that a Santa had thumped on her window too. She'd had to check.

Morwenna stood in the kitchen, clattering cups, making tea.

She picked up the phone to ring Tamsin and Ruan. She needed to warn them too, once Jim had gone.

But her sleuth brain had found something else to analyse, a distraction, just for now.

Jane was out on a date. Dinner. Morwenna had always thought that Jim would make a lovely boyfriend for Jane. But Jim was in her living room, stroking the cat.

So who was Jane out having dinner with?

FRIDAY 19 DECEMBER

16

Morwenna noticed that Louise had thrown herself into Christmas with all the force of a woman with something on her mind. She was clearly worried sick that Steve might be mistakenly charged for killing Pawly and banged up for manslaughter. Her fears had taken over her life now.

'It might be our last ever Christmas together,' she had confided in Morwenna nervously. 'I'm going to make sure we enjoy it.'

To that end, the library was booming out a CD of Christmas songs played on a Hammond organ. Several homemade mince pies stood on a dish, shedding icing sugar, the mincemeat burned at the edges of the pastry, and there was some Christmas punch with a few apple segments floating on top.

Next to some plastic cups, Louise had put up a sign that read: 'Merry Christmas from all at Seal Bay library. Help Yourself.' By eleven-thirty, no one had touched them. At twelve, Donald turned up early, refusing the refreshments on the grounds that he had brought ham sandwiches, and proceeded to talk about his theory that Lady Elizabeth should be questioned by a medium about Pawly's killer.

Perhaps the ghost had done it herself...

At half twelve, Morwenna was about to leave when Susan and Barb arrived. They were full of excitement: there had been developments.

Susan pushed a mince pie into her mouth. 'Hasn't Jane Choy spoken to you, Morwenna? She's up on Pettarock Head.'

'Oh?' Morwenna tugged on her duffel coat. 'Why?'

'The bloke who's selling the Christmas cards in the pop-up shop told us.' Barb poured Christmas punch into a plastic cup, swigged it and pulled a face. 'This needs to be sweeter, Louise.'

'Oh.' Louise had been absent-minded all morning. 'I thought the lemonade would sweeten it.'

'Not if you have a sweet tooth like Barb.' Susan reached for another mince pie to satisfy her own sweet tooth. 'These are nice, Louise. A bit of clotted cream on top would help, though.'

'I never thought of that.' Louise was miles away.

'What's happened at Pengellen Manor?' Donald asked. 'I was just wondering if Lady Elizabeth has had anything to do with Pawly's fall.'

'Does she do burglary as well?' Barb cackled.

'And break windows?' Susan added.

'What?' Morwenna had resolved to cycle up to the Pengellens' and find out for herself.

'The police are up at the manor. They got broken into overnight,' Susan explained.

'Who by?' Louise asked.

'What was taken?' Donald added.

The sisters turned to Morwenna. 'I thought you'd know,' Susan said.

Barb agreed. 'You'd better get up there dreckly and find out.'

'Yes, I will.' Morwenna grabbed her bag and was gone. The last thing she heard was Louise saying, 'Have another mince pie, Susan.'

* * *

Dark clouds hung low and the wind that whistled in from the sea had ice in it as Morwenna pedalled up Pettarock Head, feeling the electric motor kick in. Down on the beach two figures stood close to the waves. A man in a dark coat was moving a woman in a pale dress into position. Morwenna thought she was standing ankle-deep in the water. She lifted her arms like a bird, and he began to take photos. Morwenna made a mental note that Justin and Fernanda were still in Seal Bay. She wanted to find an opportunity to chat to them again.

When she arrived at the manor, there were two police cars parked at angles on the gravel drive. She pushed her bicycle towards the door and wondered what excuse she could use to get inside the house and look around. On the left-hand side of the house, a first-floor mullion window appeared to be broken; Morwenna stood back and looked at it. The pane nearest to an iron drainpipe was smashed. It was clear how the burglar had got in. She took hold of the drainpipe to see if it would budge, but it was firm enough to carry quite a weight. A man or woman could have shinned up it without too much difficulty if they were fit.

The door was ajar. Morwenna didn't need an excuse to let herself in, sidling into the warm hallway, gazing around for clues.

A tall man wearing a smart suit came from the large room. He held out a hand with perfectly manicured fingernails and a wedding band with a single diamond in it. 'Morwenna.'

She shook it. 'Julian. The door was open—'

'Jane's upstairs.' Julian seemed to be one step ahead of her. 'I expect you've come to see her.'

'Would that be OK?' Morwenna asked.

'We need all the help we can get.' Julian's handsome face looked tired. 'I know you sometimes resolve these things.'

'Things?'

'Pawly fell down our steps and the case was closed, but the police want to open it again. No one has a clue if it was an accident or if we're all suspects, Pippa, me too.' Julian sighed. 'Now someone broke in last night.'

'Did you see anything?' Morwenna asked.

'Pippa and I slept through it,' Julian said. 'The burglar got through the library window. Of course, he didn't take any books.' He gave a cynical laugh.

'What was taken?'

'Money. Jewellery. He took the safe from my office where I keep valuables.'

'How did he – or she – manage to take a safe?'

Julian looked sheepish. 'It was a small one. It wasn't bolted down.'

'Anything else?' Morwenna asked.

'No. He was in and out quickly. He left something behind, though.'

'What?' Morwenna was interested.

'A mince pie and a carrot. He left them on the windowsill before he climbed out.'

'People leave mince pies and carrots for Santa.' Morwenna recalled the masked face at her window. 'He was leaving a clue.'

'And there was a Christmas card,' Julian added.

'With a crossed-through greeting.'

'How do you know that?'

'Several of us have had one.' Morwenna was thoughtful. 'Do you mind if I go upstairs?'

'Jane's up there with the detective chief inspector,' Julian said.

'Oh, by the way.' Morwenna was on the bottom stair. 'Who was here at home last night?'

'Me, Pippa, Tristan.'

'Not Seb, Tristan's friend?'

'No, he's hooked up with a Seal Bay girl. He spends most nights in the flat over her shop.'

'Becca.' Morwenna paused. 'Tell me about Seb, Julian. Have he and Tristan been friends for long?'

'Tristan went to uni in London. LSE. He met Seb there. Yes, they've been friends for years.'

'What does Seb do?'

'He's in between jobs.' Julian pushed a hand through smooth grey hair. 'He seems to live off his wits a bit. There's always some scheme he believes will make his fortune. He told us a few days ago that he was worried about the rent on his flat in London. Tristan offered to put him up if things get tough.'

'What about his parents?'

'Poor as church mice.' Julian gave a small laugh. 'I think his father's a vicar in Swindon.'

'But he and Becca seem happy.' Morwenna wondered if Seb had another girlfriend in London. 'I assume he's single?'

'He is now,' Julian explained. 'He was married until a couple of years ago. It was a disaster. He moved out – his ex kept the flat. I think he was depressed by the whole thing. Tristan didn't say, but I know he's given him a lot of support.'

'And where's Tristan now?'

'At the tearoom.' Julian almost smiled. 'He's got something going with your daughter.'

'Right. Thanks.' Morwenna had the information she needed.

She took the stairs two at a time, along the corridor that led to the library. Jane and Blessed were inside, talking. Three forensic officers were busy, taking photos, collecting trace evidence.

Blessed said, 'Hello, Morwenna. I wondered when you'd show up. Can you stay in the doorway, please? The officers are busy.'

Jane approached and placed a hand on her arm. 'Are you OK? After last night?'

'Yes, thanks. How was the date?'

'Nice.' Jane looked a little embarrassed. 'Jim told me he looked around your garden, and he went back again to check this morning. With so much mud around, he thought there might be a footprint. Or some residual evidence of the person in the mask, at least – but there was nothing. We're working with a sly character.'

'Right. Given the face at my window and the mince pie and carrot left behind here, can we assume we're looking for the same person who pushed Pawly?'

'It's best not to assume anything, but down at the nick we're working on the assumption that the two things might well be linked. Put it this way, the Pengellens are being targeted for some reason,' Blessed said smoothly. 'It does seem to add up, the ongoing Santa theme. What's more interesting is the behaviour of our Santa.'

Morwenna nodded. 'Arrogant, cocky. He or she's playing games with us.'

'I agree. There's definitely a sense of a showman at work. Sometimes a criminal will return to the scene of the crime to revisit their handiwork or remember how good it felt when they committed the crime.' Blessed walked towards the door and stood with Jane and Morwenna, their heads close. 'It follows that the Santa would come back here to burgle the place.' She kept her voice low. 'But what sort of person are we looking for?'

'Someone who's controlling, or who needs to feel good about themselves?' Morwenna suggested.

'A local person,' Jane said. 'Someone who knows Seal Bay. Who knows the Pengellens' movements.'

'Of course, we can't rule out it being an inside job,' Blessed suggested. 'Staged to look like someone else had done it.'

'How can we find out?' Morwenna shook her head. 'Were there no clues?'

'Nothing yet. There might be a few shreds of material, synthetic Santa hair, a thread of red coat. We'll find something,' Jane said.

'Right, I'll leave you to it,' Morwenna said. 'Can we talk later?'

'I'll text you,' Jane said.

'We're reopening the Pawly case.' Blessed raised an eyebrow. 'You can have your laptop back. I'm going to finish off here, then I'm off to ask Justin for his camera. I need those photos from him.'

'Great,' Morwenna called over her shoulder as she hurried downstairs.

* * *

It was easier riding downhill, although the wind from the sea buffeted the bicycle and pushed her sideways. She turned the corner, heading towards town, and recognised the man and woman who were standing at the side of the road by a large black car. Justin was putting photographic equipment into the boot. Fernanda stood next to him, swathed in a large coat. As Morwenna slowed down, she noticed the model's eyelids were painted with green glitter. Her lip gloss was like red glass. Morwenna gave her broadest grin.

'Hello. It's good to see you.'

'Oh?' Justin didn't recognise her.

'I'm Morwenna from the tearoom.' She shook Justin's hand, then turned to Fernanda. 'I'm Tamsin's mother.'

Fernanda said something in Spanish and looked away. Morwenna wasn't put off.

'Are you doing a photo shoot?'

Fernanda didn't answer. Justin said, 'We have an assignment to complete by the new year. The sea's perfect, just the mood I'm looking for.'

'How exciting. You must enjoy your job so much. I know I would.' Morwenna sounded impressed. 'I've often wondered though... It must be so hard for the poor models. It's the story of our lives, we women have to suffer, all that cold wind, rough skin, chapped nipples.' She turned to Fernanda. 'How do you cope, dressed in nothing but cheesecloth, with the wind whistling through? The goosepimples.'

Fernanda looked away. 'I am professional.'

'You must be.' Morwenna noticed her shiny earrings again. Diamonds glittering around a single ruby. 'Are you staying until Christmas?' she gushed. 'Oh, I hope so. We have some fun in Seal Bay at Christmas. And I'm part of a swimming group. We swim in the ocean on Sunday mornings.' She looked suddenly excited as she turned to Fernanda. 'You could come.'

'No, thank you.' Fernanda didn't smile. *'Odio este maldito lugar frío.'*

'You're right, it does get cold this time of year.' Morwenna had enough basic Spanish to understand that Fernanda hated the cold.

'We should go, Fernanda.' Justin wrapped an arm around her. 'It was nice to meet you...' He'd forgotten Morwenna's name already. She pretended she hadn't noticed.

'You too. Do come in the tearoom some time soon. We're doing a lovely festive hot chocolate.'

Fernanda moved her mouth in disgust. 'The teashop where your daughter is?' She turned to Julian. *'Prefiero morir.'*

Morwenna translated. She'd rather die. 'I think we've had enough death in Seal Bay already,' she quipped as she adjusted her bicycle beneath her and took off, the wind lifting and rearranging her hair. She noticed a police car arriving at the beach; Blessed was at the wheel. She was here to demand Justin's camera.

'On that morbid note, take care. See you soon. *Feliz Navidad.*'

17

Morwenna was up to her usual sleuthing tricks, analysing everything she'd seen and heard as she rode towards the Proper Ansom Tearoom. Fernanda was a strange one; she was moody, unhappy in her work. She could see why Tristan and the Mexican model hadn't lasted long: Tristan seemed good-natured, full of fun. Justin was pleasant, although Morwenna wondered if there was more to him than met the eye.

She reached the tearoom and secured her bike. As she peered through the window, Tamsin was doing great business. Almost every table was occupied. Tristan was sitting at a table near the window with Seb and Becca, enjoying lunch. He lifted a hand and waved hello. Sheppy was at the other end of the room with a petite young woman with yellow hair. She wore thin jeans and a cropped jumper with sleeves that extended beyond her wrists, her fingers just visible. She didn't look particularly interested in the part-nibbled pasty on her plate. Or in Sheppy, who appeared to be talking nineteen to the dozen while she rummaged in her bag for her phone. Morwenna assumed that she was Courtenay.

All the other tables were full, despite it being well after two. Tamsin was at the counter, taking payment.

As Morwenna rushed inside to the warmth generated by radiators, hot food and well-wrapped bodies, she almost bumped into Imogen, who was carrying a tray piled with pasties. She greeted her with a grin, inhaling the savoury smell of onions and pastry before taking the only available seat, next to Sheppy. He seemed delighted to see her.

'All right?' Sheppy looked pleased with himself. 'Morwenna, I was telling you about Courtenay. Well, here she is.'

'Hello, Courtenay.' Morwenna held out a hand. 'Pleased to meet you.'

'Hiya.' Courtenay offered limp fingers with lots of rings, fake stones. She didn't look awake yet. She pushed back her yellow fringe, her red-painted nails bitten.

'Morwenna's my friend. It's her teashop, hers and Tam's and her mum's.' Sheppy was looking at Courtenay's half-eaten pasty. 'Do you want that? If it's going begging.'

'I'm not really hungry.' Courtenay reached for her mug of tea distractedly and took a sip. 'It's a nice place you've got here, Morwenna. It's friendly. I've done waitressing. I come from Newport Pagnell. There wasn't much work for me there, so I came here to find a job. Cornwall's supposed to be a nice place.'

'It's the wrong time of year for finding work here,' Morwenna said. 'Summer's the best.'

'Oh, I'm all right for now,' Courtenay said. 'I've got enough money to keep me going.'

Morwenna raised an eyebrow. 'You're living at the Camp Dynamo site, aren't you?'

'I came here a couple of months ago. Someone recommended it.' Courtenay chewed a nail. 'I got fed up with my parents telling me to get off my backside, and one thing led to another, and I ended up here.'

'That's nice.' Morwenna observed Courtenay carefully; she couldn't be older than her early twenties. She didn't look as if she took much care of herself though.

Sheppy had almost finished her pasty. 'I treated Courtenay to lunch. I'm doing all right for myself. There's work out there if you look, I told Courtenay. The Smugglers gig is going great, going from table to table doing card tricks for tips. People are very generous at Christmas.'

'No jobs behind the bar there though. I asked the manager,' Courtenay said.

'I'm working at The Quilkin Emporium being Santa Claus. All those kiddies telling me what they want for Christmas and I'm like "Ho, ho, ho, I'll bring you a train set, don't you worry, sunshine," and the kids are mad for it. I love being Father Christmas.'

Morwenna said, 'I might bring Elowen. When are you working?'

'This weekend, during the day, right up until Christmas Eve. They are mad busy,' Sheppy said. 'Yeh, bring your granddaughter. We'll have a joke and ask her what she wants for Christmas. They've got some lovely girlie toys in there.'

'Elowen wants football boots,' Morwenna said.

'I'll make sure she gets something nice,' Sheppy promised. 'I'm good with kids.'

'I know you are.' Morwenna recalled Sheppy during the summer in his juggler costume and his magician's suit. He was a talented performer who had a lovely way with children.

'How old is she, your granddaughter?' Courtenay asked.

'Seven last October,' Morwenna said. 'Growing up fast.'

Courtenay turned to Sheppy. 'Can you get me a bar of chocolate? Do they do chocolate here?'

'We've got hot chocolate. Would that do?' Morwenna felt sorry for her. She was all skin and bone.

'Oh, yes, please.'

Morwenna caught Tamsin's eye. She had just finished talking to a customer and she weaved between the tables, stopping to chat to Tristan. Morwenna saw him squeeze her hand.

She said, 'Hi, Mum. Sorry it's taken me so long to get over. We're so busy today. And Elowen will be back from school soon. Carole's picking her up. Thank goodness they break up today.'

Morwenna indicated Courtenay. 'Can I have a hot chocolate for Courtenay?'

'Of course. I'll do it,' Tamsin said. 'Imogen's busy; she's on the phone. She's the best thing since sliced bread, but – well – she's given me a bit of a problem.'

'What's happened?'

'Her grandmother's unwell. She lives in Penzance. The whole family want to go there for Christmas and she's asked if it would be all right. It would mean her going away tomorrow and I'd be short-handed. I'd have no one to work through until Christmas Eve. We're just frantic here. So, Mum, I was wondering if you'd be able to help out.'

'You need a waitress, Tam?' Sheppy was lightning quick. 'That's mint. Courtenay's done waitressing. She'll step in.'

'I'll work all next week.' Courtenay was suddenly wide awake. 'Any shifts you want.'

Tamsin looked at Sheppy. 'Is she a friend of yours?'

'Courtenay, meet Tam,' Sheppy said. 'She could be your new boss.'

'Could you fill in for Imogen? Can you supply references?' Tamsin asked.

'I've got one from my last employer in Newport Pagnell,' Courtenay said. 'It was a fast-food cafe.'

'That would be incredible.' Tamsin turned to Morwenna. 'It's been a lucky day for all of us.'

Morwenna was interested. 'Oh?'

'Well, Seb's just treated Becca and Tristan to lunch. He bought a lottery ticket in the Sue Ryder shop yesterday and he won.'

'Did he?' Morwenna looked surprised. 'How much?'

'A thousand pounds. He's promised Becca a great Christmas present.' Tamsin looked around, catching Tristan's eye. They exchanged smiles. 'Tristan and I are meeting up tonight. And guess what? I'm going surfing with him first thing tomorrow. The waves will be really good.'

'I'd love to be able to surf,' Courtenay said. 'I'm no good in the water.'

Sheppy tried to look alluring. 'I'll teach you.'

Tamsin dragged her eyes from Tristan. 'So, Courtenay, yes, please. It would be great to have you working for us. That's good luck all around. I'll open up tomorrow at half nine. Can you be here by then?'

'Definitely. I won't let you down,' Courtenay promised.

'I told you this was a nice place.' Sheppy looked pleased.

'I'm delighted,' Tamsin agreed. 'Imogen will be pleased too. I'll get you that hot chocolate, Courtenay—'

'Oh, hang on, I can't now.' Courtenay was staring at her phone, thumbing a text. 'I have to go. Sorry, something's come up.'

'Like what?' Sheppy asked, but Courtenay was on her feet, grabbing her cloth bag, moving towards the door.

'I'll see you later,' she called, although it wasn't clear whether she was addressing Sheppy or Tamsin. The door clanged and she was gone.

'You win some, you lose some.' Sheppy made a face. 'She's a nice girl, Courtenay, but I'm not sure she's keen on me.'

'You'll find someone who's right,' Morwenna said.

'Well, if the hot chocolate's going spare, I'll have it,' Sheppy said, ever the optimist.

'Of course. And I'll tell Imogen the good news,' Tamsin said. She hurried back towards the counter.

Morwenna's eyebrows knotted. She said, 'Sheppy, I'm just going to chat with someone over there.' She indicated Tristan's table. 'I won't be a minute.'

Sheppy spotted Tamsin approaching with a steaming mug. 'Knock yourself out,' he said.

Morwenna moved swiftly towards Tristan's table in full sleuthing mode and patted his arm. 'I'm sorry to hear about the burglary.'

Tristan stretched lithe limbs. Morwenna could see why Tamsin found him so attractive, with his easy manner and unassuming good humour. He seemed completely unaware of the effect of his tousled blond hair and direct blue gaze. Morwenna was reminded of Ruan. She shook herself. Tristan was saying something.

'...Mum was upset, because it had been her mother's necklace. I mean, money's only money, but the diamond was sentimental.'

'Your dad's got insurance though,' Seb said.

'Thank goodness.' Tristan nodded. 'The worrying thing is the Santa card, as if someone was sending a warning. Mum's got someone out to put better locks on all the windows next to the drainpipe where the burglar broke in. It must have been a professional. Or a gang of them.'

Becca shuddered. 'I'm so glad I'm not on my own all night.' She took Seb's hand. 'I feel safer with you staying round. Mind you, all those phone calls are a pain.'

'Phone calls?' Morwenna asked.

Becca brought his fingers to her lips. She was clearly besotted. 'Seb's sister's expecting a baby. He's on the phone half the time talking to his dad about it. Apparently, Phoebe's waters broke last night and Seb spent an hour in the bathroom chatting about how labour was progressing.'

'She's still not had it, poor thing.' Seb winced. His fingers moved to the chain around his neck, a dog-tag pendant with sapphires set in it.

'Well, that's exciting. I love babies,' Morwenna said encouragingly. 'You'll be an uncle, Seb.'

'I will.'

'Where does your sister live?'

'Near Swindon. Wroughton. My parents live there too.'

'So,' Morwenna said. 'What is it, do you know? A boy or a girl?'

'It's my first nephew,' Seb said proudly. 'Phoebe's decided on a name already. She's going to call him Arthur.'

'A kingly name. Arthur was Cornish,' Morwenna said.

'He was. So was Tristan: he was a Cornish knight,' Tristan said.

'Seb said he might go up to Swindon after Christmas to see the baby. He wants me to go with him,' Becca said proudly.

'You'll be taking little Arthur his first Christmas present from his Uncle Seb,' Morwenna said.

Seb nodded. 'I might get him a teddy bear to cuddle up to. You know those giant ones.'

'It's a good job you won the charity lottery ticket,' Morwenna said, watching his reaction.

'It is,' Seb said awkwardly. 'Did Tam tell you?'

'She did. That's a stroke of luck, just before Christmas.'

'Definitely. Seb only popped in to browse the second-hand books,' Tristan teased.

'I'll have to get myself a lottery ticket. I could do with a windfall.' Morwenna met Seb's eyes meaningfully. 'Is it a big prize every week?'

'Just leading up to Christmas.' Seb reached for his mug and drained the last of the coffee. 'We should go, Becca. The gift shop's closed and we've been gone for over an hour.'

'You're right.' Becca stood up slowly. 'I have a business to run.'

'I'll help,' Seb offered and Becca reached for his hand.

'I don't know what I'd do without him.'

Seb seemed about to reply, but he didn't get the chance. Tamsin shouted, 'Mum,' and was dodging through spaces between tables, her face anxious, waving her phone. She turned to Tristan. 'Can you do me a massive favour?'

'Anything,' Tristan said calmly. 'What do you need?'

Tamsin's hand rested on his shoulder as her words tumbled. 'I have to go out. Now. Can you just hold the fort for half an hour? Imogen will be fine waiting on the tables. Zach's good on his own in the kitchen and we're quiet again now. So you could just stay at the counter, take money, keep an eye.'

'Of course.' Tristan picked up on her tension. 'What's happened?'

'The school rang. It's probably nothing but – Mum, would you come with me?'

'Of course.' Morwenna's brow furrowed. 'Is Elowen all right?'

'Fine.' Tamsin nodded. 'I'll tell you about it when we're on our way. Thanks, Tristan.'

Morwenna reached for her coat and bag, calling a quick goodbye to Sheppy, who was looking for something else to eat. Tamsin grabbed her arm and they hurried outside.

'The secretary rang from the school.' Tamsin's eyes were filled with fear. 'Apparently someone just called to say they were picking Elowen up early for a dentist's appointment.'

'What?' Morwenna was surprised. 'She doesn't have an appointment.'

'And what's worse...' Tamsin was dragging Morwenna along, panting '...the woman who rang claimed to be you.'

18

Morwenna and Tamsin reached the school, a brick building surrounded by tall railings, and crossed the playground where a few parents had already started to congregate. Without stopping to chat, they hurried inside. The reception area had been refurbished a few years ago, and had a wooden desk, white walls and a shiny blue and white school sign with a Cornish coat of arms and the motto 'One and All.'

There was a display of photos: children doing gymnastics, performing in the Christmas show. There was a sign saying, 'You are Unique: YOU Matter' and another, 'We Are All Part of One World Community'. The woman behind the desk adjusted green-framed glasses. 'Hello, Tamsin.'

Tamsin dropped both hands on the desk. 'Where's Elowen? Is she all right?'

'Hi, Daphne,' Morwenna said calmly. 'Thank you for calling. We'll take Elowen home with us.'

Daphne was smart in a crisp white blouse with a bow at the neck. 'She's still in class with Ms Stark. The bell doesn't ring for another fifteen minutes. But the woman who claimed to be you on the phone, Morwenna, said she'd pick her up outside at three o'clock.'

'That's now,' Morwenna said, glancing at the clock. It was two minutes past. Without another word, she belted through the door and out, towards the road.

Carole Taylor had just arrived at the railings. She greeted Morwenna with a puzzled face. 'All right? I thought I was picking Elowen up today, and bringing her back with Britney. It's their last day. We were going to have hot chocolate.'

'Sorry.' Morwenna was staring round frantically. 'Something's come up.'

'Has Elowen been fighting again?' Carole began, then she noticed Morwenna's troubled expression. 'What's happened?'

'I'm not sure.' Morwenna was scrutinising the groups of parents, looking for a clue: someone she didn't recognise, a woman alone who might be waiting for a child. Anything suspicious. She heard the roar of an engine and a car pulled away on the other side of the road. It was a black Ford Galaxy, the windows smoked glass. She couldn't see the driver, but her instincts screamed that someone had been waiting for Elowen.

She took a breath to calm herself. Perhaps it was easily explained. 'I need to see Daphne Prowse in Reception, Carole. Is it all right if Tam and Elowen meet you up at the tearoom?' Morwenna gave a smile that said everything was quite normal and disappeared back into the school.

At the desk, Tamsin was still talking to Daphne. 'So did the woman who rang sound like Mum?'

'To be honest, Tamsin, I couldn't be sure at all. The voice was muffled. We get a lot of calls from mobiles where the reception is bad.'

'So what did the woman who was supposed to be me say, Daphne?' Morwenna asked.

'She was very polite, a bit reticent. Odd. She said she was Morwenna Mutton, Elowen's grandma. I thought that was a bit funny, because I know you're Elowen's gran. You'd never tell me that.'

'Right,' Morwenna said.

'She said that Elowen had a dentist's appointment at half three and she'd probably have forgotten, so would I remind her and send her out at three and she'd be waiting across the road.'

'Thank goodness you didn't.' Tamsin closed her eyes.

Daphne frowned. 'It's our policy not to allow children out unaccompanied. I told the woman she'd have to come to the desk, and she said it might be difficult to park the car.'

'To park?' Morwenna was surprised. 'I haven't driven a car in five years.'

'I know,' Daphne said. 'I've had a word with Ms Stark and Elowen's still in class. She hasn't been told anything. I rang you straight away, Tamsin.'

'Thank you.' Relief flooded Tamsin's face. 'I'll take her home as soon as she comes out.' She turned to Morwenna. 'Mum, I have a date with Tristan tonight but I'm going to change our plans. We'll stay in. He won't mind. I want to include Elowen, not make her feel like an outsider, so Tristan can come up to the flat and we'll cook pizza. I'll invite Becca and Seb round. We'll play games. Tristan will love it – he can't wait to get to know Elowen better. He's always saying that.'

'I think that's wise, Tam,' Morwenna said. 'And you and Tristan are surfing tomorrow, dawn patrol?'

'Yes, first light, before we open up.' Tamsin remembered: her head had been full of worries about Elowen. 'I haven't surfed in ages. I'll have to get my wetsuit out.'

'And what about Elowen?' Morwenna asked.

'Dad's coming round at seven-thirty. He's bringing her to the beach to watch. She loves the surf.'

'I'll come along,' Morwenna said. 'We can all have breakfast afterwards.'

'It's a plan.' Tamsin watched Morwenna pull out her phone. 'Who are you ringing?'

'Jane,' Morwenna said quickly. She said, 'Hi, Jane. Can you pop down to the school? Someone's phoned, pretending to be me. They might have been trying to get access to Elowen. What? Thanks – yes, I'll see you soon.'

'What's happening?' Tamsin asked, her face serious.

'Jane's coming over with Jim Hobbs.' Morwenna turned to Daphne. 'They'll ask you what happened.'

'Of course,' Daphne said professionally.

'I don't want Elowen to know any of this,' Tamsin blurted. 'I don't want her upset.'

'Absolutely,' Morwenna agreed. 'Just take her straight home. I'll wait here and talk to Jane. Carole's going to meet you at the tearoom with Britney.'

'Right.' Tamsin looked relieved. 'Thanks, Mum.'

'Try to enjoy yourselves if you can. I'll see you tomorrow, first thing.' Morwenna hugged her daughter. 'Try not to worry. Jane will sort things out. It's probably just a prank.'

'What if it isn't?' Tamsin asked worriedly.

'We stick together,' Morwenna said, and the screeching sound of the school bell drowned her words. Tamsin took off down the corridor towards the classroom and Morwenna breathed out slowly to calm her thoughts.

Whoever killed Pawly – and Morwenna was fairly sure he had been killed now – had probably also burgled the Pengellens' home and sent the Santa cards. Now, was he or she trying to get to Morwenna and her family through

Elowen? But why, and how was it all connected? She had to find out.

* * *

Two hours later, Morwenna sat in her living room, Brenda on her knee, staring into the leaping flames of the log fire. Jane had given her the laptop back. The photos from the party were still there, although Jane hadn't mentioned them. She and Jim had gone back to the tearoom afterwards, with the intention of taking a break, but Morwenna knew full well that they wanted to check that Tamsin and Elowen were all right.

Jane had been furious at the idea of someone impersonating Morwenna. She was treating the incident seriously, attempted abduction. Blessed had turned up moments later, saying the police were looking at CCTV footage near the school. There was no clear view of a Ford Galaxy.

More officers had been drafted in to increase the search of the area. She promised Morwenna that someone would be apprehended, and soon. The grim look on her face convinced Morwenna that she meant business. But Morwenna couldn't help the anxiety that gnawed at her stomach.

Her thoughts drifted to her mother, who was going on a date with her new beau, Vernon Lewis. It worried her that she'd never met him, that she knew nothing about him. She picked up her phone and pressed a button.

'Mum. All right? Are you excited about the date?'

'I'm looking forward to it.' Lamorna's voice came back, breathless. 'I'm wearing a little pink number. It's a bit short, but I've still got the legs for it. Vernon's picking me up at – what is it now – oh, half-five, gone. I'd better get some slap on.'

'Where is it you're going?' Morwenna asked. She knew that

Lamorna had been told it was a surprise, but she hoped she'd have a clue. It didn't feel right that her mother would be taken somewhere and Morwenna would have no idea of her whereabouts. Anything might happen.

'All I know is it's somewhere in Seal Bay.' Lamorna sighed. 'Oh, there's a lovely new restaurant on the seafront I've never been to – it's called Catch of the Tide, next to the ice-cream place, Dairy Godmother. I hope we're going there.'

'What time are you going out?' Morwenna asked.

'What's this? Twenty questions?'

'I can't wait to meet Vernon.'

'Oh, you'll like him.' Lamorna was probably fake swooning at the other end. 'He's asked me all about you.'

'Has he?' Morwenna raised an eyebrow. 'What did you tell him?'

'That you're the best daughter anyone could have and you live all by yourself in Harbour Cottages when you have a perfectly good man across the road.'

Morwenna cringed. 'Probably not a good idea to tell him that, Mum.'

'Oh, he's a keeper – almost family,' Lamorna said. 'Well, I'd better crack on. I've got to make myself look beautiful.'

'You are beautiful, Mum.' Morwenna heard Lamorna cackle with delight and the phone was silent.

She picked up her laptop and typed the name Vernon Lewis into a search engine. It was a common enough name. There was a photo of an American heavyweight boxer, his skin gleaming as he flexed his muscles. She flicked through more Vernons – an aircraft engineer, a lecturer from the University of Aukland, the proprietor of a shop selling old vinyl records in Surrey, a retired army officer. She brought up page after page for the next twenty minutes, then she saw a headline.

Man Jailed For Receiving Stolen Goods.

It was a newspaper article from the *South Wales Evening Post* in 1988. A Swansea man had been jailed following a spate of burglaries. Vernon Clifford Lewis, forty-three years old, was receiving stolen goods and selling them on. He was part of a gang who worked throughout South Wales. The judge had called Lewis a 'slippery man'.

Morwenna looked at the photo. Vernon would be the right age. Lamorna had said he was seventy-nine now. He had a serious expression – of course he would – and cold eyes. And a fox-fur moustache.

Morwenna shivered.

It could be the man her mother was dating. Morwenna hurried upstairs, finding dark clothes, a warm jacket, a black beanie to cover her hair. She was a woman on a mission.

Forty-five minutes later, she was waiting astride her bicycle in the dark on the corner of Tregenna Gardens. Her eyes were fixed on the row of terraced houses, and on the black BMW saloon parked outside her mother's house. She didn't have to wait long. Lamorna's front door opened, a slice of light illuminating the path, the soft bubble of voices audible as Vernon shepherded Lamorna down to his car and opened the door. Morwenna dragged her bicycle into someone's front garden as the BMW glided past. She was in pursuit, hoping they wouldn't notice a bicycle following not far behind them with the lights off, which she knew was extremely dangerous, but it was only half a mile into Seal Bay – she just needed to know where her mother was going. As she whizzed down Lister Hill, a plan was forming. She had money, her bank card. She'd get a table at the opposite end of the restaurant from Lamorna and Vernon, buy herself a starter and keep watch.

At the bottom of the hill, she followed Vernon and Lamorna into town. Several cars flashed headlights at her because she wasn't visible enough, but Morwenna's eyes were on the BMW.

She was dismayed to see Vernon take the road out of Seal Bay, towards Pennance Hill. Lamorna had said they were dining in town. So where was he taking her mother? She pedalled hard to keep up, feeling the electric motor do most of the work, but the BMW was hurtling into the distance.

Morwenna groaned. She was losing them.

Vernon began to indicate left. He was pulling into a layby. Morwenna knew the place. A shady parking spot off the road where couples often stopped their cars to canoodle. Some of the locals called it Lovers' Lane. The kids called it Shaggers' End. Vernon had stopped the car to woo her mother. Morwenna couldn't believe it.

Or perhaps he intended to harm her.

Morwenna whizzed forwards, braking just as the road twisted behind a huddle of bushes. The BMW was parked, lights off. She saw two shadowy figures inside, their heads together. Placing the bike down carefully, Morwenna sidled towards the car, hiding behind the back bumper, creeping round towards the passenger side. Vernon was talking: his mouth was moving. Morwenna edged closer. He leaned over and their lips met in a long kiss.

Morwenna caught her breath in shock. She definitely shouldn't be there. The image that was forming in her imagination was unthinkable.

Vernon drew back. He was talking again, holding something glittering in his hand, looking sentimental, but somehow, Morwenna thought, there was something false about his expression.

She popped her head up, out of sight, looking at Vernon's

back. He was holding Lamorna's wrist, placing something around it, kissing her hand.

Then Lamorna was saying something with a dreamy expression on her face that Morwenna didn't like one bit.

Morwenna leaned forward to look more closely. Her mother was now wearing a bracelet. Diamonds winked in the darkness. She edged even further forward, craning her neck for a better look, up on tiptoe, and fell, grabbing the door handle, sprawling on the hard ground. She saw her mother's mouth open in a scream.

Morwenna stood up, rapped the window gently with her knuckles and gave her most apologetic grin. The passenger window opened and Lamorna put a hand on her heart, panting in fear. 'Giss on!'

'Hello.' Morwenna's voice was jolly. 'I just popped out on the bike for some exercise, and I saw the car pulling into the layby. What a coincidence. I knew it had to be you.' She pushed a hand through the window to shake the hand of a smart gentleman with combed-over hair and a thick moustache, who wore an expensive gold watch with diamonds around the face. He looked absolutely terrified.

'I'm pleased to meet you at last, Vernon. I'm Morwenna, Lamorna's daughter. How do you do?'

SATURDAY 20 DECEMBER

19

The following morning, just as pale light began to creep across the horizon, Morwenna stood on the beach in hat, scarf and a thick coat at Seal Bay watching the waves roll in. The wind was chilly. Elowen clutched her hand for warmth and Ruan stood beside them, keeping the blast from their faces. They huddled together in warm coats. Morwenna's other hand held a bag with a flask and mugs.

Tamsin and Tristan were already heading towards the water in wet suits, surfboards under their arms.

Elowen said, 'Tristan says he'll teach me to surf in the summer.'

'Oh?' Morwenna met Ruan's gaze. They were both thinking the same thing: if Tristan intended to be with Tamsin in the summer, he was a serious boyfriend.

Morwenna said, 'Do you like Tristan?'

'He's funny,' Elowen said. 'Last night when we were making pizzas, I said I wanted pineapple on mine and he pretended he was going to be sick. I laughed and laughed, so did Mummy. He's nice. I like him more than Seb.'

'Why's that?' Morwenna asked.

'Seb just wants to kiss Becca all the time. I don't like boys like that.'

'You prefer someone with conversation?' Ruan said.

'Boys are silly. They're all right to play football with though. I like it best when I beat them and score goals. The coach says I'll play for England.'

'You might,' Morwenna said.

Ruan was staring towards the sea. 'It's glassy out there this morning. There's some spray coming off the top of the lip, so there must be a light offshore wind. The wave's breaking in one direction. Ideal for surfing.'

'It is.' Morwenna pointed. 'Look, the wave over there is walling up, peeling off, and, bang on cue, there's Tam, and Tristan.'

Ruan met her eyes. 'We should have brought our wetsuits and boards.'

'What?' Morwenna was surprised. 'You think we should have joined them, surfing?'

'Why not?'

'Well.' Morwenna was surprised by Ruan's sudden sense of adventure. 'Maybe in the summer we can help Tristan and Tam teach Elowen to surf. It's been ages since I rode a wave.'

'Maybe we should.' Ruan's eyes twinkled.

'I'm going to be a surfer too,' Elowen said. 'Tristan said he'd buy me a wetsuit.'

'I've got my eye on a new one,' Morwenna admitted. 'It's a funky graffiti design. The Quilkin Emporium are selling them.'

'Are they?' Ruan seemed interested.

'And they've got Santa's grotto this week.' Morwenna nudged Elowen. 'Shall we go?'

'Oh, yes, please.' Elowen gazed up at Ruan. 'Can you come, Grandad?'

'If your grandma wants me to.' Ruan was thoughtful.

'Can Grandad come, Grandma? Can he? Can he?' Elowen jumped up and down on the sand. 'Please say we can all go. I love it when Grandad comes with us.'

'If you want to, Ruan,' Morwenna said, feeling slightly relieved. There was safety in numbers. And Santas made her nervous nowadays. 'We'll go tomorrow, shall we, after my swim? About eleven-thirty? They're open on Sundays now for Christmas.'

'I'll pick you both up, shall I?' Ruan offered. 'We could have lunch somewhere afterwards.'

'Milkshakes,' Elowen yelled.

'One thing at a time,' Morwenna said.

Elowen pointed and screeched, 'Look at Mummy surfing. She's brilliant. And look at Tristan riding that big barrel of a wave.'

'They're both confident surfers,' Ruan agreed. He began to chuckle. 'You know, I'm still thinking about what you told me about Lamorna. How you sneaked up on her and her boyfriend in his car.' He shook his head. 'Pretending you were out on your bike, with no lights on, keeping fit. You're some maid.'

'I had to make something up.' Morwenna laughed. 'Poor Vernon looked shocked. He said something about being too shy to give Lamorna a present in a public place. But he could have given it to her later in the house. He must have wanted to get her on her own somewhere the stars were shining. That was some bracelet, mind. She showed it to me. It wasn't cheap paste.'

'Where did they go to dinner?' Ruan asked.

'Catch of the Tide, the seafood place. I followed them there on my bike, just to make sure she was all right.'

'With the lights on, I hope.'

'Of course,' Morwenna said.

Elowen pulled at her arm. 'Look, Grandma. Tristan's in the big wave now. And Mummy's there too.'

'It's good to see them having fun,' Ruan said. 'And we'll have fun tomorrow when we go to Santa's grotto.'

'I want a puppy for Christmas. And some new football boots,' Elowen explained, 'and a wetsuit. I want to surf like Mummy.'

'Right,' Morwenna said. 'What time is it, I wonder?'

'It must be approaching nine,' Ruan said. 'Tam's opening up at half past. I might pop in and give her a hand while she gets a shower.'

'Me too. The new waitress is starting. Courtenay. I can show her the ropes.' Morwenna was glad to help out. 'Afterwards I'll pop up to see Mum and apologise for gatecrashing her date. I want to take another look at that bracelet too.'

'Do you think Vernon stayed the night?' Ruan asked quietly.

Elowen was quick to pick up on his tone. 'Has Great-Grandma had a sleepover with her new boyfriend? Are they all kissy-kissy?' She began to laugh.

'Great-grandmas are allowed boyfriends,' Ruan said, with a tentative look at Morwenna. 'Everyone is.'

Morwenna took a shaky breath, wondering if Ruan was thinking about Pam Truscott. She didn't know how to ask him if he was attracted to her, if they were becoming close.

Elowen pointed. 'There's Mummy and Tristan again in the middle of that big wave. Look how cool they are.'

'I'd forgotten how much fun surfing was,' Morwenna mused. 'The SWANS are meeting tomorrow, but the cold weather puts people off. I wonder how many of us will turn up.'

There was the sound of an engine out at sea, a soft purring, as a motorboat bounced across the waves, bobbing on the surface. Ruan said, 'Who's that?'

'They're driving a bit quickly.' Morwenna had started to feel nervous. Something about the speed of the boat, the arc of the water. And the person at the wheel was leaning forward recklessly. It troubled her.

Tristan and Tamsin were riding waves, oblivious, as the motorboat roared towards them, not slowing. Morwenna was sure that the driver at the wheel was accelerating. There was something familiar about the hunch of his body. She heard her own voice cry out in alarm.

'Watch out,' Ruan called.

The next few seconds seemed to slow right down. Morwenna's eyes were glued to every detail. The motorboat swerved in the sea, sending up a swirl of spray, pointing the bow directly towards Tristan and Tamsin. They were oblivious at first, then they noticed the boat as it barrelled straight at them. Water shot upwards, the motorboat turned slickly and roared away into the distance.

Was that a flash of red? A glimpse of a Santa suit?

The waves continued to roll, but the sea was empty. There was no sight of surfers or surfboards. Morwenna shook visibly. 'What just happened?'

'Where's my mummy?' Elowen's voice was small.

Ruan picked his granddaughter up and hugged her. 'She's in the water, Elowen. I expect she's swimming.'

'I want Mummy.' Elowen began to struggle. 'Where is she?'

Morwenna was already on her phone, walking away from Elowen, her voice a strangled tremor in her throat. 'Jane. I need help. This is urgent. Can you get down to the beach? Get an ambulance. A lifeboat too. Tam and Tristan were surfing. A motorboat drove straight at them. No, a few seconds ago. It's gone – no, I can't see either of them.'

Her legs were jelly as she made her way back to Ruan and Elowen, breathing rapidly, trying to calm her pounding heart. Elowen pushed her head into her grandfather's chest. Morwenna stroked her hair.

'I hope Jane's quick.' Ruan looked around desperately.

'I asked her to alert the lifeboats,' Morwenna said quietly.

'Where's Mummy?' Elowen sobbed. 'Did the big boat crash into her? Where is she?'

Morwenna was ice cold now as she stared hard into the ocean, her eyes narrowed. Ruan pointed. 'Look.'

A round seal head appeared from the sea, a figure swimming towards shore. It was Tristan. He paused, looking round, and dived down again. Morwenna held her breath in fear.

Time stood still.

Two heads surfaced, their hair sleek against their faces. Tamsin and Tristan swam slowly to shore, standing in the water, staggering forward, exhausted. Morwenna ran to meet them, Ruan at her heels, Elowen in his arms.

Morwenna yelled, 'Tam, are you hurt?'

'I'm OK.' She turned to Tristan. 'The boat drove straight at us. I didn't see who it was.'

'Nor did I but' – Tristan wrapped his arms around Tamsin – 'thank goodness you're all right.'

'I just heard you shout "jump" and I jumped,' Tamsin panted. Elowen ran into her embrace. 'Don't worry, Elowen. We're fine. We're just cold.' Tamsin's teeth were chattering; the shock wasn't helping. 'I need to get in the warm.'

'I've phoned Jane,' Morwenna explained. 'I've asked for an ambulance to come and check you over.'

'I'll ring and tell the lifeboats that Tam's OK,' Ruan said, walking a few paces away.

'Thank goodness—' Tristan seemed stunned. Water dripped from his hair. Morwenna noticed the double diamond studs in one ear. His brow was creased with anxiety. 'Are you all right, Tam?'

'A bit shaken up,' Tamsin admitted. 'Can we go back and get warm? I'm supposed to be opening at half-nine. Courtenay will be there. I'll ask Zach if he'll look after things for a bit.'

'I can hold the fort,' Morwenna said.

'Thanks, Mum,' Tamsin began, but Ruan shook his head.

'Put a note on the door, Tam, and say you'll open at half-ten. Say it's staff training. This needs sorting out properly with the police. Your mother and I have to go somewhere first to check something out, but we'll be back soon. And you need to give a statement to Jane.'

'Oh, right,' Tamsin said, still wobbly and dazed as she, Tristan and Elowen started to walk towards the sea wall. Ruan lagged behind and turned to Morwenna, his face like thunder.

'What is it, Ruan?' Morwenna asked.

'Let them go. Jane will talk to them. What happened out there was attempted murder.'

'I know.'

Ruan's eyes flashed anger. 'The police will deal with it. And the paramedics will look after Tam. But we need to go to the boatyard now. The motorboat we saw out there is one of Damien's.'

'Are you sure?'

'I'm positive. It's the one I was thinking of buying. Morwenna – it was *The Swordfish*.'

* * *

Morwenna sat in Ruan's car. He finished his call to Damien, telling him to get down to the boatyard immediately, it was urgent. In a flash, he started the engine and he drove away from the seafront, accelerating down the hill. Behind him, a police car and an ambulance had arrived. Someone would be taking care of Tamsin and Elowen.

'Damien wasn't keen to come down,' Ruan said.

'You didn't tell him why.'

'I didn't.' Ruan's eyes were on the road. 'Someone tried to kill her.'

Morwenna was shaking inside her coat. 'I know, Ruan.' She was quiet for a moment. 'Are you sure it was the same motorboat?'

'Yes. I've sat in it, driven it in the water.' Ruan shook his head. 'It was the boat Pawly was trying to buy, but he didn't have enough money to pay it off. He fell out with Damien big time over it. Damien's offered it to me at a good price. But who was driving it?'

'Does Damien have keys to all the boats?'

'He does, but he leaves them in sometimes. The boatyard's locked overnight.'

'Do you think someone broke in?'

'That's what we're going to find out.' Ruan drove furiously towards Woon's. The gates were already open and he screeched through, stopping abruptly next to Damien's truck. Damien was leaning against it, bleary-eyed, looking unhappy.

Ruan said, 'He got here quick.'

He was out of the van in seconds, Morwenna behind him, marvelling at how he was a man on a mission. He said, 'All right, Damien.'

'What's going on?' Damien grumbled. 'Why did you get me out of bed?'

'It's gone nine,' Morwenna said but Damien ignored her.

'I had a skinful in The Smugglers last night.' Damien's voice was gruff. 'I needed a lie-in this morning. I don't take kindly to being dragged out of bed in the morning at the weekend. Bev was making breakfast just as you rang. This had better be good.'

'It will be.' Ruan was already walking towards the waterfront. 'Have you sold *The Swordfish* to anyone?'

'You know I haven't.' Damien sniffed. 'I promised you first refusal, mates' rates.'

'Have you lent it out?'

'No.' Damien's voice rose in irritation. 'What's this about?'

They had reached the quay. *The Swordfish* was in its usual place, flanked by bobbing boats. The keys were in the ignition.

Morwenna had never seen Ruan look so angry. His face was taut as he clambered aboard.

'Did you leave the keys in?'

'The boatyard's locked. The boat isn't going anywhere.'

'Then why's the engine warm?' Ruan snapped. 'Someone just drove this boat at Tam while she was surfing. They tried to kill her.'

'What did you say?' It was Damien's turn to look furious. 'In my boat?'

'Can you explain that?' Ruan turned to face Damien, his voice quiet and cold. Morwenna wondered if he'd grab the lapels of his jacket.

'No, I can't,' Damien said.

'I wanted to talk it through with you before the police come,' Ruan said. 'Because I can identify your boat.'

'Someone must have broken in.'

'How?' Ruan's single syllable made Morwenna shiver. She spoke up.

'Were there any signs of a break-in when you opened up?'

'I didn't see any.' Damien blinked; he was stunned and still under the influence of last night's alcohol. 'Ruan, you don't think I'd hurt your daughter?'

'I don't,' Ruan said. 'But someone wanted to. Someone stole your boat, and you've got no idea who it was. Or *have* you?'

'No.'

Morwenna indicated the security cameras. 'Won't these tell us if someone came into the boatyard?'

'I don't usually bother to turn them on.' Damien ran a hand through his hair. 'I lock and bolt this place at night. I put chains on the gate.'

'Someone took the motorboat and brought it back right under your nose.' Ruan folded his arms. 'And they tried to drive it into Tam this morning while she was surfing.'

'Well, I don't know.' Damien seemed truly baffled. 'I'm sorry, Ruan. You know me. I wouldn't do anything—' He turned to Morwenna. 'Is your girl all right?'

'She's a bit shaken. But the point is, Damien, whoever did it is still out there, on the loose. Who knows what they'll do next?' Morwenna spoke to Ruan. 'I'm certain it must be the same person who sent us the cards, who burgled the Pengellens' place, who killed Pawly. Someone who was at the Pengellens' party.' She took a deep breath. 'We have to tell Jane and Blessed. And we have to find the killer, before they do something else.'

20

'I just need to clear my head, Ruan. I'll catch you later.'

'Right. I told Blessed I'd talk to her now. It's good to know Jim Hobbs is already on his way to Woon's.'

Morwenna waved briefly as Ruan drove away. She walked slowly down the steps towards the beach, glancing at her phone: Tamsin had messaged that there were several police officers still at the tearoom, but the doors were open for business as usual and Courtenay was doing a great job. Right now, Tamsin wanted to spend some time with Elowen, who needed her mum and lots of reassurance. Lamorna was on her way over to pour a few cups of tea and keep the customers happy.

Morwenna turned for a moment to watch Ruan's van slow down outside the tearoom. Two police cars were parked outside. Rick would be there – as a DI, he'd be fully involved now. Finally, they were all going to treat Pawly's death as suspicious. More than that. Jane messaged that the police presence would be cranked up across Seal Bay. More officers would be drafted in from the Devon and Cornwall force. Ruan was desperate to talk to Blessed about *The Swordfish* and identify it as the one used to attack his child.

He was fairly convinced that Damien had nothing to do with the attempt on Tamsin and Tristan's lives. Morwenna wasn't so sure.

But she believed that the person who attacked Tamsin was also the person who'd killed Pawly.

Morwenna intended to hurry back to her family as soon as she could, but right now she was walking on the sand, her face covered with tears. She'd been holding them back since they left Woon's boatyard. It crushed her that someone had tried to kill her child and she was flooded with emotions she couldn't contain. Sobs racked her body – thank goodness no one was around on the beach to see her cry. She felt desolate, furious and miserable, all rolled into one. It made her determined to find out who had tried to hurt Tamsin. Again, she went through her list of suspects. There were people at the party she didn't know; people she hadn't even considered. And there were one or two more who needed further investigation.

The person she was looking for was on that list.

Morwenna took a deep breath and tried to steady her racing heart. Anxieties knocked and crashed; it was impossible to think straight. Being a mother and protecting her family made Morwenna a warrior. But it also made her a wimp.

Jane had been true to her word. Rows of police officers in yellow vests were scouring the beach. A message buzzed on Morwenna's phone. Jane was ready to interview her about the driver of the boat.

Morwenna was sure there was something she recognised about the figure at the wheel, but it was buried beneath so many layers of anxiety. More tears flowed and she wiped her face with her hand. Her skin was cold. To her right, the sea whispered. She turned to stare at the dull grey ocean, the dull grey sky.

What if Tamsin hadn't avoided the motorboat? What if she

and Tristan were still in the water, beneath the icy waves? Morwenna cried out loud.

Once. That was enough.

She took a deep shuddering breath and whispered, 'Pull yourself together, maid. People need you to be tough.'

Swiftly, she turned and headed back towards the tearoom. For a second, she thought she heard someone call her name far behind her, a light voice on the wind. She wasn't in the mood for conversations; she kept going.

'Morwenna.'

She stopped. Someone was definitely calling. She whirled round to see a silver-haired man in a thick overcoat, smiling and hurrying towards her. His handsome face was deeply tanned, showing off his white smile. She said, 'Barnaby.'

He grabbed her shoulders, kissing her cheek. 'It's good to see you.'

'When did you come back?'

'Last night. I'm staying at Mirador for Christmas.' His words hung on the air.

'With Pam.'

'Yes. And Simon will be back in the new year.'

'That's nice.'

There was a pause; so many unsaid words passed between them. Morwenna wasn't sure how to deal with the fact that he'd asked her to go to Barbados and she'd said yes. Then she'd said no. Since then, they'd hardly corresponded.

Barnaby broke the silence. 'So, what are you up to?'

'Not much. Walking.' Morwenna decided that Barnaby didn't need to know about the incident with Tamsin and the motorboat. Pam would have told him about Pawly. Right now, he would likely have other things on his mind.

'So, now I'm back in Seal Bay, how about we catch up? What are you doing tonight?'

'Nothing.' Morwenna answered before she'd thought about it. Her emotions were all over the place.

'Shall I call round at six-thirty? We can go for dinner.'

'I'd like that.' Morwenna took a deep breath. Her first thought was that she didn't want to sit in the house by herself fretting about what had happened, worrying about Santa faces at her window. It might take her mind off her worries. Barnaby was good company. It would be nice to find out about his travels.

'It's a date,' he said smoothly and Morwenna wondered what he meant by date. She'd simply imagined two people sharing a meal. Yes, that was what it would be.

'I'll look forward to it,' she said.

He kissed her cheek again. 'I'm parked on double yellows. I'd better be off.'

Morwenna almost said that the local police officers wouldn't care about his illegal parking today. They were in the tearoom trying to catch bigger fish. Instead, she said, 'It's good to see you.'

'You too,' he called as he jogged away in the other direction. Morwenna pushed along towards the steps that led to the road, thinking about Tamsin, about the motorboat that had hurtled towards her at breakneck speed. She'd forgotten Barnaby already.

The tearoom was packed. Morwenna sat at a table by the window, the only one unoccupied, looking around and listening to snatches of conversation. Susan and Barb Grundy were drinking tea, their eyes wide and their ears pricked up. Carole Taylor and Britney were sharing cake. They'd all heard the news and were desperate to find out more. Seb and Becca sat in the corner together, their faces anxious.

Ruan was standing at the counter, serving teas, taking payments, but every few minutes his eyes drifted to his daughter.

Even Zach, the young chef, his auburn hair pushed beneath a white cap, was helping to serve slices of cake. Rick and Jane were sitting at a table talking to Tamsin and Tristan. Morwenna heard Rick say, 'deliberate attempt on their lives... Pawly... possible murder investigation.'

Julian and Pippa arrived, ordering tea and sitting next to Rick, demanding loudly for something to be done. Julian boomed, 'Why isn't someone down at Woon's, asking him questions?' Jane was talking quietly, explaining that Jim Hobbs and a DC were there now, doing their jobs. Lamorna was sitting with Elowen, looking intently at a book – it was *Diary of a Wimpy Kid*. Lamorna was doing all the voices.

Someone beside her interrupted her thoughts. 'Good morning, Morwenna. I expect you'll be wanting a hot drink and a mince pie. On the house, of course.' She looked up to see Courtenay in a white apron, her yellow hair pinned up. She had the air of someone who'd waited on tables all her life. Morwenna reached for the tea gratefully, watched as Courtenay sauntered over to Tamsin and Rick and asked if they wanted refills. Morwenna was glad she was fitting in.

The chair opposite was scraped back, and Jane sat down. She reached over and took Morwenna's hand. 'How are you?'

'All right.'

'You're shaken.' Jane's eyes were full of compassion. 'I need to know what you saw.'

Morwenna nodded. 'What can I add to what Ruan told Blessed, Jane?'

'Try to remember anything you can about the driver of the motorboat.'

'I wish I could.'

'We're flat out in the nick. There's been a spate of burglaries all over the bay. Now this. But what's happened here is our priority. Blessed's drafted in DCs to help. If there's a link between Pawly and what happened to Tamsin and Tristan, and the Santa cards, we'll find out. We're stepping up investigations.'

'Oh?'

'Damien Woon's place is being given the once-over. Jim's asked him and Beverley to come down the nick. They might have seen something or talked to someone, and it could give us a lead.'

Morwenna felt her eyes fill. 'Who'd do this to Tam, though? Is it because of me?'

'Why would it be?' Jane pressed her hand.

'Because I was on the radio. Because Mike said that I could find the killer.'

'You look exhausted,' Jane said. 'I'm taking you home.'

'I ought to stay here and help Tam.'

'We're all over it.'

'Are you sure?'

'You'll be more help after a long rest.'

Morwenna looked around. 'All right. I'll get some sleep. I'll come back this afternoon. And I have a date tonight.'

'I heard Barnaby's back in town,' Jane said. 'It'll do you good to have some down time. We'll catch up tomorrow for a swim. And don't worry about Tamsin. We'll keep an eye on her and Tristan from now on.'

'Right.' Morwenna pushed her tea away. 'I'll chat to Ruan and Tam, tell them I'll be back later. Then – thanks, yes – a rest is just what I need.'

* * *

Morwenna slept on the sofa until half past three, Brenda curled at her feet. She woke in a panic, rushed down to the tearoom on her bicycle, and found that all was quiet, as if nothing unusual had happened. The police presence was all around, but Courtenay was dealing with customers with a reassuring smile and Tamsin was sitting with Elowen making Christmas decorations in the corner. There was a sense of peace and calm. Tamsin was confident that the police had plenty of leads and someone would be arrested in no time at all. Morwenna cycled back with a lighter heart and decided she'd better get ready for her date. She was pleased to be going out.

To help her get in a more festive mood, she put on an old CD of Christmas hits downstairs and turned it up loud enough to hear it in her bedroom. Slade, Wizzard, Wham!, Bing Crosby. She was determined to be festive tonight – it was her way of covering up her anxiety. She showered in something that smelled of sweet grapefruit and her hair, now washed, was a shiny silver waterfall with blunt ends, thanks to Faye at Mane Attraction.

Morwenna thought again about Faye and wondered if she was still a suspect. There were plenty of others. She tried to imagine Faye behind the wheel of the motorboat in a Santa suit, driving it at the unsuspecting surfers. The thought made her tremble with fear, but she went through the suspects one by one and visualised each aiming the boat at her child. She couldn't believe it. Yet someone had pushed Pawly downstairs. They could just have easily have wanted to harm her daughter.

Morwenna tugged on a sparkly red dress from the back of the wardrobe. She hadn't worn it since Ruan's fiftieth, and that was well over a dozen years ago. It still fitted her, sort of, and it looked festive. She teamed it with a silky shawl and some bright ankle boots. She was doing her best to perk up, to feel like a party animal again. She wondered where she and Barnaby were going. She should have asked.

There was some perfume on the dressing table. Tamsin had brought it back from the Caribbean before Elowen was born. It showed how little she had used it: the bottle was almost full. She sprayed it liberally and glanced at the clock; Barnaby would be here at any minute. For a second, she was seized with doubt. Why was she going out with Barnaby at all? It had felt like a good idea at the time. Now she thought she'd be happier staying in with Brenda and a cup of cocoa.

The doorbell rang. It wasn't Ruan. He usually knocked, then used his own keys. If it was Barnaby, he was early. She peered between the bedroom curtains. An E-Type Jaguar gleamed in the lamplight. She glanced across the road. Ruan's van wasn't outside number nine. He'd be down The Smugglers.

She took a deep breath, grabbed her chicken bag with her keys and her phone, and bolted downstairs, wondering why her head was full of thoughts of Ruan, if he'd care that she was out with Barnaby, if it would hurt his feelings. And in the middle of all of this, what did she truly feel for him?

21

'You look wonderful.' Barnaby's eyes swerved back to the road as he drove down the hill.

'Thank you.' Morwenna gazed out at the bay, the indigo sea illuminated and twinkling, as Barnaby's car glided along, taking corners easily. He looked good too, in a smart jacket and chinos, and he smelled of something musky. Morwenna inhaled their mingled scent and wondered what the evening would bring.

'So, where are we going?' she asked.

'Well, I hope it's all right. I haven't seen Pam to check – she's been in Truro all day buying clothes – but I've arranged something special. I know how much you love the water.'

'Are we going skinny-dipping?' Morwenna joked.

'Nothing quite so chilly.' Barnaby looked pleased with himself. The car began to descend the hill towards the harbour and Morwenna's mood descended with it. They were heading for Woon's boatyard. It was the last place she wanted to be.

'I took the spare keys to the *Pammy* and got everything ready for dinner. We'll just sail out a little, then eat. How does lobster ravioli sound with a crisp Sauvignon Blanc, followed by crème brûlée?'

'Delicious,' Morwenna said without any real conviction. Barnaby drove through the entrance to Woon's and brought the car to a stop next to several other vehicles. One of them was Damien's truck. The other was a Range Rover. Barnaby frowned. 'What's going on here?'

He slid from the Jaguar and walked across the gravel towards where the boats were moored. Morwenna followed him, hugging the shawl for warmth. Three figures were standing next to the dipping boats. Morwenna heard a light voice, a woman's. Barnaby joined them and Morwenna hesitated.

'What are you doing here, Pam?' Barnaby asked his sister.

Pam was dressed in a silver sequin off-the-shoulder dress, her hair swept up beautifully, an emerald necklace at her throat. Her laughter tinkled. 'I'm on a date. Why are you here?'

'The same.'

Morwenna noticed a handsome man behind her, wearing a dark jacket, a crisp shirt and black jeans. It was Ruan. He looked truly lovely. She took a deep breath and gazed from the man she was with now to the man who had been her partner for years. Had been. He was with Pam now. Morwenna wondered why it made her heart feel strange, in a disturbing way.

'Well, this is awkward,' Barnaby said. 'I suppose Morwenna and I could always go to The Captain's Table.'

'Just make your minds up, can you?' Damien shoved his hands in his coat pocket. 'Bev's got dinner on the table. One pair of you is going out on the *Pammy* and I have to come back and lock up at midnight.' He looked at Morwenna. 'I'm stepping up security on this place. I've got the CCTV on tonight.'

'That's good,' Ruan said.

'The boat's waiting.' Pam met Barnaby's eyes. 'Ruan and I are cooking salmon.'

'I put some lobster ravioli in the galley earlier,' Barnaby said, and Morwenna wondered if there was going to be a sibling squabble. She glanced at Ruan and saw the smile in his eyes. There seemed to be only one solution.

'Why don't we double date?' she asked. 'It might be fun.'

Ruan was quick to agree. 'It solves the problem.'

'Well, I was hoping for something quite different but...' Pam shrugged. 'I don't see why not. What do you think, Barnaby?'

Barnaby glanced at Morwenna and she nodded eagerly. He said, 'Very well, we'll share the *Pammy*.' He smiled but there was something about his expression that seemed unconvinced. But as Morwenna followed Ruan on the boat, she felt strangely excited about what the evening would bring.

* * *

Two hours later, the *Pammy* was out at sea, lilting gently as Barnaby poured more wine and a soda water for himself. He began to collect empty plates. Ruan said, 'The lobster ravioli was very nice.'

'It was,' Morwenna agreed. Everything was very nice. She met Ruan's eyes and knew he was enjoying himself. They'd always been able to communicate through glances.

'Barnaby's a good cook,' Pam said sweetly.

'He is. Oh, Ruan, do you remember those bao buns you made last year?' Morwenna's eyes shone. 'I loved those.' She noticed that Barnaby looked a little disappointed. 'The ravioli was gorgeous.'

'You can cook bao buns for me, Ruan,' Pam said, leaning over to pat his knee in a way Morwenna thought far too familiar.

She said, 'I can't cook for toffee.'

'Tam always loved your stargazy pie when she was little,' Ruan said. 'So did I.'

'You must cook a lot of fish,' Barnaby said to Ruan. 'With you being a fisherman.'

'We catch a lot of pollock,' Ruan said, matter-of-factly.

Pam batted her eyelashes. 'What's the most unusual fish you've caught?'

Ruan thought about it. 'We caught bluefin tuna once. And, of course, sometimes sharks hang about in the waters.'

'Sharks are scary.' Pam grabbed his arm. Morwenna knew the gesture was more about Ruan than sharks.

'I didn't know sharks were an issue with you, Pam,' Barnaby said. 'In Barbados, we saw tiger sharks in the ocean, and you swam every day.' He turned to Morwenna. 'It's a shame you didn't get to Barbados.'

'You're retiring soon, aren't you, Ruan?' Pam was still clutching his arm. 'I have a house in Prospect Bay. You'll have to come out and stay for a while.'

'The waters are crystal clear,' Barnaby said. 'You're a water baby, Morwenna. You'd love it.'

'I might.' She held her glass out for more wine and Barnaby filled it. Pam pushed Ruan's glass towards him, wanting him to fill that one too, although it was already half full. Barnaby poured wine to the very top.

Ruan asked, 'Isn't Barbados the land of flying fish?'

'There's so much more than just fish there.' Barnaby gazed at Morwenna. 'Green monkeys and mongoose. The rum is second to none, and the tamarind balls are quite special.'

'You'd like the beer, Ruan,' Pam added possessively. 'And I love the local spicy pepper sauces.' She snuggled closer. 'Do you have a taste for hot things?'

Ruan laughed. 'Morwenna's the fiery one.' He met her eyes and she saw a sadness there. She felt sad too. Here she was with Barnaby and Ruan was with Pam. It somehow seemed wrong.

Everyone was quiet for a moment.

'Shall we have dessert?' Morwenna decided to lift the mood. 'The crème brûlée looks good. Did you make it, Barnaby?'

'I bought it,' Barnaby said, his voice a little flat.

'Oh, Barnaby, do you like my dress?' Pam lifted her arms to show off the elegant sequined number. 'I got it this afternoon specially. It cost me an arm and a leg, but it's worth it.' She turned to Ruan. 'Do you like it, Ruan?'

'Very nice,' Ruan said politely. 'I remember that red dress you've got on, Morwenna. You wore it to my fiftieth birthday bash.'

'My goodness.' Pam sounded alarmed. 'I never keep a dress more than a couple of years.'

'Your dress is lovely, Morwenna,' Barnaby said.

'I think I got it from Mum's catalogue,' Morwenna said, thinking that Barnaby was a sweet man. He had perfect manners. 'Yours is gorgeous, Pam. It really suits you. I'd look daft in something like that.'

'Morwenna could always wear colourful things. You both look nice,' Ruan said diplomatically. Morwenna felt her face flush. The spark was still there between her and Ruan. She was beginning to realise just how fiery it was.

'Thanks.' Pam looked disappointed.

Barnaby placed dishes of crème brûlée on the table and Morwenna raised her spoon eagerly and began to tuck in. The portions were modest. Lamorna would have suggested that someone should shut the door before the food blew away in the wind.

'I'll just have a mouthful,' Pam said. 'All that cream will go straight to my hips.'

'I like a woman with an appetite.' Barnaby watched Morwenna tuck in.

Pam was looking at Ruan. 'I've never dated a fisherman before. I have to say, my tastes are changing. I used to like a man in a designer suit.' She glanced at Barnaby's jacket. 'Now I go for the more rugged type. It's sexier.'

Ruan smiled. 'Some of us are a sight to behold down The Smugglers on a Friday night though.'

'Perhaps I'll come with you next time,' Pam said, leaning towards him. For a second Morwenna wanted to throttle her. She liked Pam, but the way she was flirting with her ex made her feel more than a twinge of jealousy.

'Next Friday's Boxing Day. We could all go,' Morwenna said.

'I'll make coffee,' Barnaby stood up slowly. 'Morwenna, Ruan, would you like brandy in it?'

'A little, please,' Morwenna said. It had been a tough day. She'd have preferred being at home, talking to Ruan about what happened to Tamsin. But the double date had awakened something in her. A sense of loyalty and belonging. A sense of it being time to make her mind up.

And there were strong feelings of desire she hadn't expected to feel again. Longing, even. Morwenna wasn't sure how well she was hiding them. Yes, she needed a drink.

'Ruan's coming back to Mirador for coffee, but, yes, let's have one now,' Pam said. 'I have some Armagnac at home that I want you to try.'

Ruan nodded, but Morwenna knew it was neither a yes nor a no. He was good at being non-committal. Pam made eye contact with Barnaby, a gesture that seemed to suggest that he and Morwenna give her some time alone with Ruan.

Barnaby turned to Morwenna and said gallantly, 'Shall we take our coffee on deck? I have a warm coat you can slip on.'

Morwenna ignored the glance Ruan threw. She wasn't sure she could stay with him and Pam much longer. She needed to clear her head. There was a decision to be made, about her ex and her new beau, and it needed making soon. 'Some bracing sea air would be nice.'

Up on deck, Morwenna huddled in Barnaby's huge overcoat, clutching coffee. The wind blew her hair across her face. She wouldn't stay long – she'd freeze.

Barnaby was about to say something. He prefaced it with, 'Ruan's a nice man.'

'He is.' Morwenna gulped scalding coffee. The aftertaste of the brandy warmed her.

'Can I ask?' Barnaby was getting to the point now. 'Why did you both split up?'

'We argued all the time. Well, I argued and he sulked. It was fine before Tam grew up, then I suppose we realised that we just had each other for company and that wasn't enough.' Morwenna thought about her words. How stupid she had been to let it all go. Stupid and thoughtless and wrong.

'Oh?' Barnaby was interested. 'You seem to get on well.'

'We do. Because we live apart.' Morwenna laughed and wondered why she had. It wasn't funny. It wasn't even true. But the brandy was making her mouth say the words he wanted to hear. 'I'm fond of Ruan. But we put each other through it. Then one day we had a terrible argument. We both said things we didn't mean, and I asked him if he wanted to leave and he said he would if I wanted him to and I told him I did.' She sighed. 'There was no coming back from that one. He had his stupid dignity and I had my stupid pride, and we're both stubborn.'

Barnaby wrapped an arm around her. 'Do you regret it?'

'Not really.' Morwenna knew she was lying through her teeth. 'We get on well. We have Tam and Elowen, and he's good with my mum. We're still family, even though we live apart.'

'So, is there room for me in your life?' Barnaby asked hopefully. 'I'd like there to be.'

'I enjoy spending time with you,' Morwenna said honestly, knowing full well she hadn't answered the question.

'Can I see you again?'

'That might be nice.'

Morwenna shivered. The cold wind was in her bones, and talking about Ruan to Barnaby had left her feeling sad. She wasn't being fair to either of them. Or herself. 'It's been a lovely evening. I've really enjoyed it but—' She hated saying her next words. 'Perhaps you should take me home and leave your sister and Ruan to their Armagnac.'

'Of course.' Barnaby's arm tightened around her. 'We'll take the *Pammy* back to Woon's, and I'll run you home.'

'Thanks.' Morwenna was tired. It had been a long day. And as for Ruan, she'd leave him to work out what he needed in his life. If it was Pam Truscott, she'd give him her blessing. It was only fair.

But the evening had hit her like a bombshell. She knew what she wanted now – who she wanted, more than anything. And it wasn't Barnaby.

* * *

Barnaby drove up the hill towards Harbour Cottages. Morwenna had been deliberately chatty all the way home, to keep the atmosphere light. She felt that if she was silent, Barnaby might start thinking romantic thoughts. He slowed down outside number four, the engine idling, and his eyes met hers with an expression that meant he hoped to be invited in.

Morwenna knew the look. She was ready for bed. On her own. Or with Brenda. She gave a yawn, just to make the point.

Barnaby said, 'Can I ring you?'

'That'd be nice.' Morwenna pecked his cheek. 'It's been a lovely evening. I always enjoy your company.' She hoped that would communicate that she liked him, but she wasn't up for a passionate night. Certainly not with Barnaby. Her overriding thoughts were elsewhere, swamped with feelings of jealousy, stupidity and missed opportunity. And the need to hold the man she truly loved in her arms.

'I missed you when I was in Barbados.' Barnaby didn't want to go home. 'I thought of you a lot.'

'I assumed you were bored with me not making my mind up,' Morwenna said honestly.

'I thought you needed space.'

She exhaled, feeling sad. 'I suppose I still do. I'm sorry.'

'Pam and Ruan seem to be hitting it off well,' Barnaby said and Morwenna wondered if he was as envious as she was.

'They do.'

'If they're an item, would that make a difference? Between you and me?'

'I'm not sure.' Morwenna took his hand, more out of kindness than a romantic gesture. 'I just need time to—' She looked away for a moment and caught her breath in a strangled scream. A face was inches away, grinning through the window. A lurid Santa mask, a figure with a red hat, a dark red cloak.

Morwenna froze. Barnaby turned to see what had made her leap with fear into his arms.

The Santa made a sawing movement, a hand moving backwards across his throat. The figure stared for a moment longer, clearly aggressive despite the mask, and then pointed to Morwenna. She couldn't move.

The Santa bounded away, disappearing into the darkness. She caught her breath in a gulp.

'What just happened?' Barnaby's arms closed around her. 'Who was that? Are you all right?'

Morwenna nodded, but she was shivering. 'I'm fine. I'll just go inside.'

'I'll take you in,' Barnaby said firmly. 'We'll give your friend Jane a ring. The police officer. It was clearly a threat.'

'Yes, please.' Morwenna took a deep breath. She'd feel a lot more reassured if Jane came round to check the area.

She'd feel even better if she knew who the Santa was. Seeing the face at the window had shaken her.

Today Tamsin could have been killed. Elowen might have been abducted. Christmas was approaching fast and Morwenna was left with a dreadful feeling.

Something inevitable was cannoning towards them at an unstoppable pace, and it was bound to come to a head soon, she was sure of it.

Time was running out.

SUNDAY 21 DECEMBER

22

The next morning, six shivering SWANS assembled in wetsuits for the morning swim. Morwenna was conscious of the police presence on the beach. Blessed and Jane were already in the water, avoiding Susan and Barb, who were wrapped in towels discussing the stolen motorboat from Woon's. Louise couldn't stop asking questions about Barnaby. Morwenna regretted mentioning the double date.

Lamorna was there too, but she had no intention of getting wet. She was dressed in a rose-coloured faux-fur coat and hat, with one sleeve pulled back far enough for the diamond bracelet to twinkle on her wrist. There was only one subject she wanted to discuss.

'The police need to find whoever it was who tried to kill my granddaughter and kidnap my great-granddaughter. And lock them up. I'm too old to be dealing with people pushing me over in supermarkets, threatening my family. What's Rick Tremayne doing? Or Jane Choy and her chief inspector friend from London?' She sniffed. 'And I'm not happy about you swimming in the sea with a motorboat murderer on the loose.'

Morwenna glanced towards the ocean and was filled with foreboding. 'They've brought in detectives from Devon, Mum. Jane says they've narrowed down the list of suspects. They're working day and night to find the killer by Christmas.'

'Why Christmas?' Susan said. 'I can see why that chief woman Barnarde came down here though. London's full of crime.'

'Santa comes at Christmas,' Barb said simply.

Morwenna shivered. Something awful was going to happen soon. She knew it.

'I need to swim.' Morwenna shook with cold. Right now, she wanted to be in the water with Jane and Blessed. Jane had been wonderful last night; she'd sent Barnaby home and sat on the sofa with her and Brenda until one o'clock, discussing leads, promising tireless focus to find the Santa.

But who was he? Or she?

'And last night, Vera Eddy across the road was burgled. They took all her mum's antique jewellery. It's a good job I've got my new man to protect me.' Lamorna flashed her bracelet again. 'Tristan stayed over with Tam and Elowen to look after them. You shouldn't be by yourself, Morwenna. You should get Ruan to come over.'

'Pam's very good-looking,' Louise said meaningfully.

'Pam Truscott? She's full of Botox,' Susan said.

'Her brother does it for her. I reckon he does Botox on himself too,' Barb commented. 'Have you seen his bronze suntan? He looks like George Clooney.'

Louise shot Morwenna a meaningful look. 'They are an attractive family.'

'Unlucky, though,' Susan said. 'Money can't buy good luck.'

'How are they unlucky?' Barb asked, astonished. 'They've got a house in Barbados and that big place on top of the hill.'

'Yes, but Pam's husband died, remember.' Susan rolled her eyes for emphasis. 'On this very beach.'

'We should go in the water,' Morwenna said through chattering teeth.

'I'll watch. I'm expecting a call from my Vernon any minute,' Lamorna said by way of an excuse. She hadn't brought a costume.

Morwenna shuddered; she wasn't sure Vernon was a good choice. Again, their roles were reversed: she was playing mum. She took off towards the waves, doing her best not to think about it, trying to warm up. Jane waved as she felt the shock of the cold water penetrating her wetsuit. She was swimming towards Blessed, who'd emerged from a dive and was shouting, 'Hello, Morwenna. Are the others still gossiping?'

'I think so.' Morwenna looked around. Louise was in the water now, swimming with her chin high. Susan and Barb probably hadn't noticed that she'd gone. They were still putting the world to rights with Lamorna.

Jane swam up and placed a hand on Morwenna's shoulder. 'How are you?'

'Better for being here,' Morwenna said truthfully.

'I forgot to ask last night. How was your date with Barnaby?'

'Pleasant. We had dinner on the boat.' Morwenna shook water from her head, trying to forget how longingly Pam had looked at Ruan. 'I'm not sure what I want – it's hard to think about my love life with scary Santas everywhere.' She suddenly remembered something. 'How was your date? We never got to talk about it.'

'Ah, yes. I need to talk to you about that but...' Jane glanced over her shoulder to where Blessed was flipping over like a fish. 'I have work on my mind right now. Seal Bay's crime central at the moment. We're all over it though. We'll crack it soon. Then I'll be due some time off and we'll share our secrets.'

'We will.' Morwenna moved her arms vigorously, kicking her

legs, enjoying the feeling of being buoyed by the ocean. 'Jane, this business with Pawly. I'm stuck. I can't think who's behind all the things that have happened since he fell down the stairs. It makes no sense.'

'We're investigating all avenues and discussing it constantly back at the nick. It's a priority and Blessed wants arrests made by Christmas Eve. The current theory is that it has to be someone who had a grudge against Pawly. And they're hacked off because you're sticking your nose in.'

'But who?'

'The Pengellens are on our list. Damien Woon's a suspect. He had access to the motorboat. And Faye Brice is still firmly in the frame.'

'I don't know,' Morwenna said. 'Something's bothering me. I wish I knew what it was. Why the Santa suit? Why the burglaries? Is it about money? Is it about power? Revenge? Is it one person or a gang? I just can't get my head round it.'

'Well, let me know when you do.'

'One thing, Jane. Can you let me know anything about Vernon Lewis? From Swansea. He's my mum's new squeeze.'

'That's sweet.'

'I'm not so sure. I think he's got a criminal record.'

'I'll see what I can find out. Now make the most of your swim. Try to relax, if you can. I'd better get back to work soon. No peace for us.' Jane lifted an arm and swam athletically back to Blessed. Louise had joined them and they were splashing and talking. Morwenna rolled over, floating on her back, staring at the grey tinfoil sky overhead. Her mind was suddenly calm, empty. She closed her eyes and allowed the water to lift her, to hold her safely.

Her thoughts came quickly. Pawly. Who hated him enough to harm him?

And who had a grudge against her, badly enough to threaten her family? Was it someone who didn't want to be recognised? Someone she knew, who knew her? Or was there another reason?

Why had they burgled the Pengellens' house? Were the burglaries across the bay connected? Who would steal a boat and try to harm Tamsin? It could be either a man or a woman – driving a motorboat wasn't so difficult, once you got used to a tiller that steered the opposite way to the direction you push it. But who would have stolen it from Woon's? Morwenna let the thoughts merge, separate and come back, reforming.

The answer would come. It wasn't far away. She opened her eyes. It could be anybody in Seal Bay. There had to be a clue.

In a moment's clarity, she remembered her mobile phone: she'd taken photos of Pawly lying at the bottom of the stairs. She'd forgotten about the pictures, what with all the other photos she'd stolen from Justin, the photographer. She resolved to look at them as soon as she got home.

And she and Ruan were taking Elowen to Santa's grotto later. It promised to be a busy day.

She wondered about Ruan, if he'd stayed the night at Mirador. It was his life. So why did she feel troubled?

Christmas was only four days away now. There was no time for romantic feelings. She needed to find out who was inside the Santa suit.

Morwenna kicked her legs and looked round. Everyone was on their way back to the shore now, to safety, warmth and hot chocolate. It was time to join them.

* * *

She felt much more alert after the swim. And right now, she was cheerful, holding Elowen's hand, the little girl chattering, her other hand holding Ruan's. She was full of excitement as they entered The Quilkin Emporium with the enormous green frog over the door. Inside, the department store sparkled with lights in every corner. Quilkin's was celebrating Christmas in a big way. As they traipsed through the different departments, sales staff, both men and women, bobbed about in a variety of costumes.

In the cosmetics department, there was a smiling angel behind each counter.

The fashion department staff were dressed as glittery fairies. All the assistants in the men's department were dressed as reindeer and the food section was populated by elves in green costumes. Morwenna, Ruan and Elowen took the escalator to the first floor, where Santa's grotto was. Gold lights twinkled everywhere, and a green and red holly trail was pointing the way to the fairy grotto that led beyond an archway of red, silver and gold stars. Glittering signs proclaimed, 'Santa is here today'. He certainly was; every assistant was dressed in a red-belted suit with a beard and a red hat. Elowen's small face shone with delight.

'I know it's not the real Santa, Grandma, but I want to see him. I need to tell him exactly what football boots I want.'

'And which ones are they?' Ruan asked. He intended to buy them secretly while Elowen was in the grotto. He'd brought an empty backpack to conceal his purchases.

'Red ones.' Elowen was still skipping. 'And I want something nice for Mummy because of what happened to her and Tristan. I like Tristan. He's staying with us to keep us safe.'

'Oh?' Morwenna was interested.

'He sleeps on the couch. I heard Mummy tell him that she liked him a lot but she wasn't rushing into anything, and that means that he can't sleep in her bed until she says so.'

'I see,' Morwenna said, feeling reassured that Tamsin had taken her advice.

Ruan bought a ticket for the grotto and Elowen joined the queue, Morwenna holding her hand. Rosie Buvač was standing in front of her with Maya and two more of her brood. Ruan made his excuse and hurried away to do some secret shopping while Elowen and Maya chatted together.

Rosie leaned forward to whisper to Morwenna. 'Any news on who killed the writer?'

'The police are all over it.' Morwenna decided that was the safest answer.

'Milan thinks it was the Pengellens. That Julian is a money launderer. It's all over the bay,' Rosie said.

'I don't think so.'

'And Pippa's family were slave traders.'

'That doesn't make her a killer.'

'They probably burgled their own house to look innocent.' Rosie sighed. 'Oh, I'll be glad when Christmas is over.'

'Why?' Morwenna asked.

'All the stories you hear round the bay. At least after Christmas there won't be any Santas, so the robberies will stop. Not that we've got much to steal.' Rosie turned to Maya. 'Go on in, my bewty, it's your turn.' She put a hand to her head and looked exhausted. 'It all falls to me, getting presents, wrapping them, doing all the shopping, making the dinner. I'm bleddy worn out.'

Morwenna understood. 'You have a lovely family.'

'We're sleeping with a gurt cricket bat under the bed nowadays.' Rosie lowered her voice. 'The Colemans at the top of Lister Hill got burgled a couple of days back. They have the poshest house in our street. Libby Coleman had a lot of nice jewellery, her grandmother's.'

'Oh?'

'Milan says he'll club anyone who tries to break in. Everyone's talking about the robberies.'

'The police will find who did it.'

Rosie paused to send her second child in to see Santa; Maya was clutching a small doll in pink wrapping paper. She said, 'Well, you'd know, Morwenna. If you say so, we'll be all right.'

Morwenna's phone vibrated in her pocket and she tugged it out. There was a message from Jane.

> **JANE**
>
> there's a Vernon Lewis from Swansea who is a known fence convicted several times – he'd be in his late seventies now. this might be the man Lamorna is seeing. will talk soon.

Morwenna chewed her lip in thought – a fence was a person who dealt in stolen goods. Her heart began to thump. Vernon could be connected with the robberies. Perhaps the person in the Santa suit had arranged for Vernon to woo Lamorna. Perhaps Vernon *was* Santa. Morwenna was suddenly clutched with new fear.

Rosie's third child was on his way in to see Father Christmas. Maya said, 'Santa's really funny. He makes you laugh. He has three elves with him. They're all pretty ladies and they give you the present.'

Elowen curled her lip. 'I don't want a doll like yours.' She inspected Maya's sister's pink-wrapped present – she had a similar doll with different clothes. 'That's rubbish.'

'It's not rubbish.' Maya hugged her doll. 'Santa gave her to me.'

'I saw you with Ruan just before,' Rosie said. Morwenna knew what she was implying.

'Elowen likes to go out with her grandparents.' She took a breath, wondering how to break the news about Vernon to her mother. Or perhaps he'd reformed. Perhaps his crimes were in the past and he was innocent.

'I hear your daughter's got herself a boyfriend. She'll be all right if she can get him in her clutches.' Rosie chuckled. 'The Pengellens are well-heeled. Mind you, they're a dodgy family, fingers in all sorts of pies. Pawly said that, didn't he, before he died? Maybe that's why he got pushed.'

Morwenna didn't want to discuss it. But it made sense that what was said in Pawly's library talk would have found its way around Seal Bay. Rosie's third child came out of the grotto clutching a plastic train in blue wrapping paper. Rosie said, 'Well, I'm going to take this lot home and put my feet up. If I don't see you before, have a happy Christmas.'

'And you, too,' Morwenna replied. She watched Rosie and her children hurry away. Elowen was already on her way into the grotto.

She turned to see Ruan coming towards her, his backpack stuffed full. He looked pleased with himself. 'I could get used to Christmas shopping.'

'Oh?' Morwenna couldn't help the next words that tumbled from her lips. 'Have you bought something nice for Pam?'

Ruan looked surprised. 'Should I have?'

'She's your girlfriend.'

Morwenna was trying out the waters. In her heart, she believed that Ruan still loved her. Her sleuthing instinct told her so. But Pam was rich and gorgeous, and it was a known fact that some men were superficial where that was concerned. Perhaps Ruan was no different. Perhaps, given new options, he was tired of waiting for Morwenna. Perhaps he'd changed his mind.

'We just see each other sometimes.' Ruan didn't look convinced. A smile broke out on his face. 'Last night was funny, the four of us double dating.'

'Funny?' That wasn't the word Morwenna would have used. Embarrassing might have been a better one. She remembered the brandy, the rising feelings of lust for her ex, and she felt suddenly awkward. It had been the night where she'd made her mind up, finally. But it was probably too late.

'Pam was impressed that you and I get on so well.'

'Why wouldn't we?' Morwenna asked, a little edgily.

'She expected us to be teazy.' Ruan remembered something. 'Talking of teazy, Damien and I exchanged words before I went back to Pam's last night.'

'Oh?' Morwenna was more focused on the 'back to Pam's' part.

'He's hassling me to buy *The Swordfish* and I haven't made my mind up. Not after what happened to Tam. I'm still worried sick about that. It was no accident.'

'I know, Ruan.' The image came back to Morwenna, the figure in the motorboat as it accelerated. She felt herself cringe automatically against the impact.

'I still might buy it. I need time to think about it.'

'And Pam?' Morwenna couldn't help herself.

'If you mean did I stay the night, no, I didn't. More importantly' – Ruan indicated his backpack – 'I've got our little heller those football boots.'

On cue, a small voice called, 'Grandma!' It was a loud squeal and Morwenna was immediately alerted to the fact that something was wrong. Morwenna turned to see Elowen running towards them clutching a round blue package that clearly contained a football. But Elowen's expression caught her eye. She looked terrified.

'What's happened?' Morwenna opened her arms and the child filled them, bursting into tears.

'I hate Santa,' Elowen sobbed. 'He's horrible.'

'Santa?' Morwenna was gripped as if by a warning; she hugged her granddaughter tightly. 'Why?'

'Not Santa in the grotto that speaks like Sheppy.' Elowen's face was streaked with tears. 'The other Santa.'

'What other Santa?' Morwenna caught her breath.

'The horrible one who grabbed me when I came out. He had a nasty voice. He said my name and pinched my arm.'

Ruan whirled round. Morwenna followed his eyes. There were Santas everywhere, behind counters, at tills, stocking shelves. They all looked the same.

'Where did he go?' Morwenna asked quickly.

'Towards the escalator.' Elowen sniffed. 'I hate him. I want to go home.'

'What did he say to you?' Ruan asked quickly.

'He said "Happy Christmas". But he said it all mean. Then he did this nasty laugh and told me to tell my grandma it would be the last one she would ever have.'

MONDAY 22 DECEMBER

23

The following morning, Morwenna messaged Louise that she'd be late for the library shift. She desperately wanted to check on Tamsin and Elowen first.

The weather was overcast, so she decided to leave the bicycle and walk down the hill. She arrived at the door of the Proper Ansom Tearoom just as Zach Barr was securing his bike outside. In term-time, Zach was a photography student, but he came from a family of cooks and Tamsin was glad of his help in the kitchen. Luckily for them both, the busy times coincided with his holidays.

'Hi, Morwenna.' Zach looked up at the sky. 'I was hoping it would snow.'

'It never snows in Cornwall,' Morwenna said.

'I know, but wouldn't it be nice? A white Christmas.'

'We're more likely to get a grey one,' Morwenna quipped.

Tamsin was at the door, unbolting it. Her expression was anxious. 'Mum. Is everything all right?'

'Hunky-dory,' Morwenna said, trying to look as positive as possible. Without meaning to, she scanned the tearoom to see if there were any Santas seated at the tables. Of course there weren't. 'I just wanted to see how things were going.'

'Elowen's off round to Britney's later. She'll be back at three.' Tamsin smiled. 'She's brilliant, you know, Courtenay. I'd like to keep her on.'

Morwenna hurried inside. Zach followed her, mumbling that he'd get started in the kitchen dreckly.

'Where's Elowen?' Morwenna asked.

'Upstairs with Tristan. He's been great. She likes him. After what happened yesterday at the grotto...'

'I messaged Jane about it last night, so it's on her radar. There are so many officers investigating around the bay now. Blessed has the photos from the Pengellens' party and she says she's narrowing down the suspects...'

Tamsin closed her eyes. 'It's been a horrible few days.'

'It has.' Morwenna squeezed her arm.

'Dad will be in later. He wants to keep an eye on me. Just like you do, Mum. Do you want a cup of tea before you go to the library?'

'I wouldn't mind,' Morwenna said. There was a sharp cry from the kitchen.

Tamsin's eyebrows came together. 'That's Zach. He's probably burned himself on the grill.'

They both rushed into the kitchen, all pristine stainless steel. Zach had already put on his white apron and cap. Morwenna saw what was wrong instantly. He was frozen to the spot, staring in horror at a plate containing a gammon hock on the worktop. A sharp kitchen knife had been inserted into it. And a blank envelope was leaning against the dish.

Tamsin picked up the card and tore it open. A cherry-cheeked Santa grinned at her. Morwenna took it and opened the card. The print read, 'Wishing you a Christmas that is merry and bright,' but a large felt pen X filled the whole page, crossing out the greeting like a mark of death.

'Who's doing this, Mum?'

'I wish I knew,' Morwenna said.

'And how did they get in?' Tamsin was visibly upset.

'I think I know.' Zach pointed miserably to the window. 'I leave the small top one open for ventilation. I'm sorry, Tam. I never thought anyone would break in.'

Morwenna said, 'I'll make us all that tea.'

'The urn's on,' Tamsin said, leading the way back into the tearoom.

The door clanged and Courtenay came in, wearing a thin denim jacket. As she tugged on her apron, Morwenna noticed a bite mark on her neck, like a purple bruise. She hoped it meant that she and Sheppy were an item now. Morwenna made a joke, pointing to her own neck. 'Low flying bats, then?'

Courtenay's hand went to the love bite and she blushed. 'My boyfriend came round last night.'

Morwenna wanted to check if it was Sheppy. 'Doesn't he live on Camp Dynamo?'

'No, he's in the army.' Courtenay's eyes shone. She was clearly smitten. 'But he comes over when he can.'

The doorbell rang again and Becca walked in with Seb on her arm. She called, 'Can we have a quick toasted sandwich each before we open up, Tam? And coffee.'

'Take a seat and I'll bring it over,' Courtenay said quickly, hurrying towards the kitchen.

'While it's quiet, I'll just go up to see Elowen,' Tamsin said. She turned to her friend. 'I'll pop in the gift shop later, Bec. There are a few things I need – Christmas presents.'

'I'll see you then.' Becca and Seb had settled themselves at a table. Seb took both her hands in his and began to whisper. Morwenna assumed it was all sweet nothings.

The door opened and two more customers came in, bringing the strong whiff of expensive fragrance with them. Justin nodded towards Morwenna in greeting, but Fernanda ignored her and went to sit down. She was wearing huge sunglasses despite there being no sign of the sun. Her hair was pulled back in a dramatic chignon. Courtenay was back in the tearoom, hovering.

'What can I get you both?'

Justin took a seat. 'Two coffees. I'll have a pastry.'

'Croissant or pain au chocolat?'

'Croissant, butter, jam.' Justin turned to Fernanda. 'Anything for you?' She shook her head.

'Hello again.' Morwenna took the opportunity. She walked over, her mug of tea in her hand. 'How's the photography going?'

'Finished at last,' Fernanda said. 'Now I can go back to London.'

'Cornwall's an amazing backdrop,' Justin said. 'We're off home tomorrow afternoon but I'm planning a return visit soon.'

'It will not be with me.' Fernanda's lip curled. 'It's too cold. And I have no reason to come back here ever again.'

'Cornwall's a photographer's dream, all the rocks and sandy beaches, the big open skies.' Justin met Morwenna's eyes. 'It's been a mixed visit, though, after what happened at the party. I'm guessing the man who fell down the steps was drunk. There are so many rumours.'

'I don't know,' Morwenna said.

'I want to go back to Mexico soon,' Fernanda said. 'It is warmer there. *El clima es calido. Los hombres son más amables.*'

'The men are nice here too,' Morwenna said, understanding her words, but Fernanda turned away, showing Morwenna the nape of her neck and the twinkle of the ruby and diamonds in one ear. For a moment, Morwenna couldn't pull her gaze away. There was something about her earring that caught her attention. She'd noticed it before: something wasn't quite right.

Then she took her tea to the table and pulled out her phone, searching through her photos to examine the pictures of Pawly, sprawled at the bottom of the stairs.

She stared at the images, looking for clues. Pawly was in a twisted heap. The sight of him lying there made her shudder. She enlarged the photo, although it turned her stomach. Pawly was lying on dark stone steps, a mince pie in his hand. There was no blood. She enlarged the picture as far as it would go and focused in on the detail. What was she looking at, right there, next to the mince pie? A thread? A speck of dust? Or something else?

'All right?' There was a light voice in her ear. 'You're an early bird this morning, maid.' Morwenna glanced up.

'Hello, Mum.' She looked from Lamorna to her mother's companion, swathed in an expensive overcoat, a trilby perched on his comb-over. She narrowed her eyes and said, 'Hello again, Vernon.'

Vernon nodded a greeting as they sat down opposite. Lamorna said, 'Vernon picked me up this morning to take me to breakfast. He wants to meet Tam and Elowen.'

'Why?' Morwenna heard the suspicion in her voice.

Lamorna threaded an arm through Vernon's. 'Because they're my family.' She rested her head against his arm and closed her eyes. Morwenna saw the glint of the bracelet on her wrist.

Vernon gave a little cough. 'I'll be going home in a few days.'

'Where's home?' Morwenna asked.

'Wales.' Lamorna pulled a sad face. 'But you'll come back and see me, won't you, Vern?'

'Of course. Nothing could stop me. I only came to Cornwall for a few days' rest. It's been a bit of a whirlwind.' His fingers went to his moustache.

'You're staying at The Fisherman's Knot?' Morwenna was watching his every move. 'That's very plush.'

'It's hard being on your own. Especially at this time of year.' Vernon looked away. 'I lost my wife Jean a few years ago and...' He gazed lovingly at Lamorna. 'I never expected to find someone I'd care about again.'

Morwenna frowned. Vernon could certainly act. She felt her temper rise – she didn't want her mother hurt by a man who was a charlatan and a thief. Perhaps worse. She had to find out everything she could. 'So when will you come back?'

'In the new year. I'm not short of a few bob.'

I bet you're not, Morwenna thought. Instead, she said, 'Oh?'

'I've done well for myself over the years.'

'What is it you do, Vernon?'

'He's an entrepreneur. He buys and sells things. He has a gurt house in Swansea. You can see the sea from his bedroom.'

Morwenna pulled a face at the thought.

'Swansea Bay is magnificent. And it's wonderful for surfing.' Vernon's ice-blue eyes held Morwenna's.

'Surfing?' Morwenna couldn't help it. 'Do you own a motorboat, Vernon?'

Vernon frowned. 'I used to have a small boat in the marina. I sold it.'

Morwenna leaned forward, ready to ask another question, but Courtenay arrived, smiling. 'Good morning. Can I tempt you with a coffee for breakfast?'

'That would be lovely. Times two, for me and my good lady. And pastries.' Vernon gazed at Lamorna adoringly. 'This is just like France. We must go there, Lamorna.'

'Don't make any plans yet, Mum.' Morwenna stood up. She'd had enough. 'Right – I'd better get off to the library. I'll be seeing you.'

'I'll come up to yours for tea tonight.' Lamorna tried to drag her eyes from Vernon.

'Great. I was about to invite you.' Morwenna leaped at the opportunity. There were things she wanted to say to Lamorna. 'Just you, Mum. See you then.'

'Dreckly,' Lamorna said.

Morwenna made her way to the door, past Seb and Becca, who were engrossed in each other, and Justin, who was nibbling a croissant while Fernanda thumbed her phone.

She was glad to be outside, although dark clouds were hanging low. It would rain soon. She put her head down against the sea breeze and made her way through the town.

* * *

When she arrived at the library, she was surprised to see Donald there, talking to Louise and another woman. As she barged in, she called, 'I didn't think you started your shift until lunchtime, Donald.'

Donald turned in greeting, his face serious. 'Morwenna, you're just in time.'

'In time for what?' Morwenna asked.

'Oh, it's so exciting.' Louise clasped her hands together.

'This is Shaela Carmody.' Donald indicated the woman who stood beside him. She was short but regal-looking, with fluffy pink and grey hair, a long dress and Crocs. Morwenna wondered if her feet were cold. It was freezing outside.

'I know who you are,' Morwenna said. 'You write for the local paper. You do the column on spiritual healing.'

Morwenna had never read it and had no idea what spiritual healing was.

Donald was keen to elaborate. 'Spiritual healing helps us reconnect with our true selves.'

'I see,' Morwenna said, although she didn't.

Shaela began to speak, her voice soft as the sea. 'I'm much more than a simple healer though, Donald. I am an empath. I offer clairvoyance and a connection with those who have passed on to the next world.'

'She does it at the spiritual church once a week,' Louise said.

'I offer knowledge, help and comfort,' Shaela added.

'So do you want to borrow a book?' Morwenna asked. She wasn't a clairvoyant, but one look at Louise's and Donald's faces told her why Shaela was there. Morwenna wasn't impressed.

'I've asked Shaela here because of Pawly,' Donald said.

Morwenna shook her head. 'I think I should go and leave you to it. I'm not a believer.'

'Shaela thinks she can speak to Lady Elizabeth,' Louise added.

'The lady is here with us already.' Shaela's voice had become a monotone. 'I can feel her presence.'

Morwenna took out her phone and began checking messages. There was one from Jane, saying she was busier than ever, but they needed to talk urgently.

'Where is Lady Elizabeth?' Donald asked.

'I'm speaking to her now,' Shaela said.

Morwenna had no intention of being part of the medium's exercise in communicating with the beyond. She needed something to distract her.

'What does she say?' Louise was completely engrossed.

'Speak to me, Lady Pengellen,' Shaela intoned. 'Tell us what you know.'

Morwenna's thoughts went to the photos she'd taken at the scene of Pawly's death. She opened them up on her phone: Pawly, crumpled at the bottom of the steps. She wondered again how his death could be connected to all the other events that had happened recently. She went through the list of suspects in her head. Who had the strongest motive to kill him?

'I wait for you to come to me, Elizabeth. I wait for the answer to my question.' Shaela's eyes closed. Morwenna glanced at Donald and Louise. They were both gaping with surprise. She went back to her phone, skimming through the pictures, making them bigger, staring at the detail, the marks on the stone steps around Pawly.

'She speaks to us now,' Shaela whimpered, then continued in a slightly thinner voice. 'I am Elizabeth. If you wish to discover the truth about the writer who visited this library—'

Morwenna tried not to laugh.

Louise grabbed Morwenna's hand. 'She means Pawly.'

Morwenna ignored her and examined the photo. Pawly on the ground, his hand holding a mince pie, his twisted body. The space around him. Something was scratching in her sleuthing brain. Something really important.

Shaela was in full flow now. 'The truth is like a light, shining all around. He was murdered. And if you follow the light, you will discover the identity of the person who pushed him.'

'He was pushed,' Louise gasped.

'We need to find the light,' Donald whispered.

'I've got it.' Morwenna held her breath. 'The light.'

She didn't believe in mediums for one minute, but the answer was there, sparkling, right next to Pawly's sprawled body, next to the hand that held the mince pie. It was a diamond, a tiny sparkling chip of light. Someone must be missing one. Who had been wearing diamond jewellery?

The answer snapped together in her head. Of course. It was clear as the light from the tiny diamond next to his fingers.

Pawly had been pushed. And now Morwenna knew exactly who had pushed him.

24

'I've checked your Vernon Lewis out,' Jane said as she stood with Morwenna and Blessed at The Blue Dolphin Guest House. Blessed rapped at the door. 'He's done time. He's a well-known fence, good at shifting stolen goods. If Lamorna was my mother, I wouldn't like her to be around someone like him.'

'It'll break her heart,' Morwenna said sadly.

'I don't think he's violent though. There's no history of it.' Jane glanced at Blessed and knocked again. Carole opened the door and her face puckered in a frown.

'Morwenna? What's going on?'

Blessed showed her ID. 'We're here to talk to one of your guests. Which room is Fernanda Pérez in?'

'Number ten. But what—?' Carole began.

Blessed walked in without another word and Jane followed. Morwenna met Carole's gaze and gave her a reassuring smile, then rushed up after the police officers. Jane was already banging on a door.

It opened and Fernanda stood there, looking miserable. She certainly wasn't surprised.

'Morwenna?' Jane turned abruptly.

'Have you lost a diamond from your earring?' Morwenna asked, just as Fernanda turned her head. Indeed, a glittering stone was missing.

'We have photographic evidence that your diamond was discovered next to the body of Pawly Yelland—' Blessed began.

'I knew you'd come.' Fernanda shrugged as if it was inevitable. 'It's because of what happened at Tristan's party. What more can I say?'

Jane began to read the caution and Blessed led Fernanda past a shocked Carole. Upstairs, Justin rushed from his room and shouted something encouraging. Fernanda ignored him.

Jane watched as Blessed helped Fernanda into the police car. She said, 'Well done, Morwenna. It's over. We can all sleep easy in our beds now.'

'I don't get it.' Morwenna frowned. 'Why would she try to kill Tam? And kidnap Elowen?'

'Jealousy? Hatred? Who knows? We'll question her down at the nick.'

'Let me know what you find out.' A gnawing feeling still worried Morwenna.

'Well, I'd best get off.' Jane gave a small sigh. 'I can forget about my evening off now.'

She leaped in the car with Blessed, and they drove away.

Morwenna began to walk home. It was almost six o'clock; she wondered if Ruan might be down The Smugglers. Or if he'd gone to see Pam.

It was none of her business.

Her phone rang; she tugged it from her pocket and put it to her ear. 'Hello? Oh, Barnaby. No, I'm busy this evening. Mum's coming round. Yes, it was fun, double dating. What...? Just me? OK. Wednesday evening, yes, that's great. It's Christmas Eve, I know. Fine. We're not going on the boat again, ha ha, no. Yes, of course, thanks. Bye, Barnaby – bye.'

Another date with Barnaby. Morwenna probably should have said no, but she needed to think positive thoughts. Recent events had made her weary, worn her down.

As she arrived at her front door, she saw Lamorna in the distance, trudging along slowly. Talking of weary, her mother looked as though she had the weight of the world on her shoulders. As she came closer, Lamorna waved.

'This bleddy hill will kill me one of these days.'

'Come on in, Mum,' Morwenna said encouragingly. 'I'll get the kettle on for a cuppa.'

'Cuppa my butt,' Lamorna said as she reached the door. 'Have you got any white wine?'

'I might have half a bottle of Pinot Grigio left in the fridge.'

'Well, let's knock it back. It's Christmas. I need cheering up. I'm going to miss my fella when he goes back to Wales.' Lamorna took off towards the living room as Morwenna closed the door. By the time she reached her mother, she was sitting on the sofa, feet up, Brenda already on her knee. She threw out an arm. 'I like my wine well chilled. Like my men.'

Morwenna saw the bracelet and felt sad. She hated having to upset her mother. But she had to say what she had to say.

Morwenna traipsed into the kitchen and began to pour wine into two glasses. She called, 'You can stay over, Mum, if you drink too much.'

'I might,' Lamorna laughed. 'Mind you, there are burglars about in Seal Bay.'

'I've heard.'

'They won't get much from my house. Everything I have of value, I'm wearing. Oh, by the way, did I tell you they caught the kid who pushed me over in the shop? He tried it again on another woman and she pushed him back. The manager of the corner shop grabbed him. He was only nine years old. Tall for his age, mind – trying to rob purses to buy Christmas presents for his family. Poor as a church mouse.'

Morwenna felt sorry for the child. But she breathed out relief. He wasn't a suspect. Besides, Fernanda was in custody, so everything was all right now.

Morwenna knew it wasn't. Fernanda dressed as Santa? Threatening Elowen in Quilkin's? It didn't make sense.

Lamorna leaned forward. 'Which reminds me, Vernon's coming over on Christmas Eve with a special gift. He wants me to open it before he leaves. I asked him to stay for Christmas Day, but he can't. I'd have loved him to join us for lunch.'

'In the tearoom.'

'No, haven't you heard?' Lamorna looked up as Morwenna handed her a glass of wine. She took a gulp. 'Mmm. That hits the spot. No, Tristan's offered to take us all out.'

'All of us? Where?'

'Me, you, Ruan, Tam, Elowen. The Pengellens are going to London for Christmas Day. Tristan's borrowing his father's boat. We're going to have Christmas lunch at sea.'

'Oh, that sounds nice.' Morwenna wasn't sure she felt safe on the sea any more.

'I told Tam, he's a keeper, that Tristan. Mind you, there's some bad stories about Julian and Pippa going around Seal Bay. Their halos have slipped right down their necks – no wonder they're going away for Christmas Day.'

'I wouldn't listen to gossip, Mum.' Morwenna wondered how she was going to explain about Vernon to Lamorna.

'So is it time for dinner, maid? I'm bleddy starving,' Lamorna cackled, finishing her wine in two gulps.

'Come to table, Mum,' Morwenna said. 'I'll pour you another

glass. And you're definitely stopping over. This is going to be a girls' night in.'

* * *

By ten-thirty, a second wine bottle was empty. Lamorna had drunk more than her fair share. Brenda had already padded upstairs to lie on Morwenna's bed, a sign that she thought everyone else should be asleep. Morwenna was tired and Lamorna looked all in, but she wanted to talk.

'There's nothing like the love of a good man.'

'Do you think so?'

'I do. I've had some lovely men in my life but for some reason they never lasted. Your dad, Freddie. The charmer. Morrie Edwards who asked me to marry him eight times, and Harry Woon who could snog for England.'

Morwenna had heard it all before.

'Daniel Kitto. We'd have still been together but for...' Tears shone in Lamorna's eyes. The wine was making her weepy.

'You're ready for bed, Mum.'

'Dreckly.' Lamorna leaned on her hand. 'But now I have Vern, I think I've found the one.'

Morwenna wondered if this was time to say her piece. 'The thing is—'

'You should make your mind up about the men in your life. Barnaby seems a nice man. He's well heeled. And Ruan. You know he'll always be in your heart.'

'Mum, I think you need—'

'The love of a good man,' Lamorna repeated, swaying a little. 'That's everything in life. Don't you agree?'

'Not really. I mean, there are other things – independence, being fit and able-bodied and happy. Yes, being happy, Mum, that's much more important.' Morwenna wondered why she was waving her hands and speaking too loudly. She'd had three glasses of Pinot Grigio, that was why. More than usual for a Monday evening.

'A good man ticks all of those boxes.'

'Yes, but what exactly is a *good* man?' Morwenna was off. 'I'm not sure I've met one. Good man? That's a contradiction, isn't it, a paradox?'

'You're a cynic. Vernon's a good man.'

'Is he?' Morwenna countered. 'Mum, he's just a man who—'

'He makes me feel like a real woman.'

'How can a man do that? He can't – he doesn't have magic powers. What is a *real* woman anyway? We're *all* real women. We don't need a man to...'

'That's not true, we *do*. He showers me with gifts and he says nice things.'

'That's superficial, Mum. It's not real.'

'Oh, Morwenna, when did you become a misandrist?'

'A what?' Morwenna laughed. She had no idea her mother knew the word.

'It's a woman who hates men. Vernon told me. He said you were the sort of woman who makes a man feel emasculated.'

'He said that? Vernon?'

'He reads lots of clever books.'

'That's not all he does, Mum.'

'Yes, you're a misandrist. No wonder Ruan's going out with Pam Truscott.'

'What?' Morwenna caught her breath.

'You're too independent, Morwenna. It's my fault. I brought you up with no man in your life and—'

'That's rubbish. You brought me up just fine. And if Ruan

wants to go out with Pam, he's welcome.' Morwenna knew she didn't mean a word of it.

'You're getting on a bit now, though. You don't want to get to my age and be all alone.'

'I have Tam and Elowen, and Ruan and I are all right as we are...'

'You'll regret it, you'll see.' Lamorna reached for her glass and sucked at the empty dregs.

'I'll regret it, Mum?' Morwenna was furious. Her mother had hit a nerve: Lamorna was absolutely right about Ruan. She yelled, 'At least if I picked a partner, it wouldn't be a dodgy man who deals in—'

'Are you calling Vernon dodgy?'

'Too right I am. He's a criminal.'

'No, he's not. He cares for me. We might be falling in love. He gives me jewellery.'

'Stolen jewellery.'

'What? Are you calling my Vernon a thief?'

'I'm calling him a fence.'

'You're just jealous.'

'Of Vernon? No way.'

'Because he and I are an item now, and I know a good thing when I see it. And you've got two men who love you and you can't make up your mind.'

Morwenna reeled as if from a punch. 'But you pick terrible men. You always have.'

'What did you say?' Lamorna looked aghast.

'And Vernon's the worst. He's been in prison. He's dangerous. He's a thief. I bet he burgled the Pengellens'—' Morwenna stopped. She'd gone too far.

'What?' Lamorna's eyes were filled with shock. Or she'd drunk too much wine.

Morwenna was immediately sorry. 'What I'm saying, Mum, is that he—'

There was a rap at the door. Two sharp knocks. Morwenna thought instantly of the person in the Santa suit and caught her breath.

Lamorna whispered, 'Who can that be? It's past eleven.'

'I've no idea.' Morwenna held her breath.

The knock came again, this time more urgent. Morwenna padded into the hall. She called, 'Who is it?'

The answer came at once. 'Ruan.'

She opened the door and he hurried in, closing it behind him, slumping back against it. Blood was trickling down his face.

'What's happened?' Morwenna asked, then she saw the deep gash on his forehead. Her voice rose with fear. 'What's happened to you?' Before he had chance to answer, she had grabbed his sleeve and was leading him to the kitchen, sitting him down on her chair, pouring cool boiled water from the kettle into a basin, grabbing kitchen roll. She began to soak up the blood.

Ruan winced. 'It's not much.'

'Should we get an ambulance? Ring Jane?' Lamorna was already panicking. 'Ruan, do you need to go to hospital?'

'It's not that bad. After all, I drove up here.' He sat still for a while as Morwenna cleaned his wound.

'So what happened?' Morwenna asked as she worked.

Ruan took a deep breath to steady himself. 'I went to The Smugglers for a drink. Milan Buvač was there, a few of the other fishermen. The pub was quiet though. Most of the usual crowd had stayed away. I felt like a shandy and a chat. But it was all talk of burglaries and how the Pengellens staged Pawly Yelland's fall down the stairs to shut him up. People were pinning it on them. So I left. Then I heard a scuffle in an alleyway, so I went to check what was going on and someone hit me.'

'The cut's not too bad.' Morwenna held the damp paper against the wound. Blood seeped through. She couldn't help the feeling that gripped her – what if it had been worse? What if Ruan was still lying in the alleyway, unconscious? She said, 'I'm so glad you're all right.'

'Thanks. Head wounds always bleed a lot,' Ruan mumbled. 'I was stunned for a bit, but I'm OK.'

'I hope you gave the person a good bashing back,' Lamorna said.

'I lashed out – my hand connected – they ran away. I didn't see who it was.' Ruan winced again as Morwenna applied more pressure. His hair was red from the blood, but the bleeding was stopping.

'It's clean. It looks all right.' Morwenna was still concerned. 'Do you want to pop to A & E and see if it needs a stitch?'

Ruan gave a slight shake of his head. 'There will be queues at this time of night. It'll heal.'

Morwenna applied more damp kitchen roll. 'I should call Jane.' She recalled that Fernanda was at the police station being questioned. So who had hit Ruan? Again, that nagging feeling was bothering her.

'Don't disturb her,' Ruan said. 'I'll live.'

'Who do you think it was?' Morwenna asked, allowing her hand to linger against his face. She suppressed the urge to stroke his hair.

'I've no idea. A random, maybe. A chancer looking for a wallet to rob.'

'Or the Santa?' Lamorna said, glancing anxiously at Morwenna.

'Or someone who has a grudge,' Morwenna wondered.

'No one has a grudge against Ruan,' Lamorna said protectively. 'Everyone in Seal Bay likes him.'

'Except for one person, clearly.' Morwenna was thoughtful. 'Someone clouted him hard.' She dabbed at the cut again, troubled. 'Yes, it's stopped bleeding. And it's not deep. You got off lightly.'

'Stay and have a brandy,' Lamorna said. 'Medicinal. I'll have one too.'

'I might just do that.' Ruan turned to Morwenna. 'I know what's going on in your mind. You're making connections. You think whoever hit me pushed Pawly, stole the motorboat from Woon's and burgled the Pengellens' home.'

'And Vera Eddy's place from across the road in Tregenna Gardens. She's had some lovely antique jewellery stolen,' Lamorna added.

'But Fernanda was arrested this evening for pushing Pawly downstairs.' Morwenna took a deep breath. 'Perhaps she holds the key to what's going on. Oh, I hope she spills the beans and someone's arrested soon. Then we'll be able to have a really happy Christmas.'

TUESDAY 23 DECEMBER

25

The news came in dribs and drabs. Morwenna had a phone call in the library from Jane mid-morning. The sparkling speck next to Pawly's fallen body was indeed a chip of diamond. And Fernanda had admitted responsibility for Pawly's death.

Jane was interested in where the diamond was now. It had completely disappeared. The most likely scenario was that it had stuck to Pawly's clothing when his body was taken away. It certainly hadn't been visible in any of the photos the SOCO team took. And as Jane knew, the scenes of crime officers rarely missed a thing.

Fernanda had killed Pawly. Morwenna couldn't work out why, though. There was no clear motive. But it followed that she must have attacked Tamsin too. And tried to harm Elowen. She was jealous and angry. Surely the rest of the jigsaw could be put together now. And the case finally closed.

But what had driven Fernanda to do it?

There were whisperings in the library from Susan and Barb that the detectives had found Pawly's murderer, but there were no more details than that.

Morwenna popped into the tearoom to see Tamsin and Elowen at lunchtime. Courtenay had everything under control and was weaving between tables carrying trays, wearing a neck scarf that badly disguised new love bites. She brought Morwenna a cup of tea as she sat with Elowen, who was drawing a picture of her family at Christmas. She was keen to explain it.

'This is me and Mummy and you and Great-Grandma, and this is Grandad and Tristan, and we're on the boat for Christmas on the sea. Tristan's boat is called *The Penis*.'

'*The Phoenix*, Elowen.' Tamsin sat down with a coffee. 'We're going to have a buffet Christmas lunch. It's going to be wonderful.'

'I've got a football game before that,' Elowen said. 'Grandad's taking me.'

'On Christmas morning?' Morwenna was surprised.

'Apparently it's a tradition in the bay to hold a five-a-side game first thing on the twenty-fifth. They've been doing it since the end of World War One.' Tamsin lowered her voice. 'Is Dad all right, Mum? I heard from Grandma that he had a bash on the head last night, and he came round yours to get it fixed.'

'It's not as bad as it might have been,' Morwenna said. 'He's made of tough stuff, your dad.'

'Who'd do that?'

'I expect it was a random after his wallet,' Morwenna said quickly. 'He can take care of himself.'

Tamsin shook her head. 'What's the world coming to?'

Morwenna smiled at such old words from a young person. 'And the kid who pushed Mum over in the shop was after a bit of pocket money. At Christmas, poor people are even more desperate. It's a shame all round.'

Courtenay placed three rounds of sandwiches on the table.

Tamsin said, 'That was quick. Thanks, Courtenay. And say thanks to Zach.'

'I wasn't expecting to be fed.' Morwenna was delighted.

'And guess what else?' Courtenay looked so much healthier nowadays. 'Tristan's asked me to be in charge of serving the buffet on his boat on Christmas Day. And I can eat what I like while I'm there. It's better than being on my own. I get paid for it too.'

Morwenna glanced at the love bites visible beneath the scarf. 'Isn't your boyfriend with you for Christmas?'

'No, he's in the army. That's the problem with going out with a soldier.' Courtenay pulled a face. 'But guess what else I'm doing? Tam's a great boss.'

'I'm having a soirée tomorrow, a Christmas Eve buffet for friends and family,' Tamsin said. 'Just nibbles and wine. Courtenay and Zach will serve the food. Sheppy's doing card tricks. Dad's coming and so's Grandma and her new man. You'll be there, won't you, Mum?'

'I have a date with Barnaby.'

'Bring him. I think Dad's bringing Pam. Lots of people are coming. Seb and Becca, Julian and Pippa were invited, but they're off to London. I'm going to ask Louise and Jane and Blessed and Rick Tremayne.' Tamsin looked pleased with herself. 'We need to celebrate now Pawly's killer's in custody. Who'd have thought it was Fernanda?'

'Indeed.' Morwenna still wasn't convinced. 'Yes, I'll ring Barnaby. I'm sure he'll be delighted.'

'So am I,' Courtenay said. 'Do you know, a week ago, nothing was going right. My boyfriend was telling me to get myself a job and now he'll be over the moon. Thanks, Tam.' She turned on her heel and moved efficiently to another table.

Tamsin said, 'She's a gem.' She gazed at Elowen's drawing. 'That's a lovely picture. Is that all of us on the boat? And what's that little thing in the water? Is it a fish? Oh, I know, it's someone swimming.'

Elowen shook her dark hair. 'No, it's a motorboat. It's zooming along too fast. The driver's going to crash when we're on *The Penis*.'

'*The Phoenix*,' Tamsin said again emphatically. 'And it's not going to crash, I promise you. There will be no more crashes. The bad lady who drove the boat is with the police.'

'And where's Tristan now?' Morwenna asked.

'He's up at his house, doing some work. He's able to do a lot remotely, so he won't need to go to London so often. But we might go up to his flat in the new year, take Elowen and show her the sights.' Tamsin reached for her sandwich.

'I want to go on the London Eye.' Elowen was still scribbling. 'And see where the king lives.'

'Everything's working out.' Tamsin stared into the distance. 'Seb's trying to find work here too. Becca said he wants to move down permanently. It's going to be a great new year for us both. It's good to have relationships that are really going somewhere for once.'

Morwenna examined her daughter's face. Tamsin looked happier than she had been in a long while. As ever, Morwenna hoped in her heart that everything would go well for her now.

The doorbell tinkled and Carole Taylor hurried in, her hand gripping little Britney's. As soon as Britney saw Elowen she squealed with recognition and the girls hugged. Elowen shared her felt pens and a chair, and they began drawing a new picture.

Carole sat down heavily on the spare chair and lowered her voice. 'Morwenna, I need to talk to you. How did you know that Mexican model killed Pawly? She was under my roof, in the boarding house. She could have killed me, and Vic and Britney. I mean – I was in the same house as a murderer.'

'It was Fernanda, yes. I worked it out.'

'I hear she's admitted pushing Pawly downstairs.' Carole checked to see if Britney and Elowen were listening, but they were busy drawing.

'What about her boyfriend, the photographer?' Tamsin asked. 'Was he involved too?'

'He knew nothing about it. He's not her boyfriend though. They had separate rooms. They're professionals. Mind you,' Carole's voice was confidential, 'I was always a bit suspicious of her.'

'Why?' Morwenna asked.

'She didn't eat breakfast.'

'That's hardly a reason,' Tamsin said.

'I heard her crying in her room a few times, as if she was really upset about something. I expect it was guilt.' Carole turned to Tamsin. 'She was Tristan's ex, wasn't she? Didn't he break her heart?'

'I don't know much about it,' Tamsin said. 'He met her in London and they went out a few times. He wasn't really into her but...'

'But what?' Morwenna asked.

'When he stopped seeing her, she wrote him lots of letters and sent him cards, trying to get back with him.'

'Cards?' Morwenna thought about the Santa cards.

'And Tristan didn't invite her to the party. Nor did Pippa or Julian. They each thought the other had, but Fernanda invited herself.'

'She was a woman obsessed, then?' Carole said.

'I wonder why she pushed *Pawly*? It doesn't make sense,' Morwenna said.

'The police will find out.' Tamsin said. 'Let's hope that's the end of it.'

'Oh, I do hope so. We need a bit of peace in Seal Bay.' Carole noticed Morwenna's sandwich. She hadn't touched it yet. 'Ooooh, that looks appetising. Waitress?' Courtenay appeared at Carole's shoulder, ready to take an order. 'Two more of those sandwiches, please, and tell Zach to put extra mayo on them. And two chocolate milkshakes.'

'Coming up.' Courtenay dashed off.

Morwenna reached for her tea. 'Right. I might just pop next door to Becca's. I've got some Christmas shopping to do.'

But she was still thinking about Fernanda's arrest. And all the loose ends that were far from being tied.

* * *

An hour later, Morwenna was browsing in The Celtic Knot gift shop. She wanted to buy something special for Lamorna and Tamsin – and Tristan was a member of the family too now. She wandered around the shop, lit with gold fairy lights, and began to examine a few pieces of jewellery. She couldn't buy Lamorna jewellery – Vernon already had that covered – but Lamorna was keen on scented candles.

Her fingers touched a silver St Christopher necklace. Surfers wore them for luck and, after the incident, Tristan needed luck. A silk shawl for Tamsin, a light scarf for Courtenay to cover up the marks on her neck. Louise liked scarves too.

Besides, she was in sleuthing mode again. There was someone she wanted to talk to.

'Can I help?' A smooth male voice came from behind her shoulder.

'Ah.' Morwenna whirled round. 'Seb.'

Seb asked, 'How are you, Morwenna?'

'Good.' Morwenna made small talk deliberately. 'How's the nephew?'

'Six pounds ten ounces. He looks just like me, apparently. He's Arthur Sebastian.' Seb looked proud. 'And Phoebe's doing well.'

'Did you get him that teddy bear?'

'I did. I had it sent up specially.' Seb pushed a hand through his hair. 'I'm in charge today. Becca's having a lie-down. She's got a bit of a headache.'

'Oh, sorry to hear it.'

'I said I'd look after the shop,' Seb said, his expression earnest. 'I'm giving up the flat in London, moving here permanently.'

'That's nice,' Morwenna said, interested.

'It's me and Becca from now on. I want to make this shop really work.'

'It's a lovely shop.' Morwenna wanted to encourage him to talk. 'I'm sure you'll do well. Things can be a bit tight during the winter months though.'

'Becca said that. I'm trying to find a job and earn some extra cash. We might expand, get more surfer stuff. We could get a loan. I could even ask Tristan.'

'He's a good friend,' Morwenna said.

'It's nice that he and Tam are planning a future together.' Seb fingered the dog-tag pendant around his neck. 'Oh, did you know that?'

'I guessed.'

'I'm making a new start down here with Becca. I'd kill for that girl.'

'There's probably no need.' Morwenna made a mental note of his words.

'A turn of phrase,' Seb said sweetly. 'Do you want any help with your shopping?'

'I'll just take these.' Morwenna handed him the presents she'd just chosen and Seb scanned the prices.

He glanced up. 'Can I ask you something, Morwenna?'

'You can.'

'I heard on the grapevine you're friends with the policewoman. So – the person who pushed the writer downstairs has been arrested, right?'

'I think they're questioning someone,' Morwenna said.

'But I heard there was evidence that she was the killer.'

'Nothing's proven.' Morwenna's gaze was direct. 'Why the interest, Seb?'

Seb spoke quickly. 'There have been burglaries. People are saying that they're linked to whoever pushed Pawly. I was just thinking about the shop. I might get some extra security.'

'It's probably a good idea,' Morwenna said, handing her card over to pay. 'I hope Becca feels better soon.'

'Me too,' Seb said. He gave her a receipt. 'Mind you, I'm enjoying being here in the shop. It feels good to be king of my own castle.'

'I bet it does,' Morwenna said. 'I'll see you tomorrow.'

'At Tam's buffet evening. We'll be there,' Seb said.

Morwenna made her way out of the shop and into the street, her head full of thoughts and suspicions. The skies were dark overhead, the clouds low. She hurried towards the hill. She wanted to be home before the rain came in.

26

Back home, Morwenna busied herself, wrapping presents and writing cards. She put the Christmas hits CD on again: Chris Rea, Aled Jones, Mud. She found herself singing along. Her heart felt lighter. It was a couple of days until Christmas, and she began to count her blessings. There would be a party tomorrow night with her daughter. A family Christmas on a boat, no cooking to do.

And, most importantly, the horrendous time wondering who had killed Pawly was over. She had to believe it was, for her family's sake, although there was the small matter of Vernon. Perhaps he'd leave for Swansea and never come back. Jane said he was on her radar. Morwenna was sure he'd be arrested soon.

It had been a stressful time. Tamsin had been threatened, Ruan had been attacked, someone had impersonated her on the phone in order to take Elowen out of school. Morwenna was relieved the person who'd done it was in custody.

Her mind was working overtime as she tied bits of string around gifts and added tags. Why would Fernanda Pérez – that was her name – do those awful things? It didn't make sense.

Morwenna tried to recall some of her words in Spanish. What had she said?

'I hate Tristan. I hate him so much. *Ojalá el cabrón estuviera muerto.*'

I wish the bastard was dead.

Morwenna thought about it as she tied the last knot and put the presents in the corner beneath the little tree. Something that felt like doubt wriggled behind her thoughts.

She'd hardly gone to town on decorations this year. There were a couple of strings of lights shaped like berries. Some yellow stars. Definitely no mistletoe.

Brenda was asleep on the sofa. Morwenna glanced at the clock. Four-thirty. She was looking forward to a quiet night in. A shower, a healthy meal, an early night. She wondered what was bothering her, what was wriggling at the back of her mind. It was to do with Fernanda's arrest. She couldn't work out what her motive would have been.

She was about to go upstairs when there was a light tap at the front door. Not Ruan. She wasn't expecting anyone. She went to open it.

Jane was standing in the doorway in uniform; behind her, the skies were dark already and a night frost was glistening on the path.

'Morwenna, can I come in? There's something I need to talk to you about. I want you to hear it from me.'

'Oh?'

Jane marched into the living room and sat down next to Brenda, who opened one eye but didn't budge. 'Are you all ready for Christmas?'

'I am. We have a buffet at Tam's tomorrow evening.'

'I'll be there.' Jane took a deep breath, as if she was about to make an announcement.

'Is this a social call, Jane? If it is, I'll put the kettle on and get the biscuits out.'

'No, it isn't. I know there's been some speculation in the bay today about Fernanda Pérez.' Jane took her hat off and patted her hair, tied back neatly. 'You know the diamond you photographed matches exactly the one she lost in her earring.'

'You told me. But what if it was a coincidence, her diamond falling out? I've been worried about that.'

'She admitted to it, Morwenna.'

'What did she do exactly?'

'She pushed him downstairs.'

'Really?' Morwenna breathed out relief.

'But it was a mistake,' Jane began. 'Fernanda's in tears at the nick. She's given a statement and we'll charge her.'

'A mistake?'

'Well.' Jane frowned. 'This is where it starts getting complicated. She used to be Tristan Pengellen's girlfriend. You know that?'

'Tam said.'

'She was obsessive. She stalked him. She sent him cards, rang him all the time.'

'Did he report that?'

'Not at all, he just rode the wave.' Jane half smiled. 'He's a surfer.'

'So why would she kill Pawly?'

'Mistaken identity. Fernanda invited herself to the Pengellens' party and brought a friend with her in the hope that she could convince Tristan to take her back. Then she discovered he had a new girlfriend.'

'Tam.'

'And she was angry. Jealous.'

'I still don't get it,' Morwenna said.

'Tristan and Tamsin, Becca and Seb went for a tour of the house. Fernanda saw Becca and Seb peel off into a bedroom. She went looking for Tristan and Tamsin, and saw Pawly in his Santa costume. She assumed it was Tristan, by himself. He was wearing a Santa costume too, and from behind, in the dim light, she couldn't tell the difference. In her statement, she says she saw Tristan walking down the darkened corridor towards the steps. She called his name and he ignored her. Of course, he didn't ignore her. Pawly probably had no idea that someone was calling to him when they were shouting Tristan's name.'

'Oh?' Morwenna was beginning to understand.

'He was just a man in a Santa suit in the wrong place at the wrong time. But Fernanda thought Tristan was deliberately snubbing her. She lost her temper, rushed after him and pushed him. He fell. The diamond must have tumbled from her earring. She watched him fall, ran back to Justin Kidd, who'd gone to get them both a drink under the misapprehension that she'd popped off to the ladies' room and – there you are.'

'Poor Pawly.'

'It's sad.'

'I told you Ruan and I heard a sound from the stairs. Like a thud in the corridor outside, as if something had fallen. A wallop. Then footsteps.'

'The thing is, Fernanda doesn't know it yet, but we're about to charge her with the whole caboodle. It makes sense. She was obsessed with Tristan. She stayed on in Seal Bay to do a modelling shoot with her photographer, but it was a cover.'

'A cover?'

'She wanted revenge on Tristan. And Tamsin. And that means you and your family. That's what I came here to tell you.'

'So you think—?' Morwenna was piecing it together. 'She rang the school, trying to take Elowen? She sent the cards, burgled the Pengellens'? To get revenge on Tristan, she targeted Tam and me and Elowen and Ruan?'

'Exactly.'

'She stole the motorboat and attempted to run Tristan and Tam down? And she could have been the one who hit Ruan when he came out of The Smugglers.'

'It makes sense. Fernanda had the motive and the opportunity. She had her own room at The Blue Dolphin. Justin wouldn't have had a clue what she was up to after dark when he wasn't there.'

'I suppose so,' Morwenna said, but she wasn't sure. It didn't feel right.

'So we'll give her a night in the cell, we'll talk to her tomorrow morning and see if she spills the beans. If she does, that's attempted murder, abduction, burglary. We could be charging her with all of it tomorrow.' Jane exhaled. 'Then we can get on with Christmas.'

'Yes.' Morwenna was still imagining Fernanda aiming a motorboat at her daughter, dressed in a Santa Claus suit.

'Well done, Morwenna.'

Morwenna shrugged. 'I didn't do much.'

'Spotting the diamond was all down to you.'

'Don't tell Louise and Donald,' Morwenna said. 'They'll think the ghost of Lady Elizabeth solved the case.' She put on Shaela Carmody's psychic voice. 'If you follow the light, you will discover the person who pushed him.'

'What do you mean?' Jane asked.

'Oh, it's nothing. Another time,' Morwenna said. 'Fancy it being Fernanda, though.'

'Her mind was unbalanced in a moment of jealous anger, I suppose.' Jane pulled out her phone and glanced at the time.

'And the burglaries around the bay?'

'That's a difficult one. I might have a chat with Vernon Lewis tomorrow night. Unofficially.' Jane grinned. 'I'd like that cup of tea now, if you're offering.'

'A celebration, I suppose.'

'Exactly. And I can go back to the nick and fill in the paperwork, then tomorrow morning I'll pop into Bay Radio and tell Mike Sheridan. Rick will be a happy man.'

'Poor Pawly. Poor Fernanda. It's a shame all round.'

'It was a case of one Santa costume too many,' Jane said sadly.

'It was.' Morwenna remembered her own Santa costume. Ruan's too. She said, 'The safest person at that party was the man in the Rudolphkini.' She gave a smile, but it was the sad end to a sad story. 'I'll get you that tea.'

* * *

Morwenna went to bed early and woke around half-three. Her feet were numb because Brenda was sleeping on them. The cat had become a heavyweight. When she'd first adopted Brenda, she'd been thin and malnourished. She certainly wasn't skinny now.

She rolled over and realised that it was Christmas Eve. She opened her eyes and stared into blackness. Today would go quickly. It was the last day in the library before the festivities. Louise would be in a good mood. There would be no chance of Steve being locked up now. She'd bring in more platefuls of charred mince pies to celebrate. Susan and Barb would be bound to pop in for an update on the current crime situation.

Morwenna was looking forward to the buffet later. Things were really working out, business-wise. Just over a year ago, selling up the tearooms to a pizza takeaway chain had been on the cards. Now Tamsin was employing Zach and Courtenay. And

Elowen had a real bond with Tristan. They could become a real happy family one day. She might even be a grandmother again.

Morwenna hugged the pillow. Brenda didn't move a muscle. The image of Barnaby popped into her head. She'd phoned him last thing; he'd been delighted to be invited to Tamsin's buffet. And yes, Pam was going. Ruan had asked her.

Ruan. Morwenna wasn't going to think about him. She wasn't even going to ask herself why she wasn't going to think about him. All those powerful, stirring feelings had exhausted her. But he'd come to her first when his head was bleeding. He hadn't gone to Pam.

She'd been his first port of call as a nurse, that was all. The thought gave her no comfort.

Morwenna wriggled and thought of the special present she'd arranged for Elowen. After all these years, Elowen would get what she wanted most. She imagined her little face on Christmas afternoon, how delighted she'd be. She could be a little heller, Elowen – but she'd been through a lot in the past two years. She deserved to be spoiled a bit.

Lamorna worried her. Morwenna heard herself groan out loud. She'd be at the buffet with Vernon, then he was off back to Swansea. What if Lamorna didn't see him again – if he didn't contact her? He'd break her heart. But what if he did stay in touch? He was a fence – the bracelet he'd given Lamorna was probably stolen. Jane would be there tonight. She'd almost certainly take him in for questioning about the burglaries.

Morwenna's thoughts moved to Fernanda Pérez. She'd be sitting in a cold cell now, all alone. No wonder she cried at night, knowing that she'd accidentally pushed Pawly to his death. She must have been racked with guilt. Yes, Fernanda had been sullen, angry, difficult. She'd been obsessed with Tristan and come to Seal Bay hoping to win him back. *What woman hadn't felt strongly about a man who didn't return her feelings?* Morwenna thought. But Fernanda had let her anger take over.

Later, she'd be questioned about all the other offences. Somehow, Morwenna didn't see her as the type who'd burgle a manor house and drive a boat straight at her ex. It didn't feel right that she'd dress as Santa and stand outside a window. But Jane had sounded convinced.

She couldn't sleep. A glass of water might help. Morwenna slipped out of bed, into her dressing gown and padded downstairs. She moved on soft feet into the kitchen and poured herself a drink from the jug in the fridge. Sipping cold water felt comforting somehow.

She took the glass into the living room and sat down on the sofa. The room held residual warmth and she was glad of it. The little tree had been switched off, the fairy lights too, but the presents were wrapped and stowed safely beneath it and Morwenna felt a moment's gratitude. She was lucky. She had friends, family, people she loved. She had her health. Her cat.

Brenda was in the living room, staring at her with the round eyes of a cat who wasn't happy. Morwenna assumed she was after treats. She said, 'What do you want, Bren? Go back to bed.'

The cat continued to stare, her expression frozen. Morwenna listened to the silence for a moment, then she heard a sound. A scuffle, a noise outside the window, someone moving in the garden.

Morwenna held her breath. It was a fox, another animal. What else could it be? She shivered. There it was again, the distinct sound of someone behind the glass.

She tiptoed to the window, lifting the curtain, pulling it back a tiny amount, peeking through. Outside there was nothing but darkness. Kneeling down, she lifted the bottom of the curtains – if anyone was there, she didn't want to be seen. She stared into the garden, looking at shadows of plants and bushes that moved like witches. She let the curtain drop and took a deep breath.

'There's no one there, Bren. We're being silly.'

For some reason she recalled that Milan and Rosie Buvač slept with a cricket bat under the bed. She checked both doors were locked and bolted, front and back, then she went to the kitchen, found the cast-iron frying pan and climbed the stairs to the bedroom, Brenda at her heels.

WEDNESDAY 24 DECEMBER

27

It was Christmas Eve, a festive morning in Seal Bay library. Louise had brought the home-made mince pies in again to celebrate, but she'd also bought crisps and a Dundee cake. The Grundy sisters set up a stall in the corner of the library and munched their way through most of the refreshments that were meant for customers. They were hard-selling knitted goods, accosting whoever came in. Business was brisk, with so many Seal Bay residents wanting to borrow a book or an audiobook and discuss the Mexican model who'd pushed Seal Bay's resident writer downstairs. After the last customer left, clutching a copy of *Murder on the Orient Express*, Morwenna did her best to steer the conversation towards something positive.

'I was thinking,' she said to Louise. 'After Christmas, when Pawly's funeral's over, perhaps we could think about dedicating the local history section to him. The Pawly Yelland Collection.'

'Yes, we could feature other ones about Cornish heritage too.' Louise clapped her hands. 'And we could put a photo up to commemorate him.' A tear glistened in her eye.

Susan and Barb looked up. 'I was wondering if the RNLI would name a boat after him,' Susan suggested.

'Or maybe Damien Woon could rename one of his boats *The Pawly*,' Barb said.

'Bad idea.' Susan shook her head. 'You remember what Pawly said about Damien during his talk?'

'Ah, there was no love lost between those two,' Barb agreed. 'He can be a funny tuss, Damien. I think he doesn't like women much.'

Susan lowered her voice. 'Except for the maid he's got, the artist woman, Beverley. She's all over him like a rash. Like Delilah was with Samson.'

'Or Cleopatra with Antony,' Barb said. 'She paints him in the nude, you know.'

'Doesn't she get cold?'

'I mean he's in the nude when she paints him,' Barb laughed.

'Oh.' Susan gazed around. The library was empty. 'Can I have another bit of that cake, Louise?'

'Help yourself,' Louise said. 'Steve's home from work in an hour, so I'm ready to celebrate properly. A few days ago, I was worried about him being banged up for pushing Pawly down the stairs.'

'You never really believed he'd done it,' Morwenna teased.

'My Steve's very possessive where I'm concerned. Another man kissing me would drive him mad with passion.'

'Like Porphyria's Lover?' Morwenna was trying to remember Browning's poem.

'Porphyria? Does she live up Lister Hill? There's a Greek family up there,' Susan said, and Louise tried not to laugh. Barb helped herself to mince pies.

Morwenna's phone vibrated. A text had come in from her mother. She read it and frowned. 'Oh, that's not good.'

'What's not good?' Susan said, trying to catch a glimpse of the text.

'My mum's current man friend's calling round. She's just texted me – listen.' Morwenna read aloud.

> LAMORNA
>
> Vernon's on his way over here. He's going to say goodbye. He's off back to Swansea soon. It might be forever. I know my heart is going to break.

'I didn't know your mother had a boyfriend,' Susan said, all ears and eyes.

'You've seen him, Susan. He's a Welshman. He always hangs around the shops in town. He has a gurt moustache.'

'Oh yes. I know the man. He's staying at The Fisherman's Knot,' Susan said.

Not much got past those two.

'I thought he might go to Tam's party,' Morwenna said to herself. She'd been secretly hoping Jane might arrest him there.

'Morwenna, do you want to pop round to Lamorna's now?' Louise said kindly. 'We're quiet here. I can hold the fort.'

'I suppose it might help if I go round. Mum will have my shoulder to cry on.' Morwenna wondered if she should ask Vernon about the burglaries, front it out. 'She's fallen for this one.'

'She liked the actor too,' Susan remembered.

'The one who died on stage,' Barb added, just to remind everyone.

'I can be up at Mum's before Vernon leaves.' Morwenna had made her mind up. She'd ask him straight. Vernon belonged behind bars. 'Thanks, Louise. I'll see you all tonight, round Tam's.'

'Oh, the buffet,' Louise said excitedly. 'I'm looking forward to it. So's Steve.'

'We could bring knitted stuff round to sell,' Susan offered.

'It's all for a good cause. Everyone needs a scarf for Christmas,' Barb added.

'I'd better be off.' Morwenna grabbed her coat and bag. 'See you dreckly.'

'Right,' Louise replied. As she sailed through the door, Morwenna could hear Louise telling the Grundy sisters how Lady Elizabeth's ghost had told Shaela Carmody that the Mexican model had killed Pawly.

Morwenna grabbed her bicycle and was on her way. The traffic in the town centre was busy today, lots of cars, people buying last-minute presents. She cycled up Lister Hill towards Tregenna Gardens and stopped outside her mother's house. There was a black BMW saloon parked outside. Vernon was there.

Morwenna imagined the scene, her mother gripping his hand for all she was worth, her mascara streaking her cheeks as she sobbed, Vernon trying to tug himself away. It wasn't going to be easy.

She rang the bell once and Lamorna opened the door almost immediately. She was dressed in a purple maxi-dress and had a rose in her hair. She met Morwenna's eyes. 'Come in. It's like the final scene from *Romeo and Juliet* in here.'

Morwenna was horrified. 'The one where they kill themselves?'

'No. I didn't know they did that. I thought it was the one where they said goodbye forever.' Lamorna led the way in. Vernon was sitting uncomfortably on the sofa, wearing a three-piece suit, clutching a mug of tea. Lamorna went to sit next to him, moving close. She took his hand in hers and leaned towards him. 'Morwenna's here to support me at this difficult time,' she said. 'You were saying, Vern.'

Vernon turned to Morwenna. 'Well, you might as well hear the speech I've rehearsed. I spent ages working out how to say it right. So, Lamorna, this is what I want to say. I didn't come to Seal Bay to fall in love.'

'Why did you come?' Morwenna asked the question directly, and Vernon looked awkward. But he ignored her: he was making his final speech. His eyes locked onto Lamorna's. 'Every moment I have spent with you has been precious. And I look forward to the new year when I can come back to you again.'

'Do you promise?'

'On my life,' Vernon said, a crack in his voice. Morwenna thought he was either a very good actor or he meant every word. Lamorna was clinging to each syllable that tumbled from his moustachioed lips.

'You were saying, Vern.'

'Lamorna, you are more precious than all the gold in the world, all the jewels. I am a rich man now, and I want to give you something to remind you of me.'

'But' – Lamorna batted her eyelashes and flourished the bracelet on her wrist – 'you have already given me this.'

'It makes me happy to see pleasure flush your cheeks when you unwrap a gift. And…' Vernon took a package from the inside pocket of his jacket. 'Every time you wear this, think of me, my love. It's valuable, but nowhere near as valuable as you.' He kissed her, longer than was necessary in company, Morwenna thought. 'Open it.'

'For me?' Lamorna looked feverish.

'I leave tonight for Swansea. It's my token of undying love.'

'Oh.' Lamorna gasped, fumbling with the wrapping paper.

She uncovered a jewellery box, in midnight blue. 'Oh.' She flipped open the lid and took out a ring. 'Oh!'

'May I put it on your finger?' Vernon's voice a whisper, he slid the ring onto the third finger of her left hand and kissed it. 'My Lamorna.'

Lamorna's face was frozen in an expression Morwenna knew well. It certainly wasn't the look of love. She'd have looked that way if Vernon had placed a venomous snake in her hand. 'What's this?'

Vernon kissed her fingers again. 'It's an antique ring, my love; a Victorian ruby and diamond three-stone ring, 18 carat gold. I want you to have it.'

Morwenna knew what was coming. Lamorna spat out the words as if she'd swallowed poison. 'This is Vera Eddy's mother's ring. The one that got stolen a few days backalong, when they were burgled. I'd know it anywhere. I've seen it on her finger.'

'No, there must be some mistake,' Vernon began, but Lamorna was on her feet.

'Where did you get this ring?' Lamorna still had it on.

'I bought it. In Seal Bay. Yesterday.'

'Where?' Lamorna glared at him. 'Where did you buy it? I want to see the receipt.'

'But I can't show you.'

'You stole it,' Lamorna said.

'No, I just – I, well, the truth is, someone passed it to me and I wanted you to have it...'

'You deceitful thieving tuss,' Lamorna said. She was furious. She looked at her finger. 'I'll take this back to Vera dreckly.'

'Please don't tell her that I—' Vernon began, but Lamorna threw him a murderous look.

'Morwenna warned me and I was teazy with her, because of you. Stolen goods, a token of your love? I'm worth more than that.

You're a bleddy criminal.' Lamorna lifted her chin in the air and strutted into the kitchen, banging the door behind her. She could be heard yelling, 'I need a brandy.'

Vernon turned to Morwenna. 'Please don't think badly of me. I really care for your mother. I fell for her in a big way, and I wanted to give her nice things.'

'Nice *stolen* things. Where did the bracelet come from, Vernon?' Morwenna put her hands on her hips.

'I don't know exactly. Somewhere in Seal Bay.'

'You don't burgle the houses yourself, then? You're just the fence?' Morwenna asked.

'I'm good at it,' Vernon admitted. 'I always have been.'

'Not that good. You've been in prison,' Morwenna reminded him.

'On and off,' Vernon said. 'It doesn't always work out, moving stolen goods on. But if you'll just let me walk away this time, I swear I won't trouble you again. I really do love your mother. I do. She's a wonderful woman. And it's made me foolish, wanting to shower her with presents.'

'Who does the burglaries, then?'

Vernon shook his head. 'I can't say. But I was brought here to look for houses that were – you know – accessible. That was when I met Lamorna. I was scouting the area and I saw the house opposite – all that greenery in the garden shields the house from the road and you could see that there's a jewellery box in the upstairs window.'

'Who do you work for?' Morwenna asked again, this time more firmly.

'It's more than my life's worth. It'd get me into a lot of trouble.' Vernon shifted his feet. 'Some of these burglars can be a bit iffy.'

'Iffy?'

'You know, they expect loyalty. I'm not allowed to grass; honour among—'

'Thieves,' Morwenna said. 'Vernon, you'll get arrested for this.'

'I'll go somewhere far away. I'll lie low.'

'You have a criminal record.'

'I do, but I can shave off my 'tache, wear glasses, get a wig.' Vernon wriggled uncomfortably. 'Please, for your mum's sake, don't tell the police. Just let me go and I'll never bother her again. Please, promise me you won't tell them.'

'She won't need to.' Lamorna was back in the room. There was no brandy glass in her hand, but she was clutching her mobile phone. 'I've done it for her.'

'What? Lamorna...' Vernon looked horrified.

'You let me down. You lied to me. I even argued with my own daughter for you. But you won't break my heart. I don't fall in love with scumbags who tell me lies,' Lamorna said bitterly. There was a silence, a pause. Lamorna glared at Vernon; she was furious. There was a knock on the door. She turned to Morwenna. 'Can you answer that, please? Jane said there was a car in the area. It'll be someone for you, Vernon.'

Morwenna gave Vernon an appraising look, to assess if he'd try to hurt Lamorna, but he had tears in his eyes. Love had indeed made him weak. It had been his downfall. She hurried to the door where PC Jim Hobbs and another officer she didn't recognise, a short woman with a heart-shaped face, were standing on the top step.

'Lamorna rang to say—' Jim began.

Morwenna stood back. 'You'd better come in.'

Jim and the other PC marched into the lounge. Morwenna heard Lamorna mutter, 'Here he is. The man you've been looking for. Vernon the fence.'

The other PC raised her voice to explain the caution. 'Vernon Lewis, you do not have to say anything. But it may harm your defence if you do not mention when questioned something which you later rely on in court. Anything you do say may be given in evidence.'

Lamorna moved swiftly to Morwenna and tucked an arm through hers. Morwenna asked, 'Are you all right, Mum?'

Lamorna watched as Vernon was escorted from the room between two officers. He gazed over his shoulder, throwing her a final look that might have melted the hardest heart.

'I'm fine.' Lamorna tilted her chin. 'I've done myself a favour. I could have fallen for him. I was loved up, a little bit. But not now. I've got no time for liars and thieves. No, my Christmas present to him is a few years in the slammer. Bleddy Vernon. He'll have to get up earlier in the morning to fool me. I'm sorry I doubted you.' She drew herself up as tall as she could. 'I've always said, Morwenna. Men like that shouldn't mess with a Mutton maid.'

'They shouldn't,' Morwenna agreed, and hugged her mother hard.

28

'Come in, Mum. Hi, Barnaby. Great to see you both.' Tamsin was dressed in a silver beaded dress, Tristan at her elbow in a dinner jacket, double diamond studs sparkling in one ear. Morwenna stepped inside the tearoom where soft lights twinkled, shmaltzy music was playing from the smart speaker and all the tables were pushed together, laden with a magnificent spread. Morwenna, wearing a long, patterned dress she'd bought years ago for a millennium party, swept in on Barnaby's arm. He looked dapper in a pale blazer and chinos, swathed in the musky aroma he always used.

She glanced around. Ruan was actually wearing a tie. He looked handsome beyond belief. Pam was spectacular too, in an emerald ballgown. Morwenna waved, and they both waved back. So many people were there, Susan and Barb Grundy in matching jumpsuits, Louise and Steve, already smooching in the centre of the room, Damien and Bev doing the same. Sheppy was wearing a dinner jacket and bow tie, a top hat; currently he was showing cards to Rick Tremayne and his wife, Sally, who gazed in awe at his incredible prestidigitation.

Jane and Blessed stood together, both stunning in pretty dresses, talking to Jim Hobbs and a young woman Morwenna didn't know. Seb and Becca were there too, speaking quietly in the corner, sharing food. The entire Buvač family, including Tommy, were digging into the food. Elowen skipped around the room in an angel costume with Maya Buvač and Britney Taylor. Carole called out to Britney not to spoil her best dress, then she went back to talking to her husband, Vic, who was reaching for one of the drinks Zach had on a tray. Lamorna was chatting to Gill Bennett, who worked in Vic's car showroom, and Donald Stewart from the library, who had Shaela Carmody on his arm.

Morwenna could tell by the way Lamorna was waving her hands that she was explaining how she'd dumped her no-good boyfriend earlier. Morwenna's gaze moved to her mother's wrist and her finger; there was no sign of stolen jewellery.

'Hi, Morwenna. Would you like some sparkling wine?' Courtenay was at her elbow; she turned to Barnaby. 'Sparkling wine, sir?'

'Thank you.' Barnaby took two glasses, one for himself and one for Morwenna. Courtenay was very smart in a black dress. She said, 'I'm really looking forward to tomorrow.'

'Buffet on the boat?' Morwenna quipped. 'It will be nice.'

'It's just me and Pam up at Mirador,' Barnaby said. 'Simon's not coming until the new year.' Morwenna wondered if he was hoping for an invitation to the Pengellens' boat.

'My boyfriend might be coming over tomorrow evening.' Courtenay's face shone. 'He said he'd surprise me on Christmas Day. I think he's going to bring me something nice.'

'He's in the army?' Morwenna remembered.

'He is. A man in uniform's gorgeous. Not that I see him in it much.'

'Oh. Where's he stationed?'

'Culdrose. It's at the other end of The Lizard, an hour away.'

'I know it,' Morwenna said thoughtfully. 'How long have you known him?'

'Seven weeks now,' Courtenay said, closing her eyes dreamily for a moment. 'He's the nicest boyfriend I've ever had.'

Morwenna's gaze moved to Sheppy, who was engaging the Grundy sisters by discovering coins behind their ears. She heard Susan Grundy say, 'How ever did you do that?'

And Barb added, 'By magic.'

'Sheppy's nice,' Morwenna said and Courtenay agreed.

'He's a great neighbour. I'm on my own most of the time in the caravan at Camp Dynamo and he brings me stuff round – food, wine. He even practises his card tricks.' She was thoughtful for a moment. 'I think Johnny's jealous of how well we get on. He's always telling me he doesn't like Sheppy.'

'Why not?' Morwenna asked. 'Sheppy's lovely.'

'He doesn't like people from the north. It's silly really.' Courtenay moved away to Bev and Damien, who stopped dancing and were reaching for drinks.

Morwenna took a sip of hers and gazed around. Tamsin and Tristan were talking; she thought they radiated something special, an ease of being together, affection. Morwenna remembered when she and Ruan had been like that. A sigh caught and stuck somewhere beneath her ribcage.

Elowen ran up to them and Tristan bent to whisper something to her, and Elowen laughed.

Barnaby asked, 'Do you want to dance?'

'Later, maybe.' Morwenna gazed at the spread. 'Those canapés look nice.'

They wandered to the table and Pam came to stand next to them, Ruan at her side. Pam swished perfect glossy hair. 'How are you, Morwenna?'

'Good, thanks,' Morwenna said.

'How are you, Ruan?' Barnaby asked, ever polite.

'Fine.' Ruan nodded. 'Happy Christmas, Barnaby.'

The men shook hands and Morwenna wondered what it meant. It seemed like a sales transaction. Ruan had swapped his ex-partner for Barnaby's sister, and they'd shaken on it. Morwenna didn't like how it felt. She told herself she was being silly.

Pam said, 'Ruan might buy *The Swordfish*.'

'Really?' Morwenna met Ruan's eyes and something passed between them. She knew the look. They had an understanding that went beyond the knowledge of anyone else in the room. No one would ever take that from them.

'I'm haggling over a price with Damien. Retirement's definitely on the cards,' Ruan said.

'It will be nice to have more time,' Pam said, as if it were her retirement she was discussing. 'For pleasure-sailing. For pleasure of all kinds.'

'That's nice,' Morwenna said. She reached for a vol-au-vent and crammed it into her mouth.

'We could all go to Barbados,' Barnaby suggested. 'The house in Prospect Bay is plenty big enough. And it's a beautiful place.'

'What do you think?' Pam grasped Ruan's hand. 'We'd have such fun. Swimming, sailing, dining out *à quatre*.'

Barnaby turned to Morwenna. 'Could we go? In the new year?'

Morwenna's mouth was full of pastry. 'We could,' she spluttered, wondering if she'd just showered him in flaky crumbs. She took a gulp of sparkling wine. 'I'm just going to chat to Jane for a minute.' She pecked Barnaby's cheek. 'I'll be back dreckly.'

She moved off, conscious of Ruan's eyes on her. She heard him saying, 'She's some maid,' and Pam agreeing too loudly.

'Oh, she's wonderful. I remember how good she was when Alex, my husband, died.'

Morwenna needed to get away from talk of double dates. Ruan filled her thoughts. There was so much sadness and regret now. It made her miserable to see him with Pam. She ought to tell him what was in her heart. But it was probably too late. Whatever happened between her and Ruan, she'd find an opportunity to talk to Barnaby later and tell him that she wouldn't go to Barbados. She liked him a lot, but not enough. It was Ruan who—

'Ow!' Morwenna felt someone clatter into the back of her legs. She swivelled round. Elowen gazed up and lifted her arms for a hug. 'Sorry, Grandma.'

'How are you, my bewty?' Morwenna planted a kiss on her forehead. 'You make a cracking angel.'

Elowen flapped her wings. 'I'm better at football. Grandad's taking me to the five-a-side game tomorrow morning, then he's bringing me to dinner on *The Pe*—'

'*The Phoenix*.'

'Right. And we're going to have a buffet lunch all together with Tristan.'

'Are you looking forward to Christmas?'

'I'm looking forward to the football mostest, then the presents, then the dinner. Have you got me a present, Grandma?'

'I have.'

'What is it?'

'Oh, I can't say.'

'Grandad won't say either, but I know he's got me football boots because he said he'd give me my present before the game and he wouldn't do that unless it was boots. I want red ones.'

'You'll get your present from me in the evening.'

'Can you come to watch me in the football, Grandma?'

'I wasn't going to. Grandad likes to take you,' Morwenna said.

'Oh, please. Please.'

'I'm off to Woon's to get on the boat first thing, but I'll pop to the park first and watch you for a bit. Is that all right?'

'It's better than nothing.' Elowen sounded just like Lamorna.

'Come on, Elowen.' Britney was tugging her wings. 'We're playing magic angels who rescue the prince from a wicked queen with icy powers and he's trapped in her kingdom of winter forever...'

'I want to be the wicked queen,' Elowen said as she and Britney hurried over to join Maya.

Morwenna reached Jane and Blessed, who were in the middle of a conversation. Jane said, 'I think Seal Bay's the perfect setting. Fireworks over the bay, shimmering lights.'

'But imagine dinner in The Shard. The firework display's spectacular from there.' Blessed turned to Morwenna. 'We were discussing the best place for New Year's Eve.'

'Oh?' Morwenna glanced at Jane meaningfully. 'Are you going away?'

Jane gulped sparkling wine. 'I'll probably be working. Mind you, Rick owes me some time off. We've been busier than ever.'

Blessed agreed. 'But it was a good day today, pulling Vernon Lewis in. We raided The Fisherman's Knot. He had a safe in his hotel room, stuffed with jewellery and money.'

'He must be part of a gang.' Morwenna was on the ball. 'Has he said who his friends are?'

'He will,' Blessed said. 'He seems frightened.'

'You should have seen the look on his face under questioning,' Jane began, 'and he's gutted that your mum shopped him. I think he'd genuinely fallen for her.'

'He had,' Morwenna agreed. She helped herself to another canapé.

'Hello.' There was a rough voice behind her. It belonged to

Rick Tremayne. 'I just wanted to say thanks, Morwenna, for all your help.'

'Have you got a cold, Rick?' Morwenna asked. His voice was croaky and his nose glowed red.

'Bleddy typical,' Rick said. 'Just in time for Christmas. Jon brought it home from college, then he gave it to Ben, then Sally got it.' He sniffed.

'I don't want it, Rick. Don't give it to me.' Blessed took a step back.

Morwenna was still fishing. 'Have you found out who Vernon's accomplices were, Rick?'

'No, but—' Rick took out an oversized hanky and blew his nose. 'We've ruled out the Mexican model. It seems that Fernanda Pérez did push Pawly Yelland. She'll be tried for that. But we can't link her to anything else.'

'Oh?' Morwenna felt her skin become cold, as if she were in water.

'Justin Kidd gave her alibis for the times and places where the burglar struck across Seal Bay. And she was having breakfast in front of witnesses when the motorboat was driven at Tristan and Tamsin. She definitely couldn't have phoned the school about Elowen because she was doing a photo shoot lower down the beach with dozens of people watching, including Susan and Barb Grundy.'

'I see.' Morwenna shivered again. 'So whoever tried to attack Tam is still out there.'

'We'll find them.' Rick patted her arm reassuringly, and Morwenna hoped he wasn't transferring germs.

'Thanks, Rick.'

Sheppy sidled between them, doffing his top hat. 'Morwenna, you're looking belting tonight. Is that a new frock?'

'I bought it in 2000,' she said.

'Ah, I'd have been one year old.'

Morwenna made a face. 'Thanks, Sheppy. That's boosted my confidence no end.'

'Never mind. I'm buzzing tonight. It's nearly Christmas and I'm getting loads of tips. So...' He produced a pack of cards. 'Pick a card, any card, any card.'

Morwenna picked one. It was the Queen of Spades.

'Memorise it,' Sheppy said. 'Now put it back in the pack.'

Morwenna did as she was told.

'Right – now I'll just say the special magic words...' He rolled his eyes. 'Sheppyisasexbomb.' Sheppy's grin widened. 'You have to say it too.'

'Sheppyisasexbomb.' Morwenna laughed.

'Glad you think so.' Sheppy beamed. 'So, here we go. Magic Sheppy is at work. Just watch me find that card for you now.' He cut the cards with deft fingers then dropped them softly. The bottom half tilted forwards and one card stuck out slightly. Sheppy flourished his top hat. 'Take your card, madam, and you should find miraculously that it's the one you selected.'

Morwenna picked it up. 'It *is*.' She was amazed. 'The Queen of Spades.'

'Sheppyisasexbomb!' Sheppy clicked his fingers, took something from behind Morwenna's ear and gave it to her. It was a gold coin, a bright foil wrapper with chocolate inside. 'Happy Christmas.'

'Happy Christmas.' Morwenna produced a purse from her bag and handed Sheppy a ten-pound note. 'You're incredible.'

'Sound.' Sheppy was delighted. 'I swear down you're the nicest person in Seal Bay. Happy Christmas, Morwenna.'

'Happy Christmas.'

Morwenna was about to put the card back in the pack and a voice at her side said, 'That's a bad card, maid.'

'Mum?' Morwenna turned to see Lamorna frowning, a full glass in her hand.

'The Queen of Spades is unlucky.' Lamorna's eyes were round with worry. 'It's a bad omen. I've heard it's the card of misfortune.'

'I don't believe that,' Morwenna said. Her eyes moved to Tamsin and Tristan, who were talking to the children. She listened in. Elowen was jumping up and down.

'Mummy, can we play upstairs in my bedroom?'

'You and Britney and Maya?'

'We want to use my bed as a boat. We're sailing to my kingdom, the land of ice. I've just taken Britney and Maya prisoner. I'm the Queen of Freezerland and I've got icy powers and I trapped all the people in winter forever.'

'Right,' Tamsin said. 'Yes, play upstairs. Only in your room, mind. Nowhere else.'

'Can you come and play with us too, Tristan?' Elowen asked. 'You can be the prince and I can tie you up and Britney loves you and wants to marry you but I get to torture her.'

'I'll come up in a bit.' Tristan ruffled Elowen's hair.

Morwenna watched Elowen and her friends scamper up the stairs, making far more noise than their small feet should have. Not far away, Seb and Becca were smooching, her arms locked around his neck. He said something to her and started searching through his pockets.

Lamorna was still at her side. 'I'm telling you, Morwenna. It's bad luck, that card.'

'I still don't believe it, Mum.'

Lamorna drifted away. Sheppy was busy showing a card trick to Jane and Blessed. Courtenay arrived at her elbow. 'Another drink?'

Morwenna took the last glass on the tray. 'Has all the sparkling wine gone?'

'There are more bottles in the kitchen. I'll just fill up.' Courtenay rushed away. Morwenna's eyes drifted to the door. Damien was saying goodbye to Ruan and Pam. She heard him mutter, 'Bev's tired. We're going home.' Beverley didn't look at all tired, despite leaning against Damien. Her hand was fondling his buttock.

Tristan came over to Morwenna. 'Are you enjoying the evening?'

'I am.' Morwenna noticed Barnaby was being buttonholed by Louise and Steve. Louise had the look on her face that told Morwenna that Barnaby was in for a grilling about romance. He met Morwenna's eyes and she winked.

'Lunch is going to be brilliant tomorrow,' Tristan said.

'It'll be wonderful, all of us on the boat.' Morwenna felt the smile stick to her face. Whoever had tried to kill Tamsin and Tristan was still out there. The person with the Santa face. It wasn't Fernanda. She knew that now. A familiar shiver went through her as she remembered the figure at the wheel of the motorboat.

What had been so familiar about the Santa?

Tristan seemed oblivious. 'We won't go too far out, but if you want to bring your wetsuit, we could go for a swim.'

'That's a good idea,' Morwenna said.

'Morwenna, I just wanted to say...' Tristan took a breath. 'Tam and I—'

'I know.'

'She's had it tough, but she's such a strong person. We get on well.'

'I know you do.'

'The fling I had with Fernanda in London wasn't anything special. I didn't know she was coming to Seal Bay. She told me Mum had invited her but—'

'Pippa hadn't. Or Julian.'

'Exactly. I'm sorry for what happened to Pawly.'

'It wasn't your fault, Tristan.'

'Rick Tremayne said she thought she was pushing me.'

'She did.' Morwenna nodded. 'Poor Pawly. He was in the wrong place at the wrong time. In the wrong costume.'

'That's so horrible. But about Tam... I'm going to spend most of my time in Seal Bay next year.' Tristan's face was earnest. 'I can work remotely.'

'That's brilliant.' Morwenna gave him her best mother-in-law smile, to show she approved. Tristan seemed good for Tamsin. She glanced around. 'Courtenay's getting more wine. I wonder if she has any soft drinks.'

There was a piercing scream from upstairs. Morwenna froze. 'What was that?' She was on her feet, thundering up the stairs, pulse thudding. 'Elowen?'

Tamsin was already in front of her, Ruan too. Tristan was at her heels. They reached Elowen's room together. More people rushed in behind them. The window was wide open and a figure was creeping through, on his way out.

He was wearing a red Santa suit.

Ruan bolted down the stairs. Morwenna heard him shout, 'Rick – Jane – Milan – let's get after him!'

Tamsin grabbed Elowen in a hug. Rosie Buvač and Carole Taylor wrapped their arms around Maya and Britney.

Elowen said, 'Santa was coming in. I was frightened. I didn't like him, Mummy. He said my name in a nasty voice.'

Maya gulped. 'Was it really Santa?'

Britney sniffed. 'He was a burglar, Mummy. He was a horrible man.'

'It's all right now,' Tamsin said to Elowen.

Tristan went over to the window. 'He's forced it open from

outside, with a crowbar or something.'

Morwenna said, 'We should go downstairs.'

They stood in the tearoom, the girls hugged in their mothers' arms, as Ruan appeared through the door. Behind him, Blessed and Jane bolted in, then Milan Buvač, then Rick.

Ruan panted, 'He's nowhere to be seen.'

'We searched the road and the alleyways behind the shops,' Rick said.

'Who's missing from the party?' Blessed asked, staring round.

'Damien went home.' Pam stood by Ruan. 'And Bev.'

Becca looked worried. 'Seb popped next door for his phone. He left it in the flat.'

Morwenna made a mental note of who was missing as Courtenay appeared with a tray of drinks. 'Anyone for sparkling wine? Fruit punch?'

Rick took one. 'Jim Hobbs is driving a patrol car round Seal Bay. He'll find the burglar. I've alerted other cars too.'

'Good,' Blessed said.

Britney started to cry again. 'I don't like Santa, Mummy.'

'Nor do I,' Carole said with a wild look at Vic. 'That man could have hurt the girls.'

'If it was a man,' Jane said.

Barnaby turned to Tristan and Ruan. 'Can we fix the window? Make sure no one comes back?'

'After Pengellen Manor got burgled, we had someone upgrade the locks,' Tristan said. 'I can ring the guy who fitted them, but I don't suppose he can do much tonight.'

'My van's outside. I've got a toolkit. We can sort something,' Ruan said.

'I'll help,' Barnaby offered. They were on their way out into the brisk wind, almost bumping into Seb, who was coming the other way holding up his phone. He stared around. 'Have I missed something?'

'Someone tried to break in.' Becca was in his arms.

Tamsin lifted Elowen and hugged her. 'You can sleep in my bed tonight.'

'Can I sleep in your bed, Mummy?' Britney asked and Carole glanced at Vic.

Vic said, 'We'll make sure you're safe, love. We've got a burglar alarm.'

'Don't worry, we'll pick him or her up tonight,' Jane whispered in Morwenna's ear. 'Blessed and I are going to drive around Seal Bay for a couple of hours. We've only had a small glass of wine. We'll scour the place.'

'Thanks.' Morwenna's brows knitted. 'Who on earth is behind all this?'

She saw Barb turn to Susan and mutter, 'It's the Santa again.'

'I'm staying with you tonight.' Lamorna came over and grabbed Morwenna's arm as if it were a shield. 'I told you that Queen of Spades card was bad luck, maid. It's come to something, hasn't it, when Santa climbing through the window on Christmas Eve fills us all with fear?'

THURSDAY 25 DECEMBER

29

Morwenna woke on Christmas Day to the sound of someone belting out 'Santa Baby' at the top of a warbling voice. Lamorna was in the kitchen, clanking cutlery, feeling festive. After last night's shenanigans, Morwenna thought the choice of song wasn't great.

She clambered into her dressing gown and pottered downstairs. Lamorna was pouring coffee. 'I thought we'd start the day with a serious caffeine kick. We'll need it.'

Brenda was trying to lap cream from a bowl. Morwenna watched for a moment and knitted her brows. 'What's she got there, Mum?'

'Only a little clotted cream,' Lamorna said. 'It *is* Christmas, even for cats.'

'It's not good for her.' Morwenna picked the bowl up and put it in the sink.

'She's just like me, loves all the calories. I intend to eat everything that's bad for me today. It's a chance for us to enjoy ourselves. Especially after last night's shocker. Ruined my evening, that did. Tam's messaged on the family WhatsApp.'

'Oh?' Morwenna hadn't looked at her phone. 'What's she saying?'

'Tristan's got that bloke he knows to come out and make the tearoom windows secure. He's paying him double. But at least Tam can go out today with an easy mind. And Ruan's there now. Apparently, Elowen's running around in new red football boots.'

'She'll have some nice presents today.' Morwenna smiled at the thought of what she was going to give her. At that moment, a heaviness sat on her shoulders, that feeling of dread, that the Santa was still out there. Jane hadn't messaged to say they'd caught someone.

She sat at the table as Lamorna placed a plate of beans on toast in front of her and one for herself. Lamorna tucked in.

'Mum, I'd have been OK with a bowl of cereal.'

'You need something filling. We're getting on that boat at eleven, then we're out at sea. It'll be chilly on deck.'

'I know. But we'll be cosy below.' Morwenna reached for a cup of coffee. It tasted strong and bitter. Lamorna had doubled up on the grains.

'I'm wearing my glittery jumpsuit. What are you wearing?'

'I hadn't thought about it. Something warm.' Morwenna couldn't shake off the feeling of unease. It had wrapped its arms around her tightly.

'*The Phoenix* is a pleasure boat. It'll have luxury seats and panoramic windows and central heating. It even has a drinks bar. Julian and Pippa don't scrimp.' Lamorna looked delighted. 'Oh, I can't wait. How many of us are having dinner?'

'It's a buffet, Mum. Tristan, Tam, Elowen, me, you and Ruan. And Courtenay will serve drinks.'

'I feel like a superstar. Lamorna Mutton on a pleasure boat. Just imagine. Vernon Lewis will be eating his Christmas lunch off a tin plate in a police cell.' She sniffed. 'Oh, well, that's his lookout.'

'I suppose he made bad choices all his life.' Morwenna attacked the beans.

'And I was one of them,' Lamorna said. 'But Santa's still at large. Who do you think it is, Morwenna, beneath that red suit?'

'Someone who doesn't want to show their face.' The feeling of unease was squeezing her now. It was hard to breathe.

'It has to be *somebody*. Somebody we know. Somebody who's fallen out with Tristan.'

'Why Tristan, Mum?'

'It stands to reason. They tried to break into the tearoom. They burgled the Pengellens' house backalong. I expect there's a gang of them. Talking of which, where are the Pengellens?'

'In London for the day, with friends.'

'Oh, I see. That's why Tristan's using the boat. What about Becca and Seb? Why didn't he invite them?'

'I think Becca's cooking something for the two of them. It's their first Christmas together.'

'Seb's so jealous of Tristan. You can see that.'

'Can you?'

'Oh, yes.' Lamorna forked beans. 'Seb told me that Tristan was privileged and posh, and that it's always been that way since uni. Silver-spoon syndrome is what he called it. I told him that Tristan works hard. I've seen him on his laptop and on his phone when he's in the tearoom. Besides, the scented candles in that gift shop are overpriced. I told him if he sells stuff at that price, he and Becca will soon be millionaires.'

'So you've been shopping in The Celtic Knot, Mum,' Morwenna said. 'I know what you've got me for Christmas, then.'

'Don't you ever give up sleuthing? Nothing gets past you, maid.' Lamorna stood up. 'I'd better go and get ready, get my slap on. It's boat at eleven – drinks from twelve, buffet after that.' Lamorna was excited.

'Right. I'll grab a shower and get off.'

'Where to?' Lamorna asked. 'Tristan said he'd collect us at quarter to eleven.'

'Not me,' Morwenna said. 'I'm walking down to the park, so I can watch the first half of Elowen's five-a-side. I'll meet you at eleven, at Woon's. That's where *The Phoenix* is moored.'

'What about Ruan and Elowen?'

'Ruan's bringing her. They'll be with us by half-twelve.'

'How? I know he's special, but he can't walk on water.'

'I expect Damien will bring them out.'

'I'm not so sure. That Beverley doesn't like to let Damien out of her clutches.'

'I'll have the first shower if it's OK, Mum, then I'll get off.' Morwenna met her mother's eyes. 'Will you be all right until Tristan gets here?'

'I'll be fine.'

'If anyone tries to break in, there's a frying pan under my bed,' Morwenna said. Lamorna looked at her anxiously; she wasn't joking.

* * *

When Morwenna reached the park, her mind was packed with worries. It was Christmas Day. There would be no Santas around tomorrow. She felt it instinctively: something was going to happen today.

The five-a side-game was in full swing. Excited parents were standing along the touchline, encouraging and shouting. Morwenna spotted Ruan in a dark coat and striped scarf. She hurried over to him, squeezing between him and a large man who kept yelling, 'Go on, Oscar. Tackle. Tackle, Oscar. Mark your man.'

Ruan glanced at Morwenna. 'You made it, then.'

'I promised Elowen.'

'She's a proper good little player,' Ruan said.

They watched her for a while. She was smaller than the other children and one of only two girls. But she was plucky, red boots gleaming, dark hair flying behind her. She launched herself at a thick-set boy, taking the ball from him easily as he fell on the grass.

'Tackle her, Oscar. She's only a girl,' the man next to Morwenna bellowed.

Morwenna turned to him. 'She's never seen that as a disadvantage.'

Ruan winked. 'She's the best player on the pitch. She scored in the first five minutes.'

'What's the score now?'

'One-nil,' Ruan said. 'Ten minutes until half-time.'

'I'll stay until then, so she knows I've been here to watch her,' Morwenna decided. She felt cold. It was a chilly day, but it was fear and foreboding that made her teeth chatter.

Someone in the crowd said, 'Have you seen that little girl, the dark-haired one? She's like mustard,' and Morwenna felt a moment's glow of happiness. She tugged her phone from her pocket and took a few photos to send to Tamsin.

Elowen had the ball at her feet again and was running down the wing. Ruan said, 'Look at the footwork – she'll go straight past the defender – watch her.'

'Tackle her, Oscar,' the man beside Morwenna yelled and the thick-set boy hurled himself at her desperately, bringing her down in the mud. Elowen stayed there.

Morwenna caught her breath. 'Do you think she's hurt?' She

watched as Elowen dragged herself upright and limped slightly as she walked away. 'A year ago, there'd have been a punch-up.'

'She's learned some discipline,' Ruan said. 'Oh, I thought so. It's a penalty.'

'Rubbish, Ref. The girl dived,' the parent shouted and Morwenna ignored him.

'Look. The tall boy's going to take the penalty and Elowen's gone over to him. She's taken the ball off him. She wants to take it herself,' Ruan said excitedly. 'Go on, Elowen. You can do it, maid.'

Morwenna held her breath as Elowen placed the ball on the penalty spot and stepped back a few paces. She gripped Ruan's arm without intending to. The whistle blew and Elowen ran up to take the kick.

'She's scored,' Ruan shouted. 'Two-nil. She'll get a hat trick at this rate.'

He and Morwenna were hugging each other, leaping up and down, smiling for all they were worth. Morwenna pulled back and looked at Ruan for a moment. He was perfect in every way. She returned to watch the game, thinking sad thoughts. She said nothing more until half-time, keeping her eyes firmly on Elowen. The whistle blew and Elowen came running over.

'I scored. Did you see me, Grandma, Grandad? And I got a penalty.'

'You were great, Elowen,' Ruan enthused.

'You were.' Morwenna noticed the blood that seeped through Elowen's football sock. 'Are you hurt?'

'Nah. Oscar Richards kicked me but he couldn't hurt a fly. I've got shin pads on. I'm all right.'

Morwenna marvelled at Elowen. She seemed so grown up on the pitch. And she was resilient. The events of last night had been forgotten for the time being. Ruan reached into his shoulder bag.

'I brought you some water.' Ruan handed Elowen a drinks

bottle and wrapped a thick top around her shoulders. 'And I've got some fruit and pretzels to keep you going.'

'Proper job,' Elowen said and began to glug water.

'Give me a hug, then,' Morwenna said. 'I'm off to the boat now. I'll see you and your grandad for lunch.'

'Right.' Elowen was gazing back towards the football pitch. Her mind was elsewhere. 'I've got to go. We've got a half-time team talk.' She took off at a pace to where the team were huddled.

'Good luck,' Morwenna called after her.

Ruan met her eyes. 'She can get a quick shower and change out of her kit at the tearoom. I'll bring her over on *The Swordfish*.'

'Oh?' Morwenna asked.

'Damien and I finally agreed a price last night. He thinks I've swindled him but the boat's mine,' he said.

'Great,' Morwenna enthused. 'I bet Pam's pleased.'

'I expect so.' Ruan's breath was mist on the air. 'That was some scare we had last night at the party.'

'The man with the Santa face?' Morwenna was suddenly cold again. 'He's still out there, Ruan.'

'The police will pick him up soon.'

'I hope so. Jane messaged earlier. The police are still out in Seal Bay, following leads. I just can't help wondering—'

'What?'

Morwenna saw the image again. The driver of the motorboat. Something about the body shape. The way he or she leaned forward.

Who did it remind her of?

'Nothing.'

'They're kicking off.' Ruan glanced towards the pitch where the referee was blowing a whistle. Elowen waved briefly and was running to take her place.

'Right.' Morwenna touched his arm gently. 'I'll see you dreckly, then.' She turned to go. 'I hope she gets the hat trick.'

'She will.' Ruan rested a hand on her shoulder. 'Morwenna, I can see it in your eyes. You're worried.'

'I am.'

'The police are searching all over the bay. Jane knows where we are. It'll be fine.'

For a moment, she thought he was going to wrap her in the warmth of his arms. She needed the comfort of it.

But Elowen passed the ball again and Ruan shouted out encouragement. Morwenna patted his arm once and wandered away, leaving the sound of excited voices behind her on the wind. There was a huge cheer and she hoped Elowen had scored again.

She huddled inside her coat. The wind was raw, but the sky was clear. It would be lovely on the boat. She thought briefly about Barnaby. She'd arranged to see him on Boxing Day. To that end, she'd bought him a knitted hat in lambswool that would keep him warm in winter.

Then she'd wish him the best and say it was over between them. They'd be friends.

Just as she was friends with Ruan.

Friends? Morwenna wasn't sure what word to use. At times, she thought they were so much closer than that. But now Pam was on the scene, he had other choices. Ruan didn't seem to want to say much about Pam, and she didn't want to ask.

She supposed that things had changed forever: they were Tam's parents, Elowen's grandparents, and that was it. They met for parties. They helped each other out, as friends.

Everything would be different in the new year. Pam and Ruan. Barnaby and someone else, perhaps, but not Morwenna. He was not the piece of jigsaw that would fit snugly in her life, where Ruan had once been. She knew what it was, in her heart.

Barnaby wasn't Ruan.

Oh, well.

Morwenna took a breath of cold salty air. The sea was in sight as she walked down the hill to the boatyard. She checked her phone. It was eleven o'clock. She wasn't early.

There were two cars parked in Woon's boatyard: Tristan's, and Damien's truck. A group of figures were huddled around *The Phoenix*, talking. Morwenna joined them.

'I'm bleddy furious,' Damien was shouting. 'The yard was locked. I've no idea how anyone could have got in.'

'What's happened?' Morwenna asked.

'Someone broke in again,' Lamorna was quick to explain. 'In the early hours.'

'Damien's called the police,' Tristan said.

'It's my fault,' Damien grumbled. 'I forgot to switch the CCTV on again last night.' He pushed his hands into his pockets. '*The Maverick*'s one of my best motorboats. I've just overhauled it.'

'Did you leave the keys in?' Morwenna asked.

Damien huffed, 'I didn't expect anyone to break in and steal it, did I? There were chains on the gate.'

'How could someone have got in?'

'Over the top, I suppose.' Damien frowned. 'I just hope Rick Tremayne and his merry men can find it.'

Morwenna said, 'I expect it'll be out on the water somewhere,' and Damien threw her a murderous look.

'Who'd steal my boat?' Damien sniffed, the cold making his nose red. 'All this funny business, all the burglaries and what happened at Tamsin's party last night. Now my boatyard gets broken into again. What are the bleddy police doing?'

'Jane said they're scouring the bay right now.' Morwenna tried to look hopeful. 'Huge numbers of them. They'll pick him up soon.'

'Well, if I see anyone in a Santa suit, I won't be responsible for what I do. I'll give him some bleddy Christmas present,' Damien said beneath his breath.

'Talking of Christmas,' Tristan said tactfully. 'We have a party arranged.'

'Right, let's get you all on board, then you can start her up, Tristan, and be off on your Christmas jolly,' Damien said without interest.

'What are you doing for Christmas dinner?' Tamsin asked politely.

'Bev's cooking.' Damien rubbed his hands together to keep warm. 'She's got Buck's Fizz on the go back home and pigs in blankets. I need to get off.'

'We won't keep you, then.' Lamorna glanced towards Morwenna. 'I'm looking forward to a drink on board.'

'And Dad's bringing Elowen after the game,' Tamsin said.

There was a flurry of footfall behind them as Courtenay hurried through the gate. 'Sorry I'm late,' she said. 'No buses today. I had to walk.'

'No boyfriend?' Morwenna asked.

'No. He said he'd surprise me later. I'm hoping he'll bring me a nice present.'

'Is he over at Culdrose?' Morwenna asked pointedly as they clambered aboard *The Phoenix*.

'Yes, but he's got a car. It's lovely and roomy. Well, it would be if he didn't have all his crap in the back.' Courtenay laughed. 'He even has a sleeping bag in there.'

'Oh?' Morwenna couldn't help the chill that shook her. 'Why?'

'He likes camping and the outdoor life. And swimming. He'd have loved being here today,' Courtenay said.

Morwenna was still thinking about Courtenay's words as Tristan started the motor and *The Phoenix* shuddered as they walked down spiral steps. Courtenay was still chattering. 'Tristan's asked me to start with a champagne cocktail, so I'm going to make Sgroppinos.'

'You know how to make those?' Morwenna was impressed.

'I worked in a cocktail bar in Newport Pagnell for a month. They sacked me for being late twice.' Courtenay pulled a face. 'I really want to impress Tam and Tristan. I said to Tam that if she kept me on, we could do more evening parties like we did last night. You know, engagement parties and hen nights, and I'd do all the drinks. I'd love that. Tam thinks it might work.'

'Right.' Morwenna watched as Courtenay sauntered off to the bar area and tugged off her coat. She was ready for action in a little black dress.

'She'll go far, that one,' Lamorna said. She was chewing a vol-au-vent. 'I know we haven't officially started the buffet yet, but I'm bleddy starving.'

'It's such a luxurious boat. Much bigger than the *Pammy*,' Morwenna said, taking Lamorna's arm. 'It's been really nicely furnished too – look at the leather seats.'

Damien cast off and Tristan shouted that he intended to take the boat a good distance from the shore before he dropped anchor. Morwenna and Lamorna sat down on the squashy sofa, enjoying the boat's lilting movement, the views of the sea from the panoramic windows. The floors were shiny wood, oak perhaps, and a wooden table with a glass top had already been laid out with nibbles, pretzels, nuts.

The sea rocked them from below. Morwenna leaned back in the seat and closed her eyes. Lamorna said, 'This is the life.'

'It is,' Morwenna said, relaxing into soft leather and enjoying the gentle sway. The warmth of the cabin made her feel sleepy. She could easily have nodded off. She opened her eyes and gazed at Tristan and Tamsin standing near the bar. He wore a dinner jacket, and she had on a long dress. They looked the perfect couple, their arms around each other, sharing a moment.

Beyond the windows, the ocean was dark blue and choppy, merging with a pale sky streaked with clouds. Morwenna narrowed her eyes. A speck in the distance that might have been a motorboat was speeding towards them.

She frowned; Ruan was very early.

Courtenay arrived with a tray and Tristan said, 'Time for a toast.'

'Sgroppinos,' Courtenay explained. 'Lemon sorbet, vodka and champagne.'

'Yes, please.' Lamorna took a glass in each hand, offering one to Morwenna. Courtenay had made an extra one for herself.

'A toast,' Tamsin echoed.

'To us all,' Tristan said. 'Happy Christmas. And to good times in the future.'

'To good times.' Morwenna glanced towards the ocean again. Ruan and the motorboat had disappeared. She raised her glass. *'Yeghes da!'*

'Yeghes da,' everyone chorused, and the five glasses clinked together.

Morwenna looked at each face, smiling happily, enjoying the celebrations. But a strange feeling was gnawing at her. Elowen's football game wouldn't have finished yet. And Damien's yard had been broken into again. She recalled with a shiver what happened last time. She stared towards the ocean.

Who was in the motorboat?

All of a sudden, she knew.

Her heart leaped into her mouth, and she thought she might be sick with fear.

30

Courtenay brought round another tray, second glasses of Sgroppino for everyone. Morwenna had only had a few sips of her first. She glanced nervously at the clock on the wall that led to the galley kitchen where Courtenay was busy with the food. It was ten minutes past twelve.

Where was the motorboat she'd seen before? It must have gone.

She checked her phone. Nothing from Jane. Nothing from Ruan.

Lamorna was tucking into pretzels from little gold bowls. She'd have no appetite for lunch. She lifted her second glass and said, 'I like these drinks. They're even nicer than martinis. I must get Courtenay to show me how to make them.'

Tamsin and Tristan had come to sit opposite. Morwenna needed to speak, just to calm her thumping heart. 'This certainly beats watching the repeats on TV while the turkey roasts.'

'It's nice to be here together,' Tamsin said. 'Do you think we should have invited Seb and Becca?'

'They can come another day,' Tristan suggested. 'Seb's been

preoccupied. I think he's really trying to make everything work in the gift shop.'

'After Christmas, it's hard for Cornish businesses,' Tamsin said and Tristan squeezed her hand, his way of saying that everything would be fine.

Morwenna glanced around. There was no sign of the motorboat now. She told herself she was just being jumpy. She had no reason to suspect that the worst thing in the world could happen. But her hands were shaking, nonetheless. She remembered the football game earlier, Elowen's goals. 'Did you get the photos I sent you, Tam?'

'I did. Thanks, Mum. She looks in her element, bless her,' Tamsin said. 'We must go and see her play next time, Tristan.'

'We will,' Tristan said. 'Morwenna, have you heard anything more about the intruder last night?'

'Jane and Blessed are patrolling Seal Bay.' She looked around nervously, every sinew straining.

'Well, whoever it is won't be able to wear that silly costume after today,' Tamsin said.

Morwenna froze.

There was someone watching from the spiral steps – she knew he was there before she saw him. Before she heard the low chuckle, a hollow ho, ho, ho. He was staring at her, wearing a red suit and hat, a white beard, a sack over his back. He was sitting on the staircase, not moving, just watching. She drew a sharp breath.

Tamsin and Tristan turned at the same time, following the line of her gaze. Tristan's voice was low as he said, 'Who the hell are you?' Morwenna watched the colour drain from his face.

Santa Claus didn't move. He stayed perched on the middle step as if he owned the boat. He lifted his sack and placed it between his knees. It was bulky.

The heavy feeling of foreboding had been lurching in

Morwenna's stomach for a while. She'd been hiding the truth from herself all along. At once, everything fell into place. Morwenna knew who Santa was. She knew why he was there. She recognised the broad shoulders beneath the red jacket, the long legs in boots, the glinting eyes above the beard, the hat pulled down.

It was her worst nightmare.

She said, 'What do you want, Jack?'

The familiar mocking voice hadn't changed since the last time she'd seen him at the boatyard, when she'd had to fight for her life.

'I'm Santa Claus. We Santas come to see people at Christmas and bring them presents they'll never forget.'

Tamsin knew the voice too. Her ex. The man who had tried to harm her child. Morwenna saw her reach for Tristan's hand as Jack Greenwood tugged off the hat and beard. His face was stubbly now, a little leaner. Harder. There was a new scar across the bridge of his nose and Morwenna remembered that Ruan had hit out at the person who attacked him.

His expression was cold.

Tamsin whispered, 'Why are you here?' and Morwenna heard the fear in her voice.

Jack heard it too. It gave him more power. He pushed his shoulders back, self-assured, arrogant, and narrowed his eyes. 'I've come to see you, Tam. I bet you've missed me. Where's Elowen?'

'Don't you dare,' Tamsin said, her voice low.

Morwenna's mind moved quickly, desperate to find a way out. Jack was sitting on the steps, a sack grasped in his hands, containing something large. He filled the step, blocking any escape.

Tristan looked confused. He clearly had no idea what was

going on. Tamsin squeezed his hand. She knew how dangerous her ex-boyfriend was. Last time he'd been in Seal Bay, he'd threatened Elowen, kidnapped her, demanded ransom. Morwenna could see that her daughter was trembling. She was trembling too.

Lamorna reached for Morwenna's fingers and gripped them. 'What's going on, Morwenna? Why's he here?'

Jack snickered. 'I dropped in for Christmas.' His smile fell away as he turned to Tristan. 'Very nice house, that Pengellen Manor. Some expensive stuff there. Nice boat too.'

Morwenna took a deep breath. She had no idea what to do. She needed to play for time, until an idea came to her. She said, 'What happened to you, Jack, that time? After the police came to the boatyard? You fell in the water, in the harbour. I thought you'd drowned. You said you couldn't swim.'

'I'm a champion swimmer. I always have been.' Jack's lip curled. 'But we've got some unfinished business.'

'Jack,' Tamsin began.

'This time you'll get what's coming. I owe you all.' Jack leaned back on the step, surveying each face.

Morwenna heard the quake in her voice. She couldn't stop it. Ruan would be a while yet. It terrified her, the thought of what would happen when he arrived. He'd bring Elowen on the boat, straight into danger.

She wondered if she could warn him, or get to her phone, alert Jane somehow. But the phone was in her pocket – there was no way to do it.

She had to keep Jack talking. 'Was it you, burgling all those houses in the bay?'

Jack bristled, pushing out his chest. He liked to brag. 'Yeh, I did a few houses. I had Vernon fencing for me. I met him in prison. He was useful, for a bit. I hear they locked him up. But I didn't really come here for the money, did I?' He turned his eyes on Tamsin. 'Well, Tam. Where's the kid?'

'She's not here,' Tamsin said.

'Now, let's try and work this out,' Tristan began, and Jack gave a low laugh.

'Shut up. This has got nothing to do with you. Except that it has now. You're stuck in the middle. You and your boat.'

Morwenna took a breath and tried again. 'Have you been in Seal Bay all this time? Were you the face I saw at the window? Did you speak to Elowen in the emporium? Were you the person who stole the motorboat and drove it at Tam?'

Jack stared for a moment, his eyes glinting, then he clapped slowly, three, four times. 'Aren't you the clever one? I'm glad you're here, Morwenna. I owe you big time.'

'Last time we met, you held Elowen captive at Woon's.'

'You thought I'd drowned,' Jack sneered. 'But I got away, went up country, called in a few favours. I always knew I'd come back again though.'

Morwenna's knuckles were white as she gripped Lamorna's hand tighter. 'Why did you? Come back?'

'To settle up and finish the job.' Jack's expression was ugly. 'Once and for all.'

'Did you steal Damien Woon's motorboat last night, *The Maverick*? Is that how you got here?' Morwenna knew, but she was determined to keep him talking. He had no intention of moving, so she couldn't get past him; where he sat on the spiral stairs gave her no chance of an exit.

'It's a nice boat. I might keep it. It's better than the first one I nicked. Old Woon forgot I still had keys to his place from when I worked there. And I know the place inside out.'

Morwenna's heart was thudding faster. She watched as he

moved the Santa sack between his feet again. It clanked. It contained something large.

'Who's for more drinks? I've got champagne or...' Courtenay blustered in from the galley. She stopped dead. 'Johnny?'

'Hello, Courtenay,' Jack said. There was nothing welcoming in his smile.

She was confused. 'You said you'd come home later and spend time with me.'

'And here I am now instead. We're all together, on the boat. Having a party,' Jack leered. 'Now trot off back into the kitchen and get me a bottle of champagne.'

'But—'

'Go on, get it,' Jack said, his voice icy. Courtenay looked towards Morwenna for help. Morwenna nodded imperceptibly and Courtenay scuttled away.

Everywhere was silent apart from the slight creaking of the boat on the ocean. Morwenna's glance moved to her mother, who was shaking visibly. She thought about the phone in her pocket again. There must be a way to get it out, to contact Jane.

Courtenay came back with a bottle and handed it nervously to the man in the Santa suit. Jack lifted it to his lips and took two large swigs, froth dribbling down the front. She watched him, perplexed, as if this was not the man she knew so well. He drank again.

Morwenna helped her out. 'Courtenay, this isn't Johnny,' she explained. 'He's called Jack Greenwood. He's not a soldier.'

'Why did you tell me you were in the army then?' Courtenay began.

'Shut up.' Jack spat champagne.

'He couldn't be a soldier,' Morwenna continued. 'Culdrose is a naval base. He lied.'

Jack curled his lip. He didn't care.

Morwenna carried on, her voice low. 'He's been camping in the back of his Ford Galaxy. That's the car you drive, isn't it, Jack? I saw it outside the school when you tried to abduct Elowen again. The day you got Courtenay to ring up and impersonate me, and say Elowen had an appointment.'

'I did ring them and say that, but—' Courtenay was horrified. 'Johnny and I were kidding around and he asked me if I could do voices. I said I could, and he dared me to ring the school and pretend I was you. I thought it was just a bit of fun.'

'Why would you do that?' Tamsin was shaking.

'I didn't think he'd do anything bad. I just thought it was a joke. I—' Tears tumbled from Courtenay's eyes. 'I just wanted to make him like me. I never thought—'

'Stupid bitch. They're all stupid bitches.' Jack said bitterly. 'It gets easier every time.'

'Can we talk?' Tristan said, and Jack's laugh drowned his words.

'So this is your new man, Tam? I nearly took you both out in one go, when you were on the surfboards. You got away with it that time. But not now.' Jack shifted the sack beneath his feet.

Tristan stood up. 'Surely we can sort this out—'

'Sit down.' Jack snarled. He tugged a lighter from his pocket and flicked it. A flame flashed first time. 'Don't move, any of you.'

Blood rushed to Morwenna's ears. She could hardly breathe. She knew what was in Santa's sack now. It was square, flat at the sides.

A petrol can.

Morwenna felt her heart leap as if it would burst. 'Jack, why don't you just get in the motorboat and drive away? You could—'

'Not 'til I'm done.' Jack stared into her eyes, and she saw no emotion there. 'You've got it coming, Morwenna. I had everything worked out. I would've got my hands on a lot of money for Tam's kid. I'd have been set for life. But you ruined it.'

'That's in the past.' Morwenna was about to say more, but Jack's laugh was hollow as death.

'No. This time, I'm in the driving seat.'

'Johnny.' Courtenay took a step forward. 'Johnny, please don't—'

'You're nothing.' Jack turned on her. 'A stupid slag I picked up. A bed for the night.'

'But—'

'Sit down,' Jack indicated the seat next to Morwenna with the hand that held the lighter. He opened the sack and produced the metal can. In a quick movement, he tugged off the cap and hurled liquid onto the shiny floor. Morwenna could smell the sharp stink of petrol. He stood up, throwing more petrol, flinging it towards the leather seats where it splashed and dripped.

Tamsin screamed. Courtenay ran to Morwenna and began to cry. She was blubbering.

Lamorna clutched Morwenna's hand tighter, her nails digging in her flesh. Tristan was on his feet, hurling himself towards Jack, who was slinging petrol. As if he were dancing, Jack lifted the can in the air, liquid slopping from the rim, splashing on the floor.

It all happened in a flash, in a blaze of fire.

Jack flicked the lighter. A scarlet plume shot into the air. Flames leaped from the floor, the whoosh of fire catching and blazing. There was a high scream of pain. Jack's Santa suit was burning. He rushed up the stairs onto the deck. Morwenna was behind him, tugging her mother and Courtenay, pushing Tamsin.

It took seconds.

Jack leaped into the sea and thrashed around. Tristan threw himself into the water too. His jacket was ablaze. Morwenna forced everyone else towards *The Maverick*, which was moored by the side of *The Phoenix*. She started the motor as Tamsin and Courtenay tugged a dripping Tristan into the boat. Courtenay was crying, looking around for Jack, but he'd gone. Morwenna steered the motorboat, urging it forward with everything she had. She needed to get away from *The Phoenix*, as far away as possible. The wind slapped her hair across her face, and she was shivering, teeth chattering. Her hand hurt. Her fingers were blackened, but she concentrated on driving forward as fast as she could.

She heard the sound behind her, the shuddering boom of an explosion. Quickly, she glanced over her shoulder. Plumes of grey smoke filled the sky where *The Phoenix* had been. Crimson flames, the black of burning oil, rose from the sea to the sky. Nervously, she glanced around the boat. Tristan was lying down, Tamsin talking to him gently. He was alive. Lamorna was sobbing, Courtenay snivelling in her arms, her yellow hair streaming behind her. There was no sign of Jack Greenwood.

For some reason she was aware of another motorboat nearby. It was slowing down; someone talking to her, clambering aboard. In the confusion of what was happening, Ruan's arms were around her, he was whispering that she was safe, that everything would be all right. Elowen was there too, somewhere in the background, holding onto her mother. Morwenna could hear her little voice, high-pitched.

They were at the shoreline. Morwenna's ears rang loudly. She had no idea where she was or how much time had passed. Jane was there, speaking gently, then Blessed said something, but she heard nothing.

She saw blurred shapes of people around her. That was the last thing she knew, before she closed her eyes and the beach and the sea and the sky seemed to fall away.

FRIDAY 26 DECEMBER

31

Ruan collected Morwenna from hospital the next morning and drove her home. Everyone had been kept in overnight for observation and the police had been in to ask questions. As she sat next to Ruan, huddled inside an oversized coat, she asked the questions that were on her mind.

'How's Tam? How's Mum? I didn't manage to see them before I left.'

'Tam went home earlier. They let Elowen stay with her.' Ruan's voice was soothing. 'She's fine. I'm picking Lamorna up later. I heard her telling the doctor all about her amazing daughter. You need to rest.'

'I don't.' Morwenna frowned. Her hand hurt; it was neatly bandaged. She showed it to Ruan. 'It's not much, just a bit of a blister.'

'Everyone's been lucky, the doctor said. Tristan had a burn to his shoulder but they're letting him come home today. The doctors wanted to check you all for smoke inhalation.'

'We didn't have time to inhale anything.' Morwenna met his

eyes. 'We were off that boat like a shot. I just started *The Maverick* and drove and drove for shore.'

'You did well,' Ruan said softly and Morwenna could hear his anxiety. 'By the time I got to you, you hardly knew I was there. You were in shock.'

'I knew it was you though.' Morwenna closed her eyes to shut out the images, but she could still see black smoke rising and smell the foul burning. 'You're sure Mum's OK, and Tam?'

'Everyone's fine,' Ruan said. 'I spoke to Jane at the hospital too. She sends you her love.'

'And Courtenay?'

'She's gone back to Camp Dynamo. Sheppy collected her this morning. He's buying her a pasty for lunch. They left the hospital with their arms around each other.'

'What about Jack?' Morwenna asked.

'He hasn't been found.' Ruan took a deep breath. 'If I get to him first, mind—'

'Ruan.'

'Rick has a boat out searching. It's unlikely he survived.' Ruan's eyes were on the road ahead. 'I wish I'd been on *The Phoenix*. I should've been there with you.'

'It's behind us now.' Morwenna blinked to clear her vision. She still felt tired. 'Oh, thank goodness Elowen wasn't there.' She shuddered at the memory.

'It's all right.' Ruan reached out a hand and took hers. 'Don't think about it again. Elowen doesn't know about Jack. We won't tell her. She thinks there was an accidental fire in the kitchen on *The Phoenix* and you all got off safely before the explosion. She's looking forward to this afternoon.'

'Oh?'

'Pam and Barnaby have been lovely. They're cooking

Christmas dinner up at Mirador and bringing it round to the tearoom. We're going to share it.'

'That's kind.'

'They're good people.'

'And we can give our presents,' Morwenna said. 'I have something special for Elowen.'

'She was sensational in that football match,' Ruan said.

'Did she get her hat trick?'

'She got five goals,' Ruan said proudly. 'The rest of the team were carrying her round on their shoulders.'

'The new boots are working wonders, then.' Morwenna smiled. She leaned her head on Ruan's shoulder and thought about Pam. And Barnaby. 'That's kind of them to cook lunch. I'm looking forward to us all being together. Tam, Tristan, Mum – you.'

'Let's get you home first and you can have a shower, get changed. Then we can celebrate Christmas properly.'

Morwenna was slumped against Ruan, snuggling close, her eyes heavy. Seconds later, she was asleep.

* * *

Christmas music was booming from the smart speaker as Morwenna arrived at the Proper Ansom Tearoom with Lamorna and Ruan. The tables had been pushed together to form one long dining table. Pam was in her element, adorning the surface with red and green decorations, placing napkins and crackers, crystal glasses, plates. Barnaby was unloading the food: a turkey, dishes of vegetables, a huge jug of gravy. Tamsin took a dish of potatoes from him and said, 'I'll warm them through in the oven out back.' Then she turned with a smile and kissed each cheek in turn. 'Hi, Mum. Grandma. Dad. Happy Christmas.'

Elowen ran towards Morwenna and hugged her waist. 'Happy Christmas, Grandma. Grandad bought me some football boots and they're magic. I scored five goals. And he said that the boat blew up but nobody got hurt so I shouldn't worry. Tristan said it was an old boat anyway and his dad will get a new one with the insurance.'

Morwenna kissed the dark curls. 'Are you looking forward to lunch?'

'I am. It'll be the proper job. Yesterday I had some food in the hospital with Mummy, but it was cold.' Elowen turned to Tristan. 'Tristan's got a big bandage on his shoulder. He hurt it a bit when the kitchen went on fire.'

Tristan eased himself up slowly from one of the chairs. He was wearing shorts and a T-shirt, one shoulder bandaged. Morwenna asked, 'How are you?'

'Not so bad. I'm on painkillers.' He lowered his voice. 'You were pretty amazing yesterday.'

'We all were.' Morwenna wrapped an arm around her mother. 'I don't think any of us will be able to look at Father Christmas for a while.'

'But I haven't had all my presents yet.' Elowen ran towards Ruan, who whisked her up in his arms. Morwenna gazed at them as he held her in the air.

'We'll do them after lunch,' Ruan said.

Pam asked, 'Do you want to pour everyone a drink, Ruan? There's champagne on the side.'

'And you can help me dish up, Morwenna,' Barnaby said. 'Food's nearly ready.'

'Can I have champagne too?' Elowen asked.

'You and I are having pink lemonade champagne,' Tristan said.

'I'll have the real stuff, plenty of it,' Lamorna piped up. 'My nerves are shot after yesterday. What a Christmas this has turned out to be.'

'It's not over yet, Mum,' Morwenna said, her eyes shining. 'This is the best bit. Let's sit down together and raise our glasses.'

* * *

After lunch, everyone settled down in Tamsin's flat upstairs to give presents. Tamsin and Tristan retreated to the sofa to exchange gifts. Elowen was unwrapping a present from Pam and Barnaby. It was a football shirt, and she rushed to her room to put it on. Lamorna and Morwenna had exchanged presents, the same-shaped gift in different-coloured wrappers. It was exactly the same scented candle from The Celtic Knot.

Morwenna hugged her mum. 'I have another present for you too. I've booked a table for me and you at Catch of the Tide, the fish restaurant. We're having dinner together.'

'That lovely place where I went with Vernon.'

'We'll have a proper girls' night out.'

Lamorna took her hand. 'You're the best, maid.'

Morwenna kissed her cheek. 'You're the best mum.'

'Proper job.' There were tears in Lamorna's eyes.

Ruan came over to join them. He was holding up a lambswool fisherman's jumper. 'This is from you, Morwenna? I always get a jumper.'

'It's like a hug. I want you to stay warm,' Morwenna said, her voice thick with emotion.

Ruan handed over two presents, one to Lamorna and one to Morwenna. Lamorna ripped hers open and squealed. 'It's a silk shawl. Oh, it's so sophisticated.' She hurried over to show Pam Truscott, who was in deep conversation with Barnaby as they made coffee in the kitchenette. Morwenna opened hers slowly.

She saw the neoprene material inside the paper, the squiggles, the funky graffiti pattern. She said, 'It's the wetsuit I wanted. That's kind of you, Ruan.'

Ruan's eyes gleamed. 'Happy Christmas. You gave me a scare yesterday. When I saw the boat blow up, I thought—'

'Don't, Ruan—'

Ruan said quietly, 'I realised more than ever that—'

'Ruan,' Pam called. 'Coffee's ready. Do you want brandy with yours?'

'No, thanks,' he replied quickly. His gaze caught Morwenna's and held. She took a deep breath, then rushed over to Barnaby, who handed her a small cup of coffee. There was something she had to do.

Lamorna plonked herself next to Tamsin and Tristan, giving them advice about how to keep their relationship special. Morwenna overheard every word: Lamorna had never had a relationship that had lasted for more than a few years, but Tamsin and Tristan could make theirs work forever. Elowen turned the TV on and was watching football.

Morwenna put a hand on Barnaby's arm. 'Happy Christmas.'

'Happy Christmas.' He kissed her cheek. 'How are you feeling now?'

'My hand doesn't hurt now. I'm still a bit shaken, but I'll live,' Morwenna said. 'Thanks so much for organising lunch. You've been so kind.'

'I'm happy to do it,' Barnaby said softly. 'And thanks for the hat you gave me. I have a gift for you too.'

'Oh, there's no need,' Morwenna began but Barnaby handed her a square parcel. She opened it easily. It was a diary, bound in a silver filigree design. She touched the textured cover. 'It's beautiful. Thank you.'

'The gift comes with a meaning,' Barnaby said slowly. 'It's next year's diary. It's time to write your future.'

Morwenna frowned. 'I don't understand.'

'Pam and I have been talking. We're both fond of you and Ruan, as you know. I like Ruan a lot, he's a nice guy.'

'He is,' Morwenna agreed.

'And there was a time when I thought you and I—' Barnaby paused. 'What I'm saying is that there's a new year around the corner. Pam and I have decided—'

'What have you decided?' Morwenna had no idea where this conversation was going.

'We get on well, me and you.'

'We do.'

'But you and Ruan have something unique.'

'I suppose so.' Morwenna glanced over to where Pam was talking to Ruan. She imagined that Pam was having the same conversation. Ruan met her eyes.

'You have something more than history, Morwenna. You still love him. I've always known it. The problem is, you don't seem to let yourself believe it.'

'Perhaps you're right.'

'You should give him another chance. Ruan loves you like no one else can. Not me, not anyone else. You're soulmates.'

'We are.' Morwenna thought that Barnaby was a wonderful man. She'd always known it. They'd be good friends now. She was filled with a lightness, a new happiness.

Barnaby kissed her cheek again. 'Promise me you'll give it some thought.'

'I promise,' Morwenna said. She felt her heart expand.

Barnaby walked away, sitting next to Lamorna. Morwenna heard him offer to get her another drink and she asked him if he knew how to make Sgroppinos. Of course he did.

Morwenna glanced at Ruan, who was staring at her now. She thought about Barnaby's words.

She'd been so afraid of things going wrong between them. Their relationship had hit the bump in the road from which she'd never quite recovered. But what if next time there was no bump? What if it was smooth sailing instead? What if there was a happy ever after for them, starting with the first page of the diary she held in her hands?

Her phone vibrated and she read the text message from Jane.

JANE

We're here. Can you open up?

Morwenna gave Ruan the thumbs-up sign. He knew exactly where she was going as she tumbled down the stairs to the tearoom, past the detritus left on the table from lunch, tugging open the door. Jane and Blessed stood together, their shoulders touching. Jane held something carefully in her arms and said, 'Special delivery for Elowen Pascoe.'

Morwenna put out a hand and stroked the warm silken fur. The puppy licked her fingers, gazing at her with round eyes. Jane handed the pale gold Labrador retriever over and Morwenna hugged him against her cheek.

'Do you want to come up? Barnaby's making cocktails.'

'I think we should,' Blessed agreed, taking Jane's hand, and they followed her up to the flat.

Morwenna stood in the doorway, Jane and Blessed looking over her shoulder. Barnaby was handing out cocktails. Tristan's good arm was around Tamsin. Lamorna had buttonholed Pam. Everyone else turned before Elowen did – she was still watching the television. Lamorna saw the dog and let out a soft, 'Aww.' Elowen twisted round to see what the fuss was about.

She gave a loud gasp of joy and was on her feet, running to Morwenna, her arms out to take the soft bundle.

'A puppy. I can't believe it. It's a puppy.'

'It's your puppy,' Morwenna said, swallowing a lump in her throat.

'You'll have to take proper care of him, mind,' Tamsin added from the sofa.

'I will. I will. Oh, thank you, Grandma.' Elowen lifted the little dog next to her cheek, two pairs of huge brown eyes staring gratefully. 'I love him so much. I'm going to call him Oggy.'

'What else would you call him?' Ruan said.

'This is the bestest, bestest, bestest Christmas ever,' Elowen said as she clutched the small pup against her, kissing his head over and over. 'I wanted one forever and ever, but Grandma said I couldn't have one until I was grown up. I must be grown up now.' Her eyes filled with tears.

'Perhaps we all are,' Morwenna said to herself as she glanced at Ruan and sighed deeply. She was feeling blessed.

SATURDAY 27 DECEMBER

EPILOGUE

The Swordfish sliced through the sea, leaving the swell of the surf behind. The ocean extended as far as the eye could towards a sky the colour of cornflowers, a few scraps of cloud.

Morwenna watched Ruan at the helm. He was wrapped warmly in a thick jacket, a scarf, his head covered against the cold. He looked handsome, capable. She looked out to sea and the wind blew strands of her hair, the ones that weren't tucked in the woollen hat, across her face. It occurred to her that the sea was like the future. It stretched in front of you, uncharted, and you could make your way across it as you wished, quickly, slowly, hesitantly.

You could swim, sink. Or you could ride the waves.

She called over the rumble of the motor, 'This boat was a really good choice,' and he nodded. That was Ruan. Silent, practical, rugged. She loved him as he was. Behind her, the bay was getting smaller, but she could see the curve of houses, the white expanse of sand and the stretch of road where the tearoom stood, closed this afternoon.

Tamsin and Tristan were taking Elowen to Pettarock Head for

dinner at the Pengellens'. They were back from London, ready to celebrate. Seb and Becca were going too. And Oggy, of course. Elowen intended to take him everywhere. He even slept in a small basket next to her bed. The puppy seemed devoted to her.

The Swordfish slowed down, a low chugging of the engine, then they were drifting in the open water. Ruan said, 'This looks like a good spot.'

'It does,' Morwenna agreed. She stared into the depths of the ocean. Indigo, icy cold, deep beyond her imagination. She wondered for a moment if Jack Greenwood was down there, on the seabed, still in his Santa suit.

Ruan read her thoughts. 'You don't have to worry about him any more. He's gone.'

'I hope so.'

'He couldn't have survived, could he? Not given what you told me about his condition.'

Morwenna glanced back towards the bay. 'We were about this far out. He might have made it back.'

'It's unlikely,' Ruan said. His eyes moved around the panorama of the sea. 'Look. Over there.'

'It's a fin whale,' Morwenna said. 'Oh, there are two of them.'

Ruan took her hand. 'There are two of us.'

'Here together, out at sea.' Morwenna smiled into his eyes.

'I noticed yesterday Jane and Blessed are a couple,' Ruan mused. 'I'd never have guessed.'

'I've known for a while.'

'You're a super sleuth though.'

'I'm just me,' Morwenna said. 'Ruan?'

'What is it?'

'Can I ask you about Pam?'

'What about her?'

'Did you and she—?'

'Have coffee together and put the world to rights? Yes, a few times.' Ruan wrapped his arms around her. 'She's nice to spend time with. She knows there's no one else for me but you.'

Morwenna understood. 'Barnaby's the same. He gave me a diary. He told me I should write my future with you.'

'Is that what you want?'

'The future's a long time, Ruan.'

'I hope so.'

'But we could write the first page together. Then another.'

'We could.'

They looked at each other for a moment, the whisper of the ocean in their ears. He kissed her tentatively. His lips were warm despite the cold.

Then she was kissing him properly, making up for lost time, for the years she'd wanted to kiss him, the years she'd pushed it from her mind and told herself that they were better apart.

The fear had gone now and in its place was the simple desire to kiss him and kiss him and hold him in her arms.

He pulled away to look at her. 'You're some maid.'

'I am.' Morwenna wanted to stay locked in his embrace for ever and ever. But there was one thing she needed to do first. She tugged off her hat and felt the wind lift her hair and rearrange it. She peeled her coat off, her jumper, jeans, and shivered in her wetsuit.

Ruan touched her face, his fingers gentle. 'You're going in the water, then?'

She didn't move. 'I need to try out my new wetsuit.'

'You were always a mermaid. My Cornish mermaid.'

'I am,' Morwenna said. 'Right. I'm going in.' She kissed him longer than she intended to and pulled away reluctantly. Her heart was brimming with love. 'You'll be here when I come back?'

'I'll always be here when you come back,' Ruan said simply.

She traced his features with her fingertips, then she edged carefully to the end of the boat, took a deep breath and jumped.

The impact was immediate, the crash of the water against her face, the sting of the cold as it seeped through her wetsuit. She gulped in clean air, thrashed her arms and legs and delved below again. With each dip beneath the waves, she felt warmer. Holding her breath, she dived and came up spluttering, blinking water, her head cold, her hair over her face. She had never felt happier.

Mermaid-like. With a flick of her legs, she rolled on her back and stared up at the sky.

It was a deep crystal blue. The clouds had shifted, dispersed, and the sun had come out.

* * *

MORE FROM J. R. LEIGH

Another book from J. R. Leigh, *The Cream Tea Killer*, is available to order now here:

https://mybook.to/CreamTeaKillerBackAd

ACKNOWLEDGEMENTS

Thanks to Kiran Kataria and Emma Beswetherick, whose warmth, professionalism and kindness I value so much.

Thanks to the team at Boldwood Books; to Amanda and Wendy and Marcela, to designers, editors, technicians, voice actors.

Special thanks to Sarah Ritherdon.

To Rachel Gilbey, to so many wonderful bloggers and fellow writers. The support you give goes beyond words.

To Martin, Cath, Avril, Rob, Tom, Emily, Tom's mum, Erika, Rich, Kathy N, Julie, Martin, Steve, Rose, Steve's mum, Jan, Rog, Jan M, Helen, Pat, Ken, Trish, Lexy, Rachel, John, Nik R, Pete O', Chris A, Chris's mum, Katie H, Shaz, Gracie, Mya, Frank, George, Fiona J and Jonno.

To all at the LLPP.

To Peter and the Solitary Writers, my writing buddies.

Also, my neighbours and the local community, especially Jenny, Laura, Claire, Paul and Sophie, Niranjan and all at Turmeric Kitchen.

Much thanks to Ivor Abiks at Deep Studios and to Darren and Lyndsay at PPL.

Love to family, to Angela, Ellen, Hugh, Jo, Jan, Lou, Harry, Chris, Robin, Edward, Zach, Daniel, Catalina.

So much love to my mum and dad, Irene and Tosh, who I miss more than words can say.

Love always to our Tony and Kim, to Liam, Maddie, Kayak, Joey.

And to my soulmate, Big G.

Warmest thanks always to you, my readers, wherever you are. You make this journey special.

ABOUT THE AUTHOR

J. R. Leigh is the bestselling author of *The Old Girls' Network* and *Five French Hens* and the doyenne of the 'it's never too late' genre of women's fiction. She has lived all over the UK from Liverpool to Cornwall, but currently resides in Somerset.

Would you like to read Foul Play at the Vintage Village Bake-Off, an EXCLUSIVE free short story? Sign up to J. R. Leigh's newsletter to start reading!

Visit J. R. Leigh's website: www.judyleigh.com

Follow J. R. Leigh on social media here:

- facebook.com/judyleighuk
- x.com/judyleighwriter
- instagram.com/judyrleigh
- bookbub.com/authors/judy-leigh

ALSO BY J. R. LEIGH

Five French Hens

The Old Girls' Network

Heading Over the Hill

Chasing the Sun

Lil's Bus Trip

The Golden Girls' Getaway

A Year of Mr Maybes

The Highland Hens

The Golden Oldies' Book Club

The Silver Ladies Do Lunch

The Vintage Village Bake Off

The Morwenna Mutton Mysteries Series

Foul Play at Seal Bay

Bloodshed on the Boards

The Cream Tea Killer

Mince Pies and Murder

POISON & pens

POISON & PENS IS THE HOME OF COZY MYSTERIES SO POUR YOURSELF A CUP OF TEA & GET SLEUTHING!

DISCOVER PAGE-TURNING NOVELS FROM YOUR FAVOURITE AUTHORS & MEET NEW FRIENDS

JOIN OUR FACEBOOK GROUP

BIT.LYPOISONANDPENSFB

SIGN UP TO OUR NEWSLETTER

BIT.LY/POISONANDPENSNEWS

Boldwood

Boldwood Books is an award-winning fiction publishing company seeking out the best stories from around the world.

Find out more at www.boldwoodbooks.com

Join our reader community for brilliant books, competitions and offers!

Follow us
@BoldwoodBooks
@TheBoldBookClub

Sign up to our weekly deals newsletter

https://bit.ly/BoldwoodBNewsletter

Printed in Dunstable, United Kingdom